The four boys grabbed deep breaths and scurried up the rise, racing out into the open, even
as Miller's Thompson opened up, and Reiben's
B.A.R. and every rifle in the trench fired upward, blindly, but firing. It wasn't enough to
quell the river of gunfire the Germans were
pouring into that open area, and this time when
the firing ceased, and Miller's cry of "Report!"
went unanswered, the captain did not bother
going out to look to see what had occurred. He
knew. He knew.

"Jackson!" Miller called out.

The lanky sharpshooter ambled forward. "Yes,
sir?"

"You ready to get across?"

"Good a time as any, sir."

Miller scrambled up the rise into the open and
just stood there, brazenly, presenting a perfect
target. Up on the bluff, the nearer of the two
machine-gun teams reacted as if he'd goosed
them, and began repositioning their bulky
weapon on its tripod.

"Go!" Miller hollered.

And Jackson was taking off through the open
space just as the machine-gun fire was redirected toward Miller, chewing up the
ground. . . .

saving private ryan

---

a novel
by
max allan collins

based on the
screenplay
by
robert rodat

PENGUIN BOOKS

PENGUIN BOOKS

Published by the Penguin Group
Penguin Books Ltd, 80 Strand, London WC2R 0RL, England
Penguin Putnam Inc., 375 Hudson Street, New York, New York 10014, USA
Penguin Books Australia Ltd, Ringwood, Victoria, Australia
Penguin Books Canada Ltd, 10 Alcorn Avenue, Toronto, Ontario, Canada M4V 3B2
Penguin Books India (P) Ltd, 11 Community Centre, Panchsheel Park, New Delhi – 110 017, India
Penguin Books (NZ) Ltd, Cnr Rosedale and Airborne Roads, Albany, Auckland, New Zealand
Penguin Books (South Africa) (Pty) Ltd, 24 Sturdee Avenue, Rosebank 2196 South Africa

Penguin Books Ltd, Registered Offices: 80 Strand, London WC2R 0RL, England

www.penguin.com

First published in the United States of America by Penguin Putnam Inc. 1998
Published in Great Britain in Penguin Books 1998

14

Set in Monotype Palatino
Printed in England by Clays Ltd, St Ives plc

To Master Sgt. Mahlon Collins, U.S. Army
and
Lt. (j.g.) Max A. Collins, Sr., U.S. Navy
. . . two brothers from Iowa
who made it back

A Tip of the Helmet

My thanks to Robert Rodat for his fine screenplay.

The following references were consulted in the writing of this novel: *America at D-Day* (1994), Richard Goldstein; *Axis Combat Tanks* (1977), Peter Chamberlain and Chris Ellis; *D-Day and the Invasion of Normandy* (1994), Anthony Kemp; *D-Day 1944* (1971, 1994), Theodore A. Wilson; *D-Day June 6, 1944: The Climactic Battle of World War II* (1994), Stephen E. Ambrose; *D-Day: Spearhead of Invasion* (1968), R.W. Thompson; *George C. Marshall: Organizer of Victory* (1973), Forrest C. Pogue; *The GI's War* (1988), Edwin P. Hoyt; *June 6, 1944: The Voices of D-Day* (1994), Gerald Astor; *The Longest Day* (1959), Cornelius Ryan; *Marshall, Hero for Our Times* (1982), Leonard Mosley; *No Mission Too Difficult!* (1995), Blythe Foote Finke; *The Normandy Campaign* (1976), Robert Hunt and David Mason; *Voices of D-Day* (1994), Ronald J. Drez; and *Writers on World War II* (1991), Mordecai Richler. Though not a D-Day book, Audie Murphy's classic *To Hell and Back* (1949) gave me the best feel for the day-to-day life of the combat soldier.

Also, my thanks to DreamWorks and editor Danielle Perez for this opportunity; my agent, Dominick Abel; Joe Collins for technical information; and my wife, Barb, for research assistance and support in the trenches.

PROLOGUE

———

St. Laurent Military Graveyard
June 6, 1998

Immaculately trimmed hedgerows, high enough to block all else from view, edged the pathway. Up ahead, Grandpa—in his plaid shirt and gray slacks and socks and sandals—was padding quickly down the tunnel of green, and little Jimmy—at seven, the youngest of the two brothers and two sisters (Sue, at twenty, was the oldest)—could hardly keep up.

Jimmy could hardly believe a geezer like Grandpa could move so fast, hunched over, sunlight glinting off the tufts of his white hair. Mom and Dad, and the rest of the family, were almost running, trying to catch up (though Grandma wasn't even trying), as if the old man had escaped and they were hoping to recapture him.

Then Grandpa stopped.

Like he'd run into an invisible brick wall, and Jimmy could hear his grandfather's breathing quickening, as if he were still running, ever faster, ever faster—only he wasn't: Grandpa was falling to his knees, and as he did, he sucked in wind in an awful wheeze, which made Jimmy think Grandpa was collapsing or something.

"Dad!"

Mom's voice, from behind Jimmy, carried concern, but Jimmy knew now that Grandpa hadn't fallen; it was more like he was . . . kneeling. Praying.

Pretty soon Jimmy knew why. When he came up beside his grandfather, whose eyes were riveted on the landscape that had finally revealed itself as the path sloped down, Jimmy saw an amazing abstract design, a collaboration by God and man. The green of the grass on the gently rolling hill was God's work, while the sea of white crosses, interspersed with an occasional Star of David, was man's.

To Jimmy, who at seven had only been to a cemetery one other time (and not an extraordinary cemetery like this one), it was as if everybody on earth had died and been buried here; acres and acres of green with white filled his eyes, no sky above or even to the left or right, just green, white, green, white, green, white, till the boy's eyes blurred.

Then Mom and Dad were running up and hugging Grandpa; Jimmy's brother and sisters were coming, too, and finally his grandmother—though she alone was in no hurry. Grandma, whose hair wasn't as white as Grandpa's, had a funny expression; Jimmy couldn't tell whether she was happy or sad.

Grandpa didn't have any expression at all. His

eyes were open wide, as if he were trying to fill them up with the green and white landscape. Jimmy had noticed Grandpa's eyes, before—the rest of the old man's face was pretty ordinary, kind and wrinkly like any grandfather's.

But Grandpa's eyes were frequently the way Grandma's smile was, right now—they seemed sad and happy at the same time, and never more so than right now, as they fixed themselves upon a geometrically straight line of crosses. Those eyes must have seen a lot of things in all those years, Jimmy thought.

The boy wondered if Grandpa was thinking about people who were buried in this place, friends of his. Dad said Grandpa had fought in the war here, but Jimmy didn't understand, not really. He had heard of that war in Vietnam. But this was France.

Maybe a war was fought here, once, too.

PART ONE

Omaha Beach, Normandy
June 6, 1944

1

A gunmetal gray sea clawed at the gunmetal gray sky, but the Allied Armada—its five thousand ships shades of deeper gray—moved inexorably forward, the Channel's icy waves cleaved by waves of warships. Perturbed by neither the glowering sky nor the towering whitecaps came ten lanes, twenty miles across, of sleek new attack transports, rust-pocked old freighters, converted ocean liners and steamers, tankers and tugs, Coast Guard cutters, minesweepers, motor launches, buoy-layers, and convoy upon convoy of cruisers, destroyers, and battleships.

The assault on the beaches of Normandy, however, would be the work of fifteen hundred landing craft, which would make the twelve-mile trip from the armada to the beach in three and a half endless hours. Among them, out in front, two hundred craft headed for shore in the first wave, including LCIs (Landing Craft, Infantry) carrying two hundred-some troops apiece, and the smaller LCVPs (Landing Craft, Vehicle, Personnel), each carrying a platoon of thirty, or twelve plus a jeep.

In one of the latter—a Higgins boat, named after its inventor, Andrew Jackson Higgins, Jr., who made his fortune selling speedy boats to bootleggers (and speedier ones to the Coast Guard)—Captain John H. Miller of Addley, Pennsylvania, sat with his men, "new meat" fresh out of basic.

Miller, Charlie Company, Second Ranger Battalion, was not a career soldier; his rank reflected escalating battlefield commissions, earned by surviving Arzew in North Africa, Gela in Sicily, and Salerno in Italy. He was thirty-eight years old and by far the oldest man on the flat-bottomed landing craft, a small taxi-cab of combat piloted by a single Navy coxswain, a big trough of humans with a gate waiting to empty them onto a beach that could not yet be seen.

As baby-faced as any of his men, with clean-shaven, soft features betrayed by ancient eyes, Miller—like all survivors of multiple combat campaigns—knew all too well that he was a fugitive from the law of averages. How many sevens in a row can one man roll in the same game?

His hand might have been shaking dice, at that—but it was just shaking. And this was no game. He hoped his boys had not seen his trembling hand. He stared at it, willing it to stop, forcing the fear back within him, and the flesh obeyed.

None of his boys had noticed their captain's

trembling hand; they were busy, caught up in the reigning madness as the flat bow of the boat plowed into swell after swell, a freezing spray blowing in, soaking their fatigues and the woolen ODs (olive drabs) underneath. The boat battling the waves tossed the soldiers like rag dolls, sending them smashing and tumbling into each other, slender young men fat with equipment, wearing inflatable "Mae West" life preservers, carrying various weapons (rifles, mortars, bazookas, flamethrowers), canvas bags, gas masks, first-aid kits, canteens, entrenching tools, knives, wire cutters, rations, grenades, explosives, ammo. Their helmets, laced with netting, bobbed like the heads-on-springs of carnival hula dolls. The smell of diesel oil and salty metal smudged the sea breeze.

Periodically seasickness would spread across the little ship, as if it had been spilled from a container. And containers were what the men were seeking, their barf bags (each man having been issued by the Army "Bag, vomit, one") long since filled and buried at sea. Their helmets came off and were soon brimming with the remnants of the fabulous condemned-man style meals they'd been served last night, steak dinner send-offs the Army had provided, the "Last Supper," the men had called it.

At least with the water sloshing in, cleaning the helmets out wasn't a problem. A lot of the guys were helping out the craft's pump by bailing with their helmets, anyway.

Everybody had been issued anti-seasickness pills, but many a would-be tough guy had pooh-poohed the need for them, and Private Anthony Caparzo, twenty-two, Chicago, Illinois, had bought them up for a nickel apiece, on the troop ship, throughout their several long days of waiting. Caparzo had figured to make a small fortune, selling the pills for a quarter apiece, but now—with his buddies moaning and puking around him—he just didn't have the heart for it, or the stomach.

Caparzo, full-lipped, blunt-nosed, eyes so small and dark in his pale oval face they seemed like black beads, began handing out the pills, solemn as a priest giving the Eucharist.

The boat lurched, and so did Stanley Mellish, twenty-one, Yonkers, New York. He lunged right at Caparzo, snatching the handful of pills.

"Gimme some more of those!" Mellish said after the fact. He had the soft petulant features and dark yearning eyes of a spoiled child.

"That's my entire wartime supply, you shithead!"

"Put it on the war debt." The boat bounced again. "Anyway, what the hell difference does it make? You really think we're gonna be takin' any more boat rides after this?"

Caparzo had no answer for that, but the boat responded, lifting from the water just as a fifteen-inch naval shell went streaking overhead. Soon its whistle had died, and an explosion on the unseen land ahead told them they were close. H-hour had arrived.

Those who weren't puking were praying. Mellish quickly transferred from the latter group to the former, his face turning camouflage green, his neck extending like a cannon taking aim, and the anti-seasickness pills exploding out of him, the deck their target. Bull's-eye.

Then, as Mellish hung over the side, Caparzo glanced around, and when he felt sure no one was looking, he plucked the slimy but hardly used pills from the puke puddle, found a pocket to stow them in, and wiped his hands on his soaked fatigues.

His captain had seen this, but Miller understood the secrets men kept in combat—like his own tremulous hand. Again he stared at it, as if it belonged to someone else. And again it stopped shaking.

Next to him was Sergeant Michael Horvath, Minneapolis, Minnesota, a blocky battle-scarred vet pushing thirty. Like the captain, the sergeant was discreet and may or may not have seen Miller's shaking hand. Sarge gestured to their praying, puking troops.

"Guess they don't do too much boating," Sarge said, "back in the boonies."

"It's not the old fishing hole," Miller admitted.

Miller loved these kids. On the transport ship his boys had enjoyed a final burst of adolescence, sleeping all over the place, on the decks, in and on top of and under vehicles, smoking, playing cards, horsing around, talking about their girls back home. Everybody had their individual letter from the Supreme Commander—General Eisenhower—and the kids went around signing each other's letter, like a high school yearbook. Their innocence had warmed his heart, and broken it.

One of the boys, Danny Delancey, where was he from? Cleveland? He was a sweet kid who did a pretty fair imitation of Sinatra, particularly when accompanied by a shipboard guitar, and right now was peeking over the gunwale at the Higgins boat directly off the port side.

"Heads down!" Miller barked. "There's nothin' to see!"

But before Delancey could obey that order, and as if in contradiction to the captain, the Higgins boat next door ran into a mine, setting off a huge explosion that shattered and ignited the overcast morning in a shower of fuel, fire, metal, and human debris.

Delancey fell back as he and everyone else aboard the rocking boat was showered in flaming oil, seared body parts, and metallic splinters, the burning remains clunking to deck like a hellish hailstorm. Helmets used to bail became a fire brigade as the water was used to put out the flames, aided by the sloshing in of icy Channel water, roused by the explosion.

Curses and screams accompanied the frantic but focused cleansing of the boat. Miller tossed a foot in a boot overboard, and Sarge disposed of a charred arm, with a hand that seemed outstretched in unanswered plea. Tossing body parts over the side, even as the boat pitched along, the two battle vets exchanged weary glances—no dignity for the goddamned dead in this war—and the youthful faces around them turned toward their leadership for guidance.

"Injuries?" Miller called out.

Heads shook no, all around—a small miracle with all that searing flying shrapnel. Faces were turning toward the water, where bodies, and body parts, floated.

"Heads down, I said!"

"Captain"—Delancey's eyes were like a fucking puppy dog's—"are we all gonna die?"

Miller was searching for the right words—he didn't want to bullshit these boys, but they needed something to hang onto, to take with them into battle—when Lieutenant Frank Briggs responded for him.

"Hell, no, Delancey!" Briggs said with bravado-laced cheer. "Two-thirds, tops!"

Those weren't the sort of words Miller had in mind.

"Oh, Jesus," Delancey said. The line between curses and prayers blurred in the war.

Briggs—thirty, Dallas, Texas, sturdy of build with close-set glittering eyes—cupped his mouth and hollered, his voice carrying across the water to neighboring Higgins boats. "Look at the man on your left!

Every rootin' tootin' one of you. Now look at the man on your right!"

All around the boat, the boys obeyed, numbly.

Briggs grinned. "Say a prayer for those two sons of bitches, 'cause they're not comin' back. You, on the other hand, ain't gettin' a goddamn scratch!"

Delancey smiled weakly, as if the lieutenant's words had encouraged nothing more than another urge to puke. This "pep talk" had clearly made the platoon more uneasy than ever.

"Lieutenant," Miller said to Briggs softly.

Briggs' eyes were bright. "Yes, sir?"

Miller shot him a glare. "Never answer questions directed to me. Understood?"

The light in the lieutenant's eyes dulled. "Yes, sir."

Orange-white light washed across the boat, and all eyes lifted heavenward, as if checking for angels, finding instead thousands of rockets flashing over-head, shoreward, their whoosh followed by explosions making not-too-distant thunder.

"See that?" Miller yelled. "Hear that? That's every German strong point gettin' blown to hell and gone!"

"Go LCTs!" Lieutenant Briggs called out, as if cheering from the stands of a big game. "Light 'em up like Christmas!"

"Now, get those heads back down," Miller said, even as he peered over the gunwale at the crescent-shaped, mist-shrouded shoreline, bluffs rising vaguely behind the shelf of sand and a formidable seawall, yellow cordite mingling with stirred-up dust to create a ghostly landscape.

But poking out of the sand, where the tide was way back, a mile back, sprouting like bizarre mushrooms, were imperfect rows of gatelike iron-frame structures, wooden logs wearing Teller mines for caps and crossed steel rails, all angled seaward, planted by the Jerries to tear apart landing craft on a high-tide landing. At low tide they would provide cover for foot soldiers moving across the beach—although taking shelter behind an obstacle attached to a mine was essentially hiding behind a bomb in a firefight.

A chill ran through an already bone-chilled Miller: Those underwater obstacles were supposed to be gone. He had been briefed that combat engineers, before dawn, would have removed them all.

Yet there they were, Xs of steel, like grotesque grave markers in a cemetery waiting to be filled.

The Naval barrage, it seemed to Miller, was falling short, the big shells from the big guns sending up geysers of water, black as oil. He hoped to hell, when they got there, the beach would be pocked with shell craters, as promised. That was how he had trained his men, moving in and out and around bomb craters. . . .

"Gonna be a big show!" some kid shouted.

"Piece of cake!" another said.

Caparzo leaned against the side, keeping his body

in rhythm with the rocking as the shell-stirred waters roughed their ride. "Sounds like the Midnight Limited!"

"More like a chain flush," Mellish said, managing a nervous smile.

Nearby, gangly Daniel Boone Jackson, twenty-three, Hickory Valley, Tennessee, hugged his sharp-shooter's rifle and bowed his head.

"Best make yourself right with the Lord," Jackson advised his buddies in a soothing drawl at odds with the turbulence underneath, and around, them.

Spookily, as if the Southern boy had commanded it, silence fell upon the choppy waters. The Naval barrage had lifted, leaving only the thrum of the Higgins boat engines, a sound so familiar to these passengers they had long since blotted it out. The big guns were, no doubt, readjusting to direct their fire inland. But the effect was as if the war had halted to give these boys the moment of silence they needed.

Miller knew this instant of accidental mercy was all the leeway his kids were likely to find on this cold gray morning, on the hazy shore ahead. He glanced at the coxswain, who held up three fingers.

His boys were gazing up at him. They knew this was it; they needed only their final cue.

It was not Miller's way to make speeches, so after a glance at the sergeant, and an exchange of tiny smiles that each knew might be a final farewell, the captain moved among his boys, winding through them, his manner, his voice, conversational, calm.

"Keep it simple," he soothed, "sides of the ramp, move fast, no bunchin' up. . . . Good luck, Godspeed, lock and load."

Occasionally he would grant a small smile, even a wink, now and then a shoulder pat. Several times he adjusted the inflatable life jackets the boys wore, knowing if a Mae West hiked too high and the vest inflated, a soldier getting into deep water or stepping in a shell hole was in deep shit.

"You can wind up with your head down and your legs sticking out of the water," Miller chided gently. He moved on, making eye contact, little nods, tight smiles.

"Keep sand out of the actions," he said. Many of the men had condoms snugged over their rifle barrels, an absurd sight but a rational precaution for the watery landing ahead. "Good luck, men."

The Navy's big guns started in again, but so did something else: enemy artillery and mortar fire, raining down on the approaching landing craft, plumes of water blossoming nearby, from guns that should not have survived the Allied bombardment. The nasty purr of machine guns sounded at right and left, and Miller saw tracer bullets dancing in the water and careening off the ramp and sides of the LCVP to the side of them, just a little ahead of them. Miller knew all too well that for every tracer bullet you saw, there were four more bullets you didn't. Then as water sprayed in from enemy shells, the boat lurched, running onto a sandbar, jerking all aboard rudely forward.

"Piece of cake my ass," Caparzo muttered to Mellish.

"Looks like there's a little opposition," Mellish said glumly.

And as the men stared straight ahead at the steel gate before them, a gate that would lower into a ramp and send them into battle, a sudden metallic hailstorm hammered against it.

Shit, Miller thought. He had two choices: send his men directly into the machine-gun fire that was knocking so insistently at their door, or stay put until mortar fire or an artillery shell took them all out in one fiery ball.

But the machine-gun fire was sporadic. He would find a gap, and charge through it . . . and as these thoughts swirled through his brain, the boys who were his men backed away from the bullets pounding at the barricade, jockeying for position as best they could in the cramped craft. A few of them unleashed their bladders, warm wetness mingling with the chill Channel water already soaking them.

"I'm so fuckin' seasick," said Private Brad Lewis, twenty, Bayonne, New Jersey, to anyone interested, "that beach'll be a fuckin' cure."

Pudgy Brad Lewis, a grocer's son, had never used

the word "fuck" until about three months ago; now some form of it found its way into everything he said or thought, with the exception of prayers.

"Not yet!" Miller called to the coxswain, who would lower the gate, which another barrage of machine-gun fire was battering. Miller hollered to his boys: "When that gate comes down, I want you to debark both sides of the ramp! Understood? . . . See you on the beach! Good luck!"

Every boy on the ship was listening to the same small inner voice: *It can't happen to me . . . can it?*

Then the machine-gun fire let up, and Miller hollered, "Now!" and the gate came down.

And the machine-gun fire resumed.

Miller, at the rear of the boat, heard it more than saw it—the sound of triangulated .30-caliber machine-gun fire, chewing up men and metal, his boys screaming as they died. All he saw, at first, was the metal minutiae, pink and gray matter, human dust, smoke and sparks exploding past him.

"Fuck—fuck!" Private Brad Lewis screamed. His last words.

All Miller could see was the backs of his boys, as the heavy caliber slugs exploded through them, sending sprays of blood but more so shrapnel of shovel and canteen and canvas, even rubber from rended Mae Wests. As many times as Miller had been in combat, he was not prepared for this, as in less than twenty seconds, two-thirds of his platoon was stacked up like human cordwood, only not neatly. Like the steel-rail dragon's teeth on the beach, the dead and dying were obstacles that a dozen survivors had to find their way over and around, to make their way to the ramp and hurl themselves into the water. And they were, splashing like stones, stones with frantic eyes.

Behind them Miller charged, shouting, "Go! Go!" working his voice above the machine-gun storm.

Private Delancey was screaming. The scream was neither of fear nor pain, but horror, caught as he was under a pile of corpses that had moments before been comrades. The moans and whimpers of the wounded could not be heard over the machine-gun chatter and engine thrum. Miller, staying low, kept his steel helmet between him and the gunfire. He plucked the boy from the pile—yanking him by the backpack and pulling his trapped legs out from under the bodies— a moment before machine-gun fire stitched across where the boy had just been.

Then Miller dragged the boy to the ramp and, still holding onto him, plunged himself, and Delancey, into the water, deep water, to the left of the sandbar the LCVP had rammed onto.

2

As he splashed into the water, Miller—lungs filled with cold morning air—released the boy and punched his carbon dioxide cartridges, to inflate his Mae West. This, along with his gas-mask casing, provided buoyancy, but not enough to appreciably slow his plunge. Sixty pounds of gear sank him like a rock, and a strong undercurrent pulled him to the left, as he careened down and through an underwater nightmare of foundering, drowning soldiers, the wounded ones staining the greenish-blue world with contrails of red.

With men flailing around him, releasing equipment to survive, Miller resolved to cling to his rifle even as his backpack dragged him to the sandy floor. Tumbling around him in a slow-motion underwater ballet were helmets, M–1 rifles, flamethrowers, walkie-talkies, a mortar, a bazooka, even a scaling ladder.

And as he struggled to release himself from the burden of his heavy backpack, Miller—lungs bursting, bubbles trailing from his nostrils—looked up toward the surface. Freezing though the water was, it was as if he were cooking at the bottom of an immense pot, the surface boiling with shell bursts, shrapnel splashes, and most ominously, the rain-like pitter-patter of machine-gun fire. Bullets piercing the water's skin left fizzy trails before slowing and settling gently around him on the murky, sandy bottom, harmless metal pebbles now.

Backpack off, Miller realized the floundering soldier nearest him was Private Delancey, dancing a frenzied water-retarded tarantella, impotently attempting to undo the straps of his own heavy pack. Withdrawing a trench knife from his boot, Miller slashed the boy's backpack straps, the pack joining the parade of discarded gear marching to the sandy floor.

But the kid was panicking by now, air bubbles streaming out of an open silently screaming mouth, eyes wide with fear. The captain looped an arm around the private, tight, and swam with the boy, underwater, staying below the shooting gallery that was the water's surface.

As Miller, lifeguarding Delancey, lungs bursting, moved nearer the shore, the sandy floor inclined until that bullet-riddled skin of water overhead was ever nearer. Miller punched the boy's CO_2 tubes, inflating the Mae West, and soon the captain and the private broke the surface.

They gasped for air as their ears filled with the chaotic symphony of carnage that was Omaha Beach, shells and men screaming, fire crackling as oil burned atop the water, gunfire popping like firecrackers, machine guns kissing the sand, *sppp sppp, sppp sppp.* Floating around them were landing craft and jeeps and DUKWs and rubber-skirted tanks, dead vehicles alive with flame and smoke, none of them reaching the shore, mechanical corpses among the flesh-and-blood ones.

Miller fell back into the water, a wave taking him, the terrible cacophony mercifully muted underwater; but then he gained his footing, as Delancey clung to him like a frightened child to its parent, gasping a curse or a prayer: "Jesus . . . Mary . . . Joseph . . ."

The captain waded with his human cargo through the shallow water, bullets pinging and splashing around them, bodies drifting; other soldiers around them slogged the same rough road, many without helmets or weapons, highly trained crack infantrymen arriving on the beachhead as exhausted, waterlogged, shipwrecked survivors. Miller hauled the barely conscious Delancey by a strap on his backpack, navigating their way around the steel dragon's teeth obstacles, sometimes pausing behind them, even latching on to them for support.

They were doing this when machine-gun fire wrote its name on Delancey's back; the private arched in the captain's grasp, the boy's face slack with the surprise of his death. Even in a hellish landscape like this, death had the power to amaze.

The body fell onto Miller, pinning him in two feet of water. There was no helping the boy now, and the compassionate captain made a cruel decision: he would use the boy's body as a shield. Struggling, paddling toward shore, Miller felt Delancey taking more hits, seven or eight of them, jerking violently in his grasp, puffs of blood misting the air. Miller wondered if this might not finally be the moment he should choose to go insane.

Panting with exhaustion, he paused beneath the bloody body of the boy he'd tried to save and looked around, seeing he was not alone in such thoughts, or actions: scores of other men, from other boats, were working their way grimly toward the smoke- and dust-draped shore. Some, like him, were using corpses for cover, moving past the tangled and burning wreckage of their well-planned assault, wending through wave- and surf-tossed bodies. Absurdly, dead fish by the hundreds were washing ashore, their peaceful world disrupted by man's squabble.

Nearby a soldier raised his head and winced, and rolled onto his back on the shallow water lapping the shoreline. Miller grimaced as he tossed aside the human shield, dropped his life belt, and splashed to the aid of a wounded man.

Or what he thought was a wounded man.

"Get away," the soldier snarled as Miller moved in to drag him to shore. "No, no—leave me!"

Miller understood, and wondered how many other men were pretending to be dead, in hopes the machine guns and small arms fire would seek out living targets instead.

The captain, not wanting to provide such a target, hurled himself behind another cross-steel obstacle, pressing against it for dear life as machine-gun rounds hammered the metal, whanging, ricocheting, death pounding at the door.

Several soldiers making their way to shore still wore their Mae Wests, which as they moved onto the beach would prove cumbersome. Miller was hollering to them to drop the life belts when an artillery shell, a big 88, exploded just in back of him, slamming him into the water as debris flew and smoke plumed.

When he came to, seconds later, he pushed up from the sand and the water, dripping, dizzy with concussion, and leaned into the cross-steel obstacle like a drunk propping himself up against a barroom wall. He looked into the water and saw a helmet floating there: his. He put it on, his gaze catching the water's shimmery blue-green surface, and a vaguely familiar face looked back blankly at him: the face of a man at the end of the road. Not a captain's face, not a soldier's, just the face of a man willing to crawl into his wicker basket and stay there.

His fatigues had little tears and charred patches, and anywhere his flesh was showing was nicked and bleeding, as if he'd cut himself shaving, all over. He wondered why the shooting had stopped; was the battle over?

The world was a grotesque silent film. Hundreds of dead soldiers littered the beach, staining golden sand red as yellow smoke drifted like fog; countless others, wounded, thrashed in pain and fear, writhing like worms, their mouths moving, some silently crying for help, or their mothers, others moaning, others screaming, but no sound, no sound.

Miller watched the pantomime battle continue: four soldiers trudged onto the beach—in their water-logged uniforms it was as though they were walking against a strong wind—and then two of them pitched forward, joining the other bodies, apparently cut down by machine-gun fire, but Miller couldn't hear it. Couldn't hear a thing.

He could see, though, all too well. The sand was scattered with rifles and helmets and gas masks and blankets. A Sherman tank had made it to the water's edge, only to aim its barrel at nothing, its charred bulk shrouded in flame, sending clouds of greasy black smoke roiling into the sky. Some men had made it onto the beach, and were returning fire toward the nebulous enemy in the bluffs and the cliffs that bookended them. One GI dropped to the sand and fired back at the invisible Jerries, but caught instead one of his buddies running ahead of him, killing him instantly.

The poor bastard—the living one—looked around frantically, wondering if anybody had seen what he'd done; Miller had, and their eyes met, but the captain looked away. He knew that the guilt and horror of that fuckup would follow that kid till the day he died, whether today or sixty years from now. But it would probably be today.

When he turned away, Miller suddenly stared into the face of a private, a blue-eyed boy whose expectant expression baffled the captain. A few feet away three more young privates were huddled behind an X of steel, shivering in the cold water, looking at him in that same manner.

"Huh?" Miller managed.

The blue-eyed private's mouth moved, and sound seemed to be returning; finally the cobwebs cleared and Miller understood his disorientation and impaired hearing had to do with an 88 going off under his ass.

"You say something, soldier?" Miller said.

The private said, "What now, sir?" but Miller only saw lips moving, though the rumble of war was gradually turning up its volume.

"*What?*" Miller screamed, unaware he was screaming. "*What are you saying?*"

"*I said,*" the private screamed back at the captain, "*what the hell do we do now, sir?*"

Miller glanced around, forcing himself to look past the carnage, to see beyond the catastrophe of this landing, realizing that he was not alone. These privates and many others were alive, taking shelter behind the dragon's teeth obstacles, hanging on by their figurative fingernails, but alive.

"Captain! Captain!" The familiar voice found him even as his hearing returned, more or less, to normal. On the other side of him, Miller could see Sergeant Michael Horvath, crouched behind another steel-rail barrier; from Sarge's expression, Miller gathered the man had been shouting at him for some time.

Miller granted himself a tiny millisecond smile at seeing his friend still alive, then in a voice that was all business, said, "Take these men off the beach."

One of the cluster of young privates squeaked, "Sir, what's the rallying point?"

Miller pointed toward the cliffs to one side of the bluff, a distance of perhaps two hundred meters. "Get to where they can't shoot you!"

Through the smoke and dust, beyond the dragon's teeth rising from the low-tide sands, the body-littered beach gently sloped to a shingle of gravel that rose, in stair-step fashion, to a seawall of stone and masonry. At some points along the beach, that seawall was as high as twelve or fifteen feet—but here it was a mere three or four. All along the top of the seawall was a nasty concertina snarl of barbed wire. Snugged along that seawall, ragged groups of GIs were already avoiding the machine-gun and small-arms fire pouring down from the bluffs and cliffs, struggling to dig foxholes, keeping low, tending wounded.

"The seawall!" Miller hollered to the twenty or thirty privates huddling behind obstacles in the shallow water. "You see it?"

A soldier's voice cried out: "I'm stayin' here!" It was the voice of a frightened, pouting child, who'd been lied to by his parents once too often.

"Get your asses off this beach!" Miller yelled, his voice carrying across the gunfire-riddled water. "Make room for the next wave!"

Another pitiful private's voice called out: "These are all we got between us and the Almighty!"

The boy meant the triangle of steel rail he hid behind.

Miller's voice cut through the concerto of exploding shells and the machine-gun cross fire. "Every foot of this beach is in some Kraut's crosshairs! If the machine guns don't get you, an 88 will! And this tide is rising, an inch a minute! That seawall is life . . . you're all dead here!"

No more talking. They would either follow him or not.

And Miller charged out from behind the steel-rail obstacle, rifle at the ready, splashing through the shallows, weaving around dragon's teeth and floating casualties, while dozens of men emerged from behind the obstacles, joining him in the assault, whimpering survivors suddenly soldiers again.

Boys became men as they crossed the killing zone of Omaha Beach, often dead men, but men; many of their fathers had crossed a similar no-man's-land of furious enemy fire, a war ago. Running, yelling, screaming, crawling, scrambling on hands and knees, leapfrogging positions, zigzagging, high school athletes summoning their broken-field running skills, they worked their way toward the seawall.

Men whose rifles were jammed with sand, or who had lost their weapons in the water, plucked replacement guns from the dead. Shell holes provided temporary foxholes, a knocked-out tank—one of the few that had made it this far—provided cover. And as some men were brutally cut down, dropping to the sand or the gravel as the signal from their brain to the legs was severed, the merely wounded often found themselves scooped into the arms of a fellow GI, for hauling. Others could not be helped; the sound of wounded and dying men reverting to boys echoed across the smoky beach in an eerie lullaby: *Mama! Mama! Mother! Mom!*

Miller was crouched behind an obstacle, grabbing breath; not a steel-rail hedgehog this time, but one of the angled, mine-capped logs, this one tree-trunk thick and providing decent cover. Huddled behind the obstacle next to him were a trio of wild-eyed privates clutching typewriters and cardboard boxes.

"What the hell are you doing?" Miller shouted, getting his voice over the popping gunfire.

A freckle-faced kid answered, "One Hundred and Fourth Medical Battalion, sir! Here to set up field operations!"

"Do you see anybody who could use a fucking typewriter right now?"

"No, sir."

"Get rid of that shit and find a weapon. Follow me!"

On the sand now, out of the surf, but the going still slow, Miller didn't risk firing, too many GIs up ahead of him. Many of the men were so burdened down with waterlogged gear they could barely walk let alone run, some of them shedding gear as they went.

Two kids, trotting weaponless to the sanctuary of that seawall, helped each other out of wet uniforms. They were down to trousers and T-shirts when a GI with a flamethrower next to them caught a round in the canister. Flames burst out, engulfing him and the two boys as well. The boys ran like human bonfires screaming along the beach, other soldiers staying out of their way as they dashed along in an orange and blue blur, until machine-gun fire mercifully cut them down. Now they were just three more burning obstacles to navigate.

Next to Miller a soldier muttered, "That's goin' to hell in a hurry."

Miller, the horror of that knotting his bowels, dove behind another steel-rail obstacle. He needed a moment. Just a moment . . .

"Help me outa here," a voice said.

Behind the steel-rail obstacle next door, Lieutenant Frank Briggs lay, slumped in the sand.

"Caught one low," Briggs gritted. "Something hot . . . inside me. Feels like there's a fuckin' shot put in there. . . ."

But Briggs was not alone. A pair of combat engineers were wiring the dragon's tooth Briggs was sheltered behind, working quickly and nimbly.

Miller scrambled over and shoved the nearest of the two, who was wrapping explosives around the base of the obstacle. "What the hell do you think you're doing?" Miller demanded.

"Navy Beach Battalion, sir!" The engineer was in his mid-twenties with a pale oblong face and unblinking brown eyes; he nodded to the dragon's tooth. "I gotta blow this bastard."

"Why in hell?"

"Make a hole for the tanks."

"What fucking tanks?"

The engineer returned to his work. "Orders, sir."

"All our armor is floatin' in the fucking Channel! Look around you!"

"Go away, sir!" Suddenly the engineer had a fuse lighter in his hand. "We're blowing this one."

Time for discussion seemed over; Miller grabbed

Briggs by his pack harness, leaving the stupidity behind, dragging the lieutenant into the smoky rain clouds ahead, and their deluge of bullets. A soldier running alongside Miller soon passed him, and the captain realized the GI, who was shouting, "Medic, medic, medic!" was carrying something like a rifle that was in fact his arm; the recent amputee made it to the seawall, hurling his severed arm over it as if it were a grenade and flopped to the relative safety along the wall.

In combat, such strange sights could only be witnessed, not absorbed. But Miller's mind was still in the process of cataloging the oddity for later reflection when the mortar shell landed nearby, throwing him in the air, and setting him back down again.

Miller swallowed, brain whirling, ears ringing—but at least his hearing hadn't gone this time—and checked for his legs, knowing that wounds sometimes didn't register at first, shock stifling the pain. Bullets were buzzing like stirred-up hornets all around him. His nostrils were choked with the stench of burned powder, and the acrid, greasy taste of it was in his mouth, as well.

But he was not wounded, anyway nothing more than assorted new shrapnel nicks. He grabbed Lieutenant Briggs by the pack harness strap, and scrambled to his feet, hauling Briggs toward that seawall again. Only Miller seemed stronger now, as if the impact of the mortar shell had bolstered rather than sapped him; no—it wasn't that he was stronger, but that Briggs was lighter. . . .

The lower half of the lieutenant was gone.

Woozy, Miller dropped the half-a-man, like a suitcase, and suddenly something slammed into him, *someone* slammed into him: Sarge.

And the sergeant was grabbing hold of him now, propelling him along. Then Miller got into the swing of it, hobbling with Sarge the last dozen yards as bullets pinged and popped around them.

They hurled themselves to the gravelly ground along the edge of the seawall. Miller had never been this exhausted, this spent, not in civilian life certainly, not even in battle. His eyeballs burned, his every bone ached, his muscles were a twitchy, aching, unresponsive mass.

All along the seawall, other brave, lucky, exhausted soldiers were tossing themselves to the relative safety of the seawall, up and down the beach. Still, the machine-gun and mortar fire continued, raining lead on the gravel and the sand inches away; the noise of this storm of bullets and shells was relentless. Near the seawall casualties were mounting, piling up.

"Can't tell the dead from the wounded," Miller said.

"Not without a scorecard," Sarge said.

They spoke over the constant cries of "Medic!" "Corpsman!" "Aidman!"

Along the seawall, faces were turned toward

Miller, faces belonging to soldiers largely stripped of their gear, not to mention their dignity, huddling under this scant cover. They had made men of themselves, crossing that bloody beach. But now, at a sort of rest, the scramble across the beach over, they were boys again, their precarious shelter allowing the fear to take over.

Miller looked at these scared kids, some of them weeping, out of control, and asked anyone who cared to respond to the terrible question: "Who's in command up here?"

Two answers were simultaneous: machine-gun and small-arms fire, from the pillboxes and dugouts above, said that the Jerries were in command.

But several of the young privates shouted the other awful answer to that question: "You are!" "You are, sir!"

Miller looked at Sarge and whispered, "That's what I was afraid of."

"Don't get *your* ass killed," Sarge whispered back, "or I'll be in charge."

"Hell, we don't want that," Miller said, finding a smile somewhere. "Then you would be a sorry bunch of sons of bitches. . . . You recognize where we are?"

Sarge shrugged. "About a mile from where we're supposed to be?"

Hearing this, a soldier down the seawall called out, "Nobody's where we're supposed to be!"

The private next to Sarge, a round-faced kid, said,

"He's right, sir, we're all mixed-up. We got leftovers from Fox company, Able, George, plus some Navy demo guys and beach masters."

Miller surveyed his ragged mix of regiments and companies, and, knowing that their seawall shelter was only a temporary stop on their way, repeated to himself, *That's what I was afraid of.*

3

Taking inventory of his men, Miller moved low along the seawall, with Sarge trailing after him. Amid the chaos of the living, dying, and wounded, a young radioman was keeping his head, barking into his shoe-boxlike, antenna-sprouting handset. Miller scrambled up to him, grabbing on to a shoulder. The radioman, a blond kid, craned around and found himself looking at a captain.

"Ask about our air support!" Miller demanded, shouting above the gunfire. "Tell 'em we got no goddamn air support!"

The kid nodded, turned away, relaying the message. The cough, cough, cough of mortars was followed by booming blasts and the whistling of shrapnel.

Miller grabbed the kid's shoulder again, and the radioman looked back expectantly.

"And tell 'em," Miller continued, "no heavy armor is making it onshore! The C-3 gully is not open! Ask 'em, where are the fucking DD tanks? They're no-where near the draws!''

The radioman nodded again, turned away, holler-ing into his headset. Machine-gun fire rattled from above. The boy had finished relaying his message, and Miller again grabbed him by the shoulder, pull-ing him around, saying, "And tell 'em . . .''

But the words caught in the captain's throat: the young radioman was no longer listening, having fi-nally lost his head, half of it anyway, his face shot away. The boy tumbled lifelessly to the sand, and Miller grabbed for his radio, but it, too, was bullet-riddled, shot to shit. Shaken, Miller drew back against the seawall, away from the beach where bul-lets continued kicking up little sandstorms.

Private Robert Reiben, twenty-four, Brooklyn, New York, plunged from the beach under a welcoming committee of machine-gun chatter and hurtled him-self against the seawall, between his captain and sergeant.

"I'm takin' this up with Eisenhower," he said. Rei-ben was a lanky fair-haired smart-ass whose old man was Jewish and mother Irish, explaining the kid's reddish-haired, pasty looks.

Sarge asked him, "Seen anybody else from the platoon?"

"Jackson," Reiben said, nodding down the seawall a ways. The Southern sharpshooter, his beloved

Springfield rifle in hand, had made it to temporary safety. "But that's it."

"Mellish, here, sir!" a voice called from the other direction, along the seawall.

"Caparzo, too, sir!" another voice called from the same direction.

Miller craned out enough to spot them, sharing cover; then he ducked back as Caparzo's voice continued: "Wade's back there with DeForest, but Dee's so shot to hell, he's sprung a hundred leaks."

"Where *is* Wade?" Miller called back.

"Out there on the beach," Caparzo yelled, "tryin' to plug up those holes!"

Finally, through the floating smoke and scrambling men, Miller spotted the company medic, Corporal Edward Wade, San Diego, California, at twenty-eight one of the oldest of the captain's boys. The small, dark Wade was kneeling over Private Brian DeForest, twenty-one, DeKalb, Illinois, trying to save him, despite a sucking chest wound that would seem to make the effort futile. Wade was bloody up to his elbows, his white armband spattered as if its red cross were dripping.

Wade was ignoring a senior medical officer's orders to move on to the next patient, insisting, "He's not gone, sir." As men dropped around him in the killing zone, Wade calmly piled up bodies, using them as human sandbags, to give himself some cover to keep working on his buddy.

"Wade!" Miller called from the seawall. "Wade! Aidman! *Wade!*"

But Wade either did not hear his captain or ignored him, too.

Miller shouted, "Mellish—Caparzo . . . haul Wade's ass off that beach! We're not losing our fucking medic!"

The sandbagged bodies were getting chewed up by machine-gun fire, like a saw through wood, but Wade kept at it, administering plasma. Then a slug passed through one of the corpses and caught DeForest in the side of the head, and the medic lost his patient.

"Fuck!" Wade screamed, shaking bloody fists. "Shit!"

That was when Caparzo and Mellish hauled the medic off the beach, dragging him to the seawall.

Miller turned to Sarge. "That's it? That's all of us that's left?"

"Not necessarily, sir. We got scattered pretty bad. Bound to be more of us around, somewhere."

"Not enough. Not enough."

Miller was thinking of that LCVP and how he sent his boys out into the slaughterhouse of machine-gun fire. But the harsh cough of mortars and the whistle of shrapnel was all around—no time for reflection.

"Where's DOG-1?" he asked Sarge. "Where's our damn exit?"

"Gotta be that cut on the right."

"Yeah?"

"Or maybe that one on the left?"

"No," Miller said, thinking. "Vierville is west of us. It's gotta be the one on the right."

A mortar blast hit the sand near enough the sea-wall to kill three of the huddling soldiers, ripping them to pieces.

A voice near the carnage shouted hysterically: "They're killing us! They're fucking killing us! We don't have a chance! It ain't fair!"

Miller looked toward the voice. It belonged to a corporal, an experienced "old man" like himself, probably in his late twenties. If somebody like that could come apart, these younger, inexperienced boys were like grenades with the pin out. Time to move.

"Gather firepower!" Miller announced. "Whatever you got, whatever you can find! Drag 'em in off the sand if you have to! Those weapons aren't doing any-body any good out there!"

Word was relayed up and down the seawall; hol-lers followed by a murmuring among the men, who seemed spurred by the thought of taking action. Sit-ting along this seawall, waiting for shrapnel or an exploding 88 or a ricocheting slug to catch them, had lost its appeal.

Sarge turned to Reiben. "Where's your B.A.R., Reiben?

"Bottom of the drink, Sarge." He grinned. "Bastard tried to drown me."

"Find another."

"It's in the bag, Sarge."

And the cocky bastard scrambled out onto the beach to find a replacement for his Browning Automatic Rifle. Similar actions were being taken all along the seawall, as troops, galvanized by the thought of a breakout, were gathering guns and ammo, fishing for armament, braving bullets to pull in such valuable catches as machine guns, bazookas, M-1's, and .45 automatics.

Miller had his eye on the thicket-line concertina-curl of barbed wire atop the seawall.

"We need stovepipes," he said. "That'll tear up the barbed wire and set off any mines in the ground nearby."

"Stovepipes!" Sarge called, and the word was picked up all along the line, up and down the seawall, various voices calling, "Stovepipes!" "We need Bangers!" "Bangalore torpedoes!"

Then somebody called back, "We're lookin', we're lookin'. . . . Where are those engineers? . . . Jackpot! Bangalore torpedoes!"

Elsewhere along the seawall, privates Caparzo and Mellish, joining the scavenger hunt for weapons, were hungrily eyeing a .30-caliber machine gun that lay on the sand like a child's discarded toy.

"You run faster'n I do," Mellish said.

"You're a smaller target," Caparzo said.

"You're Italian. They might take you for an ally."

"Oh, yeah?"

"Yeah. Plus, you kinda look German."

"Shove it. First one there owns the son of a bitch!"

And they both broke cover, racing out to grab the weapon, scrambling in the sand, returning moments later, holding the weapon in both their arms, grinning at each other like proud parents mutually cradling a newborn.

Elsewhere along the seawall, Sergeant Horvath had just presented Miller with a Thompson submachine gun and several spare clips.

"Hot damn," Miller said.

"So you can let 'em know we was here," Sarge said with a nod at the Thompson.

Other weapons—and men willing to use them—were gathering on either side of the captain and sergeant. A private with a flamethrower still strapped to his back reported in to Miller, staying low, as well he should.

"I'm impressed," Miller admitted with a tiny smile. "You brought that all the way in, from the other side of hell?"

More LCVP's were landing, even now. Waterspouts geysered in the sea and surf, courtesy of German 88's.

"Not by choice, sir," the boy grinned. He was a slightly goofy-looking kid with an overbite. "Buckle jammed, and I couldn't get the damn thing offa me!"

The boy proved his point by yanking on the strap.

"Don't tell 'em that when they put you up for a medal," Miller advised the private.

"No, sir."

A pair of sergeants from the 149th Engineer Combat Battalion crawled along the seawall, staying low, each with a pair of TNT-packed three-foot lengths of pipe—bangalores. When they reached Miller, the captain directed that the procedure begin. These torpedoes were designed for assembly under fire, the lengths of tubing inserted into another and another until they formed a long pole-like pipe that could be edged up on top of the seawall and threaded through the nest of barbed wire. When the bangalore blew, it would burst sideways, ripping a passageway in the concertina wire.

That, at least, was the plan.

It took many hands to accomplish this, and Miller knew that if this day, this invasion, was to succeed after all the failed planning and miscalculations by the brass, it would be thanks to ragtag teams of common soldiers, improvising desperately, like these men around him. These kids in khaki were gearing up, cleaning the sand out of weapons as best they could, working bolts, checking actions, loading ammo, kissing rosary beads. He caught a glimpse of Mellish and Caparzo grinning as they oiled the kinks out of their newly acquired machine gun. But most of them were strangers to Miller, and he loved them like the two children waiting for him at home.

The stovepipe assembly of TNT was inching toward its mark, edging up the seawall, nosing into the tangle of barbed wire. Miller watched the bangalore's progress, riveted, as Wade moved in alongside him, medic's pack at the ready, the blood wiped from his hands, though his sleeves were damply black and his palms were stained a deep terrible pink.

"Good to see you, sir," Wade said quietly.

Rock steady, this one.

"Good to be seen," Miller admitted.

"Papa loves his new baby," Reiben was saying, nearby. He was loading a B.A.R.

One of the engineer sergeants from the 149th gave Miller a thumbs-up: the bangalore was in position.

"At your discretion, Sergeant," Miller told him.

The sergeant pulled the pin on the ignition cap in the final tube, shouted, "Fire in the hole!"

"Fire in the hole!" Reiben shouted, and the cry was picked up all along the seawall as soldiers took cover.

The explosion was just another of many on this overcast morning, though it multiplied with mines it set off. When the smoke and dust cleared, a wide gap in the barbed-wire barricade provided an exit from this bloody beach.

"We're in business!" Sarge shouted. "Let's get through that hole!"

Miller heaved himself up the seawall and scrambled through the gap, a dozen men right behind him, Reiben and Mellish and Caparzo and Wade and, of course, Sarge among them, sprinting into the beach flat beyond, where waited patches of high grass and marsh, dotted with scorched areas where the bangalores had set off land mines. The soggy, swampy terrain slowed the soldiers only slightly, as they raced toward the steep, eroded slope that promised cover in its deep, winding furrows.

But the fire of the German machine guns was redirected, to track the runners and try to stop those coming through that gap in the barbed wire. Two men went down in the marsh, and another died tangled in barbed wire.

And, on the beach side of the seawall, this discouraged other soldiers who were considering making the run through that hole in the concertina tangle.

Then one private said, "Shit, if I'm gonna die, least let me be headin' uphill," and lunged over, and through the wire. That ignited the remaining troops. Two more waves of a dozen men or more broke cover to follow the private's lead in the footsteps of Miller and his men.

By that time, however, Miller and the remains of his platoon and a few other hearty soldiers were starting up the slope, sticking to the deepest furrows, which provided natural cover. Of course, the erosion furrows could just as easily cloister Germans, and surely did. But none had shown themselves thus far. . . .

As the other troops joined them, the machine-gun

fire halted, lending an eerie silence to their efforts. The GIs traversed different winding furrows of the escarpment, breaking off into little groups slinking through the maze of natural trenches, leap-frogging positions, keeping low, working their way uphill. Now and then they would pause to assess a blind turn.

A group of five soldiers in the erosion trench ahead of Reiben was doing just that; then they looked at each other, exchanged mutual shrugs of *What the hell,* and took the turn. Another group was right behind them, and Reiben, cut off from Miller and the other guys from the platoon, was bringing up the rear. But before the second group rounded that blind curve, small-arms fire so dense it sounded like an explosion ripped the silence to shreds.

Two of the first group that had rounded that corner came scurrying, screaming back, olive-drabs red-splotched, eyes popping, legs churning, colliding into the next group, knocking them over like bowling pins. Suddenly everybody was piling up in the narrow passage, clogging it, creating a bottleneck of tumbling, fumbling men, trapped among their own flailing arms and legs as if dancing to the dissonant music of small-arms fire.

This ungodly human traffic jam stopped Reiben in his tracks, and he watched with a weird sense of detachment as German potato-masher grenades came cascading from around the corner, arcing through air, four of them, eight, twelve of the damn things, plummeting down on them like tiny bombs from tiny planes.

Reiben dove in the opposite direction, hitting the dirt just as the dozen small explosions collaborated into something terrible and large. Then as he propped himself up on an elbow, alive, unwounded, a yellow-gray cloud of dirt and cordite rolled through and a dreadful red rain fell, spattering the trench, and Reiben.

Sickened, frightened, smeared with gore and dirt, he scrambled to his feet and went back the way he came. Just then a familiar voice reached out to him, and he followed it, the captain's voice, calling, "*This* way! *This* way!"

Miller, spurred by the sounds of gunfire and exploding grenades, was running up a deep rut with half a dozen soldiers following his confident lead: Sarge and Mellish and Caparzo among them. A relieved Reiben, taking a fork in the furrowed pathways, fell behind the pack. Up ahead of Miller were three privates who rounded a corner and were barely out of view when the twin thunder of exploding land mines signaled Miller to throw on the brakes.

The captain caught himself with the heel of a palm, digging a crumbly groove in a dry dirt wall; then he peered around the corner of his gully-like path and saw the sad, seared remains of two of the soldiers, tossed to either side, like fender-flung animals along a roadway.

And an equally sad sight tightened Miller's eyes: blue-yellow-brown smoke floating over and around him and his dead buddies, the third GI, eyes wide, face clenched, stood petrified with the knowledge that he was a human tree planted in a minefield.

Then came an incongruous sound: whistling. Not the whistling of artillery shells or mortar shrapnel, but human whistling, as if to summon a prize pet. The common sound, so eerie in this context, echoed down the furrow, and was followed by a voice: "Fritz! Fritz!"

A German voice.

Sure enough, a dog came charging through the narrow gully from behind them, like an apparition from a simpler, kinder time, surprising Miller and his men. They reflexively grinned at the dog, not even thinking to catch it, as it bolted right past them, a Rin Tin Tin trailing its leash, eyes bright and alert, tongue lolling. The animal took a fork away from the furrow where land mines held their terrified hostage, and Miller glimpsed a gray-coated, kettle-helmeted form dart from behind a turn in the path to take the joyfully barking, leaping German shepherd into his arms and pull the animal into safety, around the corner, out of sight.

Miller was momentarily touched by this shared humanity: here was a soldier who loved his dog, like any boy would love his dog.

This rare moment of brotherly contemplation was interrupted by the German soldier reappearing to aim his rifle and shoot the land-mine-locked GI in the side of the head. The bullet entered the boy's left ear and traveled through his brain and sent him tumbling to the ground, where he did not set off a mine.

Then the German was gone, the barks of his dog diminishing as master and mutt retreated to some unknown position.

4

Smoke drifted lazily bearing the sour fumes of powder and the appalling stench of singed hair and burned flesh as Miller paused at this fork in the trench pathways. The execution-like death of the private trapped in the minefield did not elicit a comment from the captain or the boys bunched up behind him, a motley group of muddy, bloody GIs that included the remnants of his platoon. Some things were too terrible to comment upon. Perhaps what was most terrible was the shared knowledge that in the German's place, they might have done the same.

"We're fucked!" a boy behind him was saying, trying to sound angry but the fright coming through. "The Krauts got all the exits mined!"

The slightly muffled sound of war continued as machine guns from somewhere above them sprayed the beach, and the occasional 88 shell made the earth shiver.

Sarge said to Miller, quietly, "It wasn't no picnic gettin' here, sir, but gettin' out's gonna really be a bitch."

"A son of a bitch is more like it," Miller said, and turned to give his boys a smile that he hoped didn't look as forced as it felt. "That dog, Fritz, knew the way out."

Mellish, chewing gum nervously, said, "You think that mutt knows where the mines are?"

"That hound is German personnel," Miller said matter-of-factly, "and they got to travel up and down these draws every day, don't they?"

And with that, Miller, the Thompson in his hands poised for mayhem, took off at a trot up the pathway Fritz had chosen. After the slightest hesitation, his troops followed after him, and they had gone a good distance up the inclining trench when their captain raised his hand for them to halt.

The pathway was rising to, and about to empty out into, a gap in the escarpment, the walls of the trench ending. Though their position was low, essentially placing them at a dead end, the GIs could view across the slope of thirty feet of hard, dry earth to an outcropping of rocks and dirt. It was an inviting straightaway, with one exception: the rattle of machine guns and the popping of small-arms fire blasting down at the beach had gradually risen in volume, and the *poof poof poof* of mortars sounded close by, too. Running across that gap might put Miller and his men in range, in sight, of the Germans manning those positions.

"We're at a blind angle," Sarge said as the group huddled within the walls of the trench. "Won't know what we're up against till we poke our heads out."

"Who's got a bayonet?" Miller asked, and one was passed up to him. "Who's got a mirror?"

A small shaving mirror found its way to the captain, who looked back at Mellish and said, "Say 'ah.' "

"Huh?"

"Close enough," Miller said, plucking the wad of chewing gum from the private's open mouth.

Puzzled eyes were fixed on Miller as he stuck the sticky wad to the tip of the bayonet blade and stuck the little mirror into the gum; the mirror was wobbly in its perch, but secure enough to do the job, he figured. Then, as his men grinned and nodded around him, the captain eased the bayonet out, just enough to angle it around and get a view.

A hell of a view, in the shaky little mirror: about twenty yards beyond their position, and another thirty yards to the left, rose a bluff overlooking the beach; but it also flanked the gap between their sheltering trench and that protective outcropping. Roosted there, twenty-some feet above them, were two two-man machine-gun crews, blasting down with tripod-perched MG-42's at the beach from their heavily sandbagged emplacements. Two mortar teams were firing their deadly rockets from the bluff as well, and a handful of infantry were guarding the position, popping occasional small-arms fire at the beach below, as if shooting pigeons.

Miller swallowed, and carefully angled his make-shift periscope higher, hoping he'd seen the extent of it; he hadn't.

Ten yards beyond the machine-gun nest, built into that bluff, squatted a camouflage-draped, wire-festooned, flat-headed concrete bunker, the long thick tapering snout of an 88mm cannon jutting from the wide narrow smile of the bunker's firing port. The big gun belched fire and thunder, shaking the ground, almost toppling the little bayonet-mounted mirror.

Pulling the mirror back in, Miller reported: "We got a nest on the bluff, with a pair of Hitler's zip-pers." Miller was referring to the MG-42's with their capacity of ripping through 1200 rounds per minute. "Plus two mortars, and an 88 through an embrasure to the rear of 'em."

"Position?" Sarge asked.

"Add twenty yards, left thirty."

Sarge nodded toward the outcropping. "There's our perfect firing position; we can hit their flank. But it's no walk in the sunshine."

Miller twitched a non-smile. "Let's get off our dead asses and get these draws open." He turned to the four GIs huddled nearest him and nodded to each in turn.

He spoke to the other troops gathered in the trench. "When they take off, we'll cover 'em with suppressing fire. At this angle we're not likely to hit anything, but it'll distract the bastards, keep 'em busy."

Nods from all around. Reiben patted his new B.A.R., as if soothing it.

"Those MG-42's are heavy sons of bitches," Miller told the four boys. "The Jerries shouldn't be able to jockey 'em around in time. There's some infantry up there, so you're gonna get some small arms thrown at you. Zigzag . . . don't bunch up. Weave like a drunk on New Year's . . . got it?"

Four young faces looked at him and nodded, two of the boys swallowing.

"Then go!"

Rifles in hand, the quartet of soldiers scrambled up the furrow and disappeared over the rise, dashing into the open area.

Miller blasted up toward the bluff with the Thompson, firing blindly from the trench. The others joined in and sent a firestorm in the general direction of the German position. Small-arms fire returned, intense volleys, but none of the slugs seemed directed toward the trench where Miller and the others were shooting.

That could only mean the Germans' lead was raining down on that open area where the boys had run.

When the shooting stopped, cordite scorching the air, Miller called out, "Report in!"

Silence.

The captain scrambled up the rise and ducked out for a quick look. The four sprawled, smoking, blood-soaked bodies of the boys were scattered about the open area as if they were making snow angels.

Miller dove back, as rifle shots narrowly missed him, turning dirt to dust.

Sarge greeted him with a whisper: "It's a fucking firing squad. You oughta hand out blindfolds."

Miller whispered harshly back: "You got any other ideas for getting us the hell out of here?"

The captain turned and selected four more men, saying, "You're next."

"Captain," Sarge said softly, "they're gonna have those zippers in position now. . . ."

Miller didn't acknowledge the remark. To the other troops, he said, "Let's see if we can get a better angle. . . ."

As Miller and his men repositioned themselves in the trench, the second group of four moved solemnly to the rise of the pathway.

"Go!" Miller shouted.

And the four boys grabbed deep breaths and scurried up the rise, racing out into the open, even as Miller's Thompson opened up, and Reiben's B.A.R.

and every rifle in that trench, fired upward, blindly, but firing. Jackson had positioned himself up on the rocky wall within the trench to get a shot, and one of the infantrymen crumpled under the Southern boy's dead aim.

That wasn't enough to quell the river of gunfire the Germans were pouring down into that open area, and this time, when the firing ceased, and Miller's cry of "Report!" went unanswered, the captain did not bother going out to look to see what had occurred.

He knew. He knew.

Miller looked out at the eight men who remained, and his eyes fell on Reiben's blood-speckled mug. The boy grinned suddenly and said, "Captain, is this a bad time to put in for my transfer?"

"Not at all," Miller said, managing the barest grin himself. "I'll meet you on the other side, and we'll start the paperwork."

Then he selected another three boys, as Sarge looked at him with an expression that stopped short of accusation, but conveyed to Miller the madness of what they were doing.

This caught Miller short, and he stopped and considered his options for a moment. Then he said to Reiben and the other boys, "Let's hold up a second . . . Jackson!"

The lanky sharpshooter ambled forward. "Yes, sir?"

"You ready to get across?"

"Good a time as any, sir."

"Get ready for my signal," Miller said, and he scrambled up the rise into the open and just stood there, brazenly, presenting a perfect target. Up on the bluff, the nearer of the two machine-gun teams reacted as if he'd goosed them, and began repositioning their bulky weapon on its tripod.

"Go!" Miller hollered.

And Jackson was taking off through the open space just as the machine-gun fire was redirected toward Miller, chewing up the ground, stirring dirt clouds. The captain dove back in the trench, machine-gun rounds ripping the heel off his boot. In the meantime, a zigzagging Jackson was dodging small-arms fire as he neared the outcropping of rock and dirt.

Sarge and Reiben had caught the diving captain, dragging him down into the furrow.

"Your mother would be very upset with you," Sarge said, "if she saw that kinda behavior."

"I thought you were my mother," Miller managed, breathing hard.

Then Miller called out: "Report!"

Jackson's voice returned: "Yo!"

Miller and Sarge exchanged grins. Others in the trench were smiling, too. Suddenly machine-gun fire hammered down on them, and they sunk down as low as they could in the furrow, dust and rocks flying, stirred up from the thunderous machine-gun barrage. Reiben screamed obscenities, and the others were yelling, too, and it was as if the world had gone mad.

But Miller—who figured this rapid-fire bullet storm was an expression of frustration from those pissed-off machine-gunners, at having their fire drawn away from the gap—knew that Jackson would not likely succumb to the madness of the moment.

Right about now, Miller figured, Jackson would be praying. . . .

And Jackson, standing behind the hillock of rock and dirt, rifle propped and angled toward that bluff, doing his best to tune out the noise and fury surrounding him, was in fact softly saying, "Be thou not far from me, O Lord." He was also taking careful aim at one of the German machine gunners hunkered over an MG-42 on its tripod. Motion and smoke were blurring in the crosshairs of Jackson's sharpshooter rifle.

From across the way, his captain's voice came: "Jackson—do you have a shot?"

Target steady in his crosshairs, Jackson called back: "Send over a batch!"

And the Southern sharpshooter squeezed the trigger, gently, so gently, and the rifle crack was lost in the machine-gun fire, which suddenly halted as the man firing stopped. A bullet had snapped the gunner's head back, as the bullet sped through his forehead, through his head, punching an exit out of the back of his steel helmet. The dead gunner's partner, stunned, was moving the body aside, fumbling as he took over the weapon. . . .

Down in the trench, Sarge was saying, "We're in business!"

And three more GIs, Reiben among them, scrambled from the trench and sprinted like hell. More followed, including Sarge, Mellish, and Caparzo carrying their heavy .30 caliber machine gun.

At his outcropping position, Jackson was taking aim again, and praying, "Oh, my strength, haste thee to help me," firing again, sending to hell or glory the German who'd replaced his dead partner, the Jerry pitching over, knocking the MG-42 off its tripod. Its chattering halted, the heavy machine gun tumbled down the bluff, and its barrel caught one of the GIs running below on the back of the head, dropping him unconscious to the dirt. Reiben grabbed him and dragged the man behind the outcropping.

From up on the bluff, a German voice rang out: "Die flanke! Die flanke!"

They were his last words: a classic between-the-eyes shot by Jackson made it three for three.

"Amen," Jackson said.

With the machine gun down, the German flank was wide open. Everybody picked up on Miller's wild cry and he and his spitting Thompson led his boys out from behind the outcropping they'd worked so hard to reach. Then they charged up the steep but navigable slope.

The other German machine-gun team, who had kept their aim on the beach throughout this episode, were now desperately, frantically trying to reposition the bulky weapon on its tripod. They shifted it to their flank, where the handful of supporting infantry was taking position, and mortar teams were scattering for weapons.

Miller was yelling, "Pour it in there, goddamn it! Pour it on!"

Two thirds of the way up the slope, Caparzo and Mellish were able to slam their machine gun down and open fire, raking shrieking Germans off their feet. Reiben was at the top already, advancing toward the machine-gun nest where that gun was not yet repositioned, training the deadly force of his B.A.R. on them, blowing huge holes through the sandbags and only slightly smaller ones into the pair of Germans who'd been manning the gun. Both flopped, dead, one onto the MG-42, the other across the ruptured sandbags, blood and sand seeping.

The battle was fierce and short. Miller and his boys swarmed the German position, and while a few GIs fell, every one of the Jerries went down.

That kid who'd made it to shore with a flame-thrower had the last word, spraying the area with fire, incinerating the enemy, bullets on cartridge belts on burning bodies exploding like firecrackers. Orange and blue flames licked the sky, and thick black curls of smoke accompanied them.

"Bunker!" Miller shouted.

The GIs pressed on, racing for the bunker, from which erupted scattered rifle and machine-gun fire, angling through its firing port. Two boys went down, but the rest were too fast, coming in too low, slamming themselves against the cement below the port and the shaft of the 88 muzzle.

"Grenades," Miller said, and pins were popped, pineapples lobbed over their heads, pitched right through the horizontal port, and the boys ducked and covered as multiple blasts soon followed, and dark smoke streamed out like fleeing ghosts.

"Let 'em have it!" Miller shouted, getting onto his feet, his boys following his example as he emptied his Thompson through that port, which didn't seem like a smile at all now. The GIs pounded rifle and even handgun fire through the concrete mouth into that fucking bunker, just to make goddamn good and sure. . . .

The aftermath was a dazed fever dream, as the living moved among the dead, the terror and adrenaline wearing off into numbed aftershock. The only one who didn't seem to be sleepwalking was Wade, his medic duties at the fore now; he was hurrying to the aid of wounded men, summoned by moans and cries. Some of the boys helped him out.

Limping due not to a wound but his shot-off heel,

Miller, Thompson in hand, stumbled across the charred bluff, the stink of burned hair and flesh and gunpowder no longer bothering him—he was alive. He wasn't happy; more like stunned. He had never expected to make it off that goddamn beach. That he had made it this far was more than he, or any of his men, had expected.

This shared feeling went unremarked upon. No need to express the obvious. The words didn't exist, anyway. They were here, they were alive; that was all. That was enough.

Sarge was kneeling to scoop up some dirt and shovel a handful into a small metal container, with a white slash of tape across it, inscribed in smeary blue ink, "France." Miller smiled to himself as he watched Horvath screw the tin lid back on, and stuff it back into his pack where the captain knew two other, already earth-filled tin cans waited: one marked "Africa," the other "Italy."

Reiben, walking in circles, B.A.R. hanging, was saying, "I'm not dead," over and over again, softly, a shell-shocked mantra.

Mellish had discovered a souvenir. He rose from where he had found a knife that had fallen to the ground. Its blade was wicked, its handle inscribed with a swastika.

"Hitler Youth knife," Miller informed him.

Mellish smirked. "Now it's a Shabbat challah cutter."

"What," Caparzo said, "you gonna circumcise some Germans with that thing?"

"I said a bread knife, shithead," Mellish said, tucking it into his belt. "Not that that's a bad idea. . . ."

"My God," Sarge said softly. Almost prayerfully.

Miller joined the sergeant, who was standing at the edge of the bluff looking out on the beach.

"Hell of a view," Sarge said.

On the horizon an endless row of Allied ships watched silently as landing craft after landing craft weaved through carnage and obstacles, heading inexorably for the beach, Higgins boat gates lowering, seasick troops scampering through the surf, streaming onto the sands, seeking cover behind dragon's teeth, running for the safety of the seawall through an obstacle course of flames, smoke, and the scattered refuse of the fallen. Along the shoreline dead Americans floated, bumping each other, near the shattered, burning hulks of wrecked landing craft. Tanks and bulldozers slept through it all, on their sides, snoring smoke and flame. Shells continued to burst, in the water, on shore, geysers of water, showers of dirt and sand and stone.

Yet still the American soldiers came. Nothing stopping them. Advancing.

It was a terrible landscape of destruction and death. And a magnificent testimony to the resolve of those fighting and dying here.

"Hell of a view," Miller agreed.

The tide had come way in, and—though from his vantage point, Miller couldn't tell—had gentled, breaking easily over the debris all along the scorched, disrupted beach. Helmets, smashed radios, gas masks, mine detectors, reels of wire, weapons of all stripe—rifles and machine guns and bazookas—and bodies, so many bodies, lay on the sand, the driftwood of battle carried in and out with each wave. Stenciled on the backpack of just another one of the many dead soldiers sunning on this beach was a last name: RYAN.

But, of course, from where he stood, Miller couldn't see that.

PART TWO

The Pentagon, Washington, D.C.
June 8, 1944

5

Within the limestone walls of the sprawling, fortresslike War Department building—a year-and-a-half old, the five-sided edifice was the largest office building in the world—another battalion fought the war. The rat-ta-tat-tat was not that of machine guns, however, but typewriters, and foxholes were replaced by desks, as row upon row of somber clerks served their country, typing the words "We regret to inform you . . . killed in action . . . heroic service . . ."

In its way, this duty was as harrowing as combat. These men and women—middle-aged and older, most of them, many with sons in the service, with daughters married to boys who were serving— were creating telegrams that would break the hearts of mothers, fathers, brothers and sisters, sons and daughters, all around the forty-eight states.

But typing the same words again and again can numb the senses. Still, no one in this vast chamber of an office took the work lightly, or became indifferent to the paperwork of death; no small talk or laughter, even the nervous variety, here.

And when Lucy Freemont—forty-two, a local girl, brunette, married, her husband overseas, a Navy ensign—placed a sheet of paper atop the ever-growing pile in her "OUT" box, and moved onto the next file, the name "RYAN" did not at first penetrate her boredom. She had scrolled a fresh sheet of paper in her typewriter before a second word—"IOWA"—registered upon her, and a frown tightened her sad expression into something troubled.

The terrible tedium was suddenly broken, as Lucy rustled and ruffled through the stack of papers in that "OUT" box, looking for a telegram she'd typed up a little more than an hour ago. Then she flipped through the manila-folder files and double-checked. The eyes of her coworkers followed her as she rose quickly from her desk and hurried from the typing pool.

From Lucy Freemont to the lieutenant supervising her, and to his supervising captain, the disturbing news was passed. The reaction of the female civilian clerk was mirrored by the Army men, who were visibly shaken by what she had discovered.

Lucy was out of the picture by the time Captain John McRae—twenty-eight, Peoria, Illinois, clear-eyed, square-jawed—carried the news to the next link on the chain of command.

Colonel Richard Wilson, who had lost an arm in

Sicily, was typical of General George Marshall's habit of appointing wounded officers to his staff. The colonel oversaw a bustling war room whose walls were papered in maps of Normandy and whose desks were spread with complex deployment charts. Coffee and cigarettes were the fuel of the military and civilian aides and secretaries scurrying about.

Colonel Wilson, forty-seven, Atlanta, Georgia, had the grizzled look of a combat veteran, though his uniform with its pinned-up left sleeve and chest full of ribbons looked crisp, particularly considering its wearer hadn't slept for a day and a half. He was pouring himself the latest of an endless succession of cups of coffee when Captain McRae approached him.

"Colonel," the captain said, "something's come up you should know about."

Wilson, standing near a map on the wall, pins indicating troop positions, sipped his coffee, noting the three sheets of paper the captain was holding in two hands, like notes for a speech he was about to make.

"Well, what is it, Captain?"

"Better read for yourself, sir."

The captain handed him two of three sheets. Wilson glanced at them, and the words "RYAN" and "IOWA" were on both of them. He sat at the nearest desk as the captain hovered, a third sheet ominously in hand.

"These two men died in Normandy," McRae said, leaning in. "One at Omaha Beach, the other at Utah."

"I can see that," Wilson said, reading the death notifications. "Thomas Ryan. Peter Ryan. Brothers?"

"Yes, sir. And this man . . ." He handed Wilson the third sheet of paper. ". . . This man was killed last week in New Guinea."

"Daniel Ryan," the colonel said. That word "IOWA" again. "My God . . . brothers? Three brothers, all killed in action?"

"Yes, sir. And I've just learned that this afternoon their mother will be receiving all three telegrams."

Color drained from the colonel's face. "Jesus," he said. It was almost a shout.

The bustling in the room stopped; the aides, the secretaries, froze at the colonel's uncharacteristic outburst.

"Jesus," Wilson said again, more softly now.

"There's a fourth brother in Normandy, sir."

Wilson frowned. "I don't see a fourth death notification. . . ."

"No. At least, not yet, sir. The fourth brother, James, he's the youngest, sir—parachuted in with the 101st Airborne, night before the invasion."

"Where the hell is he now?"

"We don't know, sir. Somewhere in Normandy, presumably."

"Alive?"

"We don't know that, either, sir."

Wilson covered his eyes with his hand, leaning on his elbow. Whether he was thinking or praying, his team around him couldn't say; but they provided him with the respectful silence he required.

When he noticed this, it embarrassed him, and he barked, "Get back to work," rose from the desk, nodding curtly to McRae, saying, "Come with me."

As the colonel and captain in Washington, D.C., strode from the war room, a black government sedan was tooling along a dirt road in Mansfield county, Iowa, in the rich farm country outside Peyton. Dust stirred as the sedan moved through a corridor of ripening corn, endlessly green in buttery sunlight. The black sedan—out of place in this all-American landscape, a hearse at a county fair—turned at the big metal mailbox painted with the name RYAN down a lane leading to a white farmhouse and a red barn and a green windbreak, on a manicured yard that was an island in a cornfield ocean.

Kids grew up here—boys. The evidence still remained: a tire swing in the yard, a bushel basket nailed high on the side of the barn over a hard-dirt basketball court. Those boys had no doubt sat in the porch swing now and then. It was empty now—though the wind was moving it, gently, as if two invisible young lovers were sitting there, spooning.

In the window of the farmhouse was the proudly displayed flag of blue stars—four of them, one for every member of the family in the armed services.

The mother of the four boys, Margaret, sixty, stepped onto the porch, her blue and white calico dress lifting gently in the wind's whisper. Her husband, William, was in town buying supplies; she was alone on the farm. Just how alone, she would soon know.

She had been smooth and pretty as a girl, but a life of hard work on this farm, and raising four boys into men, had grooved her face handsome. The sound of the approaching car had summoned her from her cornbread batter, and she wiped her hands on her apron as she watched the dust rising behind the black sedan.

Seeing that sedan approach her house made her uneasy, but this lane was shared by four farms. They might not be stopping here.

But they did, and as the three men stepped somberly from the car—one of them in a clerical collar—she collapsed against a post of the porch, hugging it as if it were a small child. She began to cry, knowing that she had lost one of her boys, thinking of how hard her husband would take this, never imagining this terrible news could be worse. Far worse.

By this time, half a country away, in the Pentagon, the Army Chief of Staff, General Marshall, was meeting with Colonel Wilson and the general's aide, Colonel Louis Dye.

Wilson stood to one side, in the wood-paneled, spartanly appointed office of the general, his neat-as-a-pin desk flanked by American and District of Columbia flags. The general and the colonel were poised at a nearby conference table, on their feet, reading the files on the Ryan brothers.

General Marshall, a tall, fit, weathered sixty-four, dark close-set eyes and a thin line of a mouth highlighting a ruddy, unsymmetrical, rather homely face, softly said, "Goddamn it."

He tossed the file on the conference table.

"Iowa again," he muttered. Then he demanded: "How did we let this happen, after the Sullivans?"

The question seemed to have been lobbed the captain's way, so McRae said, "Originally, all four of them were in the same company in the 29th Division, but we split them up after the Sullivans."

The five Sullivan brothers of Waterloo, Iowa, had all served on the same ship, the *Juneau*, torpedoed off Guadalcanal in November, 1942. The tragedy had alarmed and even outraged the public.

"Sir," Colonel Dye offered, "it's not even official Army policy to separate or protect brothers in any way. It's the Navy who put that rule into motion, and besides, as I say, these Ryans weren't serving together. . . ."

"Would you like to be the one who informs Surles of this?" Marshall snapped.

Brigadier General Alexander Surles headed up the War Department Bureau of Public Relations.

"Not particularly, sir," Dye admitted.

"Can't you hear him?" Marshall asked dryly. " 'The public's going to think the armed services declared open season on Iowa boys!' . . . Any contact with the fourth brother . . . what's the boy's name?"

"James," Wilson said. "No, sir. He was dropped about fifteen miles inland, near Neuville."

The thin line of Marshall's mouth twitched. "And even now that's deep behind German lines, I take it?"

"Yes, sir."

"We don't know that for sure, sir," Dye said, stepping forward. "First reports from Ike's guys at the SHAEF said the 101st got scattered to hell and gone." The colonel shrugged and spread his hands. "Misdrops all over Normandy. We had a high casualty rate, after all. He may not even have survived the jump. Even then, he's probably KIA."

Marshall said nothing; his homely face was set into a grave mask. He moved to his desk and flipped the intercom switch. "Captain Newsome, the Bixby file, please."

"Yes, General," a female replied from the intercom.

"Private Ryan could be anywhere, sir," Dye picked up again. "If we send a patrol flat-hatting around, through swarms of German reinforcements, all along our axis of advance . . . we'll be sending out death notifications to all of *their* mothers."

Marshall shook his head, seemed to sigh but no sound came out.

A businesslike, rather severely attractive dark-blond WAC entered: Captain Florence J. Newsome, Marshall's personal secretary. She handed him a manila folder, he thanked her, and she exited.

The general moved slowly to his desk, got behind it, and withdrew a worn sheet of paper from the folder. "I have a letter here, written some time ago, to a Mrs. Bixby in Boston . . . if you'll bear with me. . . ."

The colonel and the captain exchanged glances—a soldier would always "bear with" a general—as Marshall put on his reading glasses.

" 'Dear Madam,' " he read. " 'I have been shown in the files of the War Department a statement of the Adjutant General of Massachusetts that you are the mother of five sons who have died gloriously on the field of battle. I feel how weak and fruitless must be any words of mine which should attempt to beguile you from the grief of a loss so overwhelming. But I cannot refrain from tendering to you the consolation that may be found in the thanks of the Republic they have died to save.' "

Marshall put the well-worn piece of paper down on his desk, atop the folder. But he was not finished: merely finished reading.

" 'I pray that our Heavenly Father may assuage the anguish of your bereavement,' " he said from memory, " 'and leave you only the cherished memory of the loved and lost, and the solemn pride that must be yours to have laid so costly a sacrifice upon the altar of freedom.' And it is signed: 'Yours very sincerely and respectfully, Abraham Lincoln.' "

The captain and the colonel exchanged another glance; both were moved, deeply so, but neither was surprised by Marshall's feelings on this subject. This was a general who had refused to accept medals for himself for service on the home front while boys were shedding blood overseas.

The soft contours of the general's uncomely features hardened—the eyes glittered with resolve.

"If that boy is alive," Marshall said, "we're going to send somebody to find him . . . and get him the hell out of there."

That was just what Captain McRae had been hoping to hear; and, judging by the faint smile Dye was wearing, McRae suspected that the colonel, for all his attempts to discourage Marshall, felt exactly the same.

PART THREE

Normandy
June 9, 1944

6

As a convoy of jeeps, tanks, and other vehicles rumbled along nearby, Captain John Miller sat with the remnants of his platoon—privates Reiben, Caparzo, Mellish, and company medic Wade—within the scooped-out shelter of an 88-shell hole in a field of such craters, enjoying a few moments of R & R after a C-ration lunch. Their khaki green almost blending with the caked brown of the crater, Miller's men looked older to their captain, their rumpled uniforms, several days growth of beard, and half-lidded eyes telling a story of coming to age the hard way. Only Sergeant Horvath had carried this look into combat with him; and even he seemed older now. Or at least, more weary.

"You think it's true," Reiben wondered aloud, lanky frame sprawled out, holding his B.A.R. straight up like a flagpole, "that the Japs pull out your toenails with pliers, to make ya talk?"

"Wrong theater," Sarge said.

"I'm just thinkin'," Reiben said, "maybe we're lucky, not bein' in the Pacific. I hear stories about bamboo shoots and a guy's dick I wouldn't wanna repeat in such tender company."

Mellish, the youngest among them, took that as an insult and blustered, "Hey, they don't have a shoot long enough for me to even feel it."

That made everybody laugh, though muffled explosions, at some distance, cut the laughter off abruptly, the war reminding them it would be waiting for them, after their breather.

"Still," Reiben mused, "this is pure fucking torture, sittin' here, six measly miles from Caen."

"What's in Caen that's such a big hairy deal?" Sarge asked, lighting up a Lucky.

"Jesus, Sarge," Reiben said, grinning, "don't you even know what Caen's famous for?"

"Frog nuts à la mode?"

Reiben shook his head as if pitying his sergeant. "It's hard on a cultured guy like me, keepin' such unrefined company."

"We were 'tender' company a minute ago," Caparzo said, lighting up his own smoke, a Chesterfield.

Reiben chose his words carefully, painting a picture. "Caen, in historic Normandy, is noted for the manufacture, the . . . fabricatication . . . of"—the private's eyebrows flicked up and down—"lingerie."

"Yeah?" Sarge said, and farted with his lips. "So?"

"Imagine some little French number, a curvy Caen cutie pie"—Reiben traced imaginary curves in the air with one hand—"raven-black hair, blue eyes, little beauty mark near red-rouged lips. . . . After she's been spendin' all day, every day, sewing cream-colored, sheer-body nighties with gathered empire waists and silk cups, with gentle uplift." He demonstrated with a cupped hand. "What the hell you *think* she's gonna wear at night?"

"Dr. Denton's?" Sarge asked.

Reiben frowned. "Sarge, you got no romance."

"Hey," Sarge said defensively, "she works around the stuff all day. It's a busman's holiday."

"On the other hand," Mellish said, caught up in Reiben's word rhapsody, "maybe she gets a discount."

"Reiben," Miller said, genuinely interested, Thompson submachine gun cradled in his lap, "what the hell makes you such a lingerie authority?"

Pride perked the private; beneath the stubble of beard and rumpled ODs, an American kid still dwelled. "Family business, sir. Lingerie's my life. My mother's got a shop in Brooklyn. Grew up around it. From the time I could crawl, I knew about Caen lingerie. Best there is, lotta demand—men buyin' for their wives and/or girlfriends, females for their fella. . . ."

"Case you haven't heard, there's a war on," Miller said. "I kinda doubt they're still makin' lingerie down the road, there."

"Oh, Captain," Reiben said, shaking his head no, a thousand times, no, "they'll always make lingerie in Caen. It's one of the three basic needs of man—food, shelter, unmentionables."

The rest of the platoon was considering that proposition, and finding nothing in it to argue with, when Miller noticed a runner who seemed to be heading their way. The captain nodded to Caparzo to meet the runner and retrieve the message. Caparzo nodded and clambered out of the crater.

"If things hadn't been so *foobar* on the beach," Reiben said, "we'd probably be in Caen right now, hip deep in glamour pusses and silk." He smirked humorlessly, shook his head. "I mean, what the hell Einstein was it came up with this plan? Send a thousand guys fresh off the base into a fuckin' hell storm?"

"You're Rangers," Miller said flatly. "Elite trained troops."

"Yeah, sure," Mellish said. "No offense, sir, but would they send a guy from the farm league to play in the fifth game of the world series?"

"If the draft board took the first team away," Sarge said, "you bet your ass."

"Back in the states and across the Channel," Mellish continued, "they told us what it was supposed to be like, and we talked about it and everything, and we trained our asses off, simulations and that shit. But the second I jumped off that Higgins boat,

I thought, fuck a duck! Nothin' coulda prepared me for this!"

A distant explosion added a second exclamation point to Mellish's sentence. This, and his words, provided food for thought for the men in the shell crater.

Finally the medic, Wade, said, "Big show like that, they can't prepare you for." He shrugged. "Maybe they figure if you're surprised enough, the fear won't kick in so bad."

"Maybe," Mellish said. "But if that was the plan, it didn't work for shit."

Miller asked, "Hey, Reiben, tell me—if you had to hit bloody Omaha Beach again, how d'you think you'd react the second time around?"

Reiben didn't miss a beat. "By shooting myself before I ever got off the goddamn boat."

"Let me know if you need any help," Sarge said, good-naturedly, and everybody laughed a little. But the laughter was followed by solemn thoughtful nods from men who knew what Reiben meant.

Caparzo hopped into the crater. "Captain," he said, "Battalion C.O. wants you back in the rear area in a hurry."

"Maybe the war's over," Miller said, and climbed out of the hole.

"Be sure to let us know who won," Sarge said, a wry half smile dimpling his stubbly cheek.

Field headquarters, above the beach, was a dizzying swirl of vehicles and personnel and kicked-up dust, spurred by the rumble of explosions that weren't next door, but weren't far away, either. Miller wove through men and jeeps, making his way across ground pocked with the aftermath of shell fire from weapons of every size. He was heading to a sprawling, heavily damaged concrete bunker that the Americans had taken over as their HQ.

Within, the remnants of the former occupants—debris and abandoned equipment, twisted rebar, cement fragments from pebble to slab, a few dented German helmets, even a tattered Nazi flag—had been shoved over and unceremoniously piled to one side. Otherwise, the bunker complex had been tidied up, providing an orderly contrast to the chaos outside.

Miller was met by a surprisingly crisp-looking major of about forty, who the captain saluted, saying, "Miller, C Company, Second Rangers, reporting as ordered, sir."

"Go on in, Captain," the major said, gesturing, and Miller moved deeper into the complex.

Perhaps a dozen officers were bustling within the bunker, and at least as many aides, runners, and radiomen, all of them in uniforms that, while not pristine, maintained a trouser crease, at least. Within this proper military setting, the captain stuck out like the dirty, unshaven, blood-spattered sore thumb he was, but his presence brought only respectful nods and the occasional, combat-casual salute.

Seated at a small scarred wooden table, talking on

a field phone, was Lieutenant Colonel Walter Anderson, forty-two, Denver, Colorado, the commanding officer of the Second Ranger Battalion. Slender, his narrow face grooved with character, the C.O. acknowledged Miller with a nod, then motioned with a traffic-cop palm, for him to wait.

"We expected thirty-two tanks to float to the beach," Anderson was saying into the phone. "Twenty-seven went underwater. . . . I understand your problem, but if we don't get those dual drive Shermans onto the beach by oh-six-hundred, we're gonna have an entire division at Carentan with its pants down around its ankles and a target painted on its ass."

A steaming cup of coffee and a half-eaten sandwich were on the small table. Anderson ignored them.

"All right," Anderson concluded curtly, "let me know when." He slammed the field phone into the hook and spoke to a passing aide: "Hold Baker Company up at Vierville till we can get some armor up to them."

"Yes, sir," the aide said, and scurried off.

Anderson rose and strode to a large map pinned to the concrete wall, gesturing for Miller to join him, which the captain did.

"Airborne was supposed to open a door for the rest of us," the lieutenant colonel said, shaking his head as his eyes searched the map. "Instead they mis-drop, scatter all their damn sticks to the wind. . . . What's your situation, John?''

"Sector four is secured," Miller said. His manner was quick, methodical. "We took out 88's here, here and here." And he pointed to the spots on the map. "Unfortunately, this was after they'd nailed four Shermans and some trucks." He pointed to another area. "Your map indicates two minefields, but it's actually one big one."

"How did you determine that?"

"By trying to go between them."

This was Miller's way of telling his C.O. that he had taken casualties due, in part, to faulty intelligence.

"It's a mixed, high-density field," Miller reported, coolly, almost coldly. "Sprengmine 44's, Schumine 42's, Pot Mines, the A200's, and a few of those little wooden sons of bitches that our detectors can't pick up on." Miller pointed to another section of the map. "They also planted some big mushrooms in the road for tanks, Tellermine 43's, I'd say, from here all the way to the edge of the village."

"You marked them?"

"Yes, and called for engineers."

"Resistance?"

"Mainly pocket actions. I had higher support expectations. No counterfire, though." He pointed to yet another area of the map. "We encountered an understrength company with the artillery . . . Wehrmacht, 346th Infantry, von Luck Kampfgruppe."

"Prisoners?"

"Twenty-three. Turned 'em over to division MPs from the 29th."

"Well done. Our casualties?"

"Thirty-five dead. Wounded, times two, sir."

Everyone in the room had heard this, but no one looked Miller's way. Only the silence that draped the bunker indicated the horror and respect shared within these concrete walls.

"Jesus," the C.O. said finally.

"The Jerries didn't want to give up those 88's, sir," Miller said matter-of-factly.

Anderson's mouth twitched in a non-smile. "It was a tough, thankless assignment. That's why I picked you for it."

"Yes, sir."

"And I have another one for you."

"Sir?"

"It's another beauty, John." Anderson shook his head, laughed a little; there wasn't much humor in it. "This one's straight from the top."

Miller felt as if he'd been struck a blow in the pit of the stomach. "Eisenhower, sir?"

"Marshall." Anderson nodded to the little table. "Find a chair, get yourself some coffee. I'm to give you all the background. . . ."

When Miller trooped back into the crater field, a

little less than half an hour later, he was greeted by Sergeant Horvath, with a simple one word question: "Caen?"

"Not hardly. We're taking a squad up to Neuville on a mission."

Sarge pushed his helmet back, exposing his frowning forehead. "A captain leading a squad? What the hell kinda mission can that be?"

Miller grunted a laugh, smiled half a smile. "A public relations mission, Sergeant."

"What the hell . . . ?"

"Some private in the Hundred-and-First . . . three brothers bought the farm, and little brother a ticket home."

"I'll be damned. Why Neuville?"

"That's where the brass thinks he landed. He's up there somewhere, one of those poor misbegotten misdropped bastards."

Sarge blew some air out. "This ain't gonna be easy, tryin' to find one lone soldier in the middle of this big goddamn war. Findin' a fuckin' needle in a haystack."

"A haystack of needles," Miller said glumly.

Sarge nodded his head toward the crater, where the platoon's remnants still lounged. "What about Charlie Company?"

"I get the pick of the litter. Rest get folded into Baker."

Sarge's eyes popped, his jaw dropped. "Jesus Christ, they took away your company for this?"

"First of all, it's not my company, it's the Army's. . . . The C.O. reminded me of that, in case I forgot. Second of all, there's not that many of us left. Anyway, I want Reiben on B.A.R., Jackson, Wade, of course, Caparzo, Beasley . . ."

"Beasley bought it."

"Shit. Okay, that kid Mellish. We got anybody that speaks French?"

"Reiben is fluent in lingerie. Other than that, not that I know of."

"Talbot, then. His accent is for shit, but he knows his stuff."

Sarge shook his head. "Gone. This morning."

"Damn." Miller sighed. "I'll go see if I can find another victim. A French-speaking one. . . . Round up the rest, meet me at Battalion Motor Pool, on the beach."

"Yes, sir."

Above the beach a short distance, in the midst of a staging area, rose the clean, taut lines of a tent, a beacon of order in the brouhaha of roaring vehicles and babbling GIs. Moving slowly but steadily, as unnoticed as a ghost, Miller wove through this movement of men and machines, skirting as well stacks of supplies and heaps of equipment. He entered the tent, which housed that contradiction of terms, military intelligence.

At three tables were three corporals, huddled over maps like bookworms boning up for the big test. It was tedious, precise work, gridding maps, covering them in plastic; but it was not terribly dangerous, unless a stray shell should find them.

"I'm looking for Corporal Upham," Miller announced.

One of the boys raised his eyes from his map: slender, rather baby-faced, his eyes were gentle, thoughtful, and gray behind thick glasses. They refocused as he looked at Miller. A distant explosion—very distant—was enough to make him jump.

"Sir," he said, "I'm Upham."

"I understand you speak French and German."

"Yes, sir," said Corporal Tim Upham, twenty-four, Boston, Massachusetts.

Miller came closer. "How's your accent?"

Upham pushed at the bridge of his glasses, which were slipping down his unsubstantial nose. "A slight one in French. My German is clean, with a touch of the Bavarian."

"Good. I'm Captain Miller. You've been reassigned to me. Get your gear."

"Sir?"

"We're going to Neuville."

Upham smiled nervously and gestured back to his map, spread out like a tablecloth. "Uh, sir, there are Germans at Neuville.",

"That's my understanding."

"Quite a few of them, is my understanding."

Miller glowered at the kid. "Wouldn't you expect to find Germans, behind enemy lines, Corporal?"

Upham motioned to himself with both hands. "Sir, I've never been in combat. I'm afraid I'd be a liability to you, sir. I'm a mapmaker. I translate."

"I need a translator."

"You do?"

"Both of mine were killed."

Upham, who was pale to begin with, whitened further. "Sir, I haven't fired a rifle since basic training. . . ."

"It's just like riding a bicycle—you never forget."

"I never learned how to ride one of those, either. Sir . . ."

"Where's your gear stowed?"

"I'll, uh . . . I'll get it, sir."

"Good."

"Sir?"

"What?"

"Can I bring my typewriter?"

"Your typewriter."

"I'm writing a book, and I . . ."

Miller just looked at him. Was he kidding?

The nervous smile again. "Well, then . . . how 'bout a pencil?"

Miller made a small "C" of his thumb and forefinger. "A little one," he said.

Upham nodded sickly, and turned to go retrieve his gear.

"Look at the bright side, son," Miller told the boy's back. "Live through it, it's research. You'll have some good stories to tell."

Upham just looked at him. Was he kidding?

"Go, go," Miller said, shooing him off.

The other two corporals, hunkered over their maps, wore faint smiles of relief. Miller sighed and went back out into the war.

7

The dead and wounded were long gone now, the wreckage cleared, Omaha Beach a vast tableau of military history in the making. Barrage balloons hovered over the sloping sand and its swarming troops and mountain range of stacked material. Just offshore, a horde of bustling engineers were assembling the sections of a massive Mulberry harbor, towed across the Channel in treacherous weather. Ships' cranes lowered brimming cargo nets into waiting DUKWs, and tanks and bulldozers began their cumbersome crawl off the sand. On the horizon of waters that looked blue now, not gray, the thousands of disparate ships comprising the Allied Armada kept watch as explosions inland provided a rumbling reminder, for all the stunning scope of this invasion, of a campaign not yet won.

Streams of vehicles wound up the sand dunes, moving off the beach, and among them was a jeep crammed with GIs: Captain Miller (riding shotgun, navigating) and his squad of seven—Sergeant Horvath driving, Corporal Upham between the sergeant and captain, and in back, sardines, the medic Wade and privates Reiben, Caparzo, Jackson, and Mellish. Speeding along, weaving around the various other vehicles and slogging-along advancing infantryman, the jeep of GIs seemed to be leaving the bulk of the American Army behind.

Soon they were tooling down a hard-packed dirt road, stirring dust, bouncing along through sun-dappled, lushly green countryside broken up periodically by the occasional quaint stone farmhouse. This scenic route was grotesquely littered with the road-side refuse of war: twisted, burning vehicles, cars, trucks, wagons, German and American alike, abandoned equipment, and bodies carefully laid out and cloaked with mattress covers. Occasionally a dead animal, a horse or cow with spilled entrails, added to the stench of death—singed hair, burned flesh, vacated bowels—that wafted on the gentle breeze riffling roadside foliage.

Bespectacled Corporal Upham was taking this in with wide eyes bulging in an ashen, nostril-flared face, as he sat cradling a pristine M-1, nestled between Sarge and the captain, who ignored both the glorious and grotesque aspects of the scenery in favor of the map he was unfolding.

From the cramped backseat, where soldiers seasoned by bloody Omaha Beach were taking in the view calmly, came Reiben's voice: "Captain, would a question be out of line?"

"Depends on the question."

"Where are you plannin' to put Private Ryan, sir? I mean, this buggy doesn't have a rumble seat."

Miller, eyes searching the map, didn't reply.

"I mean, sir, it's just that it's kind of crowded back here."

Miller unfolded more of the map, eyes narrowing.

"I was just wondering," Reiben continued, "if maybe you're expecting to have more room on the way back."

Miller gestured to the left at a fork in the road ahead.

Sarge, following the captain's directions, asked, "We in radio contact with anybody up there?"

"Most of our radios are lost or busted," Miller said. "Somebody fucked up and sent the wrong crystals for the ones we do have left. The few that work are gettin' jammed by German signals. We're goin' in blind."

"Hell of a mission. Regular walk in the park."

"Yep. Hell of a mission."

Upham cleared his throat. "So, uh, you're all Rangers?"

Reiben, Jackson, and Caparzo glanced toward the front seat as if an insect had landed there and they wondered if it were worth swatting. Wade was watching the countryside glide by. The debris of war was easing as they moved deeper inland.

"I'm Upham," Upham said cheerfully, glancing back, offering a hand that nobody shook. "That's Corporal Upham . . . but you don't have to call me that. I know you don't stand on formality in combat."

Nobody said anything.

"I mean," Upham said, pushing his glasses up his nose, nervously smiling, "I realize all of that, uh, military etiquette kinda breaks down in battle. . . ."

Mellish fixed a ferrety gaze upon the new meat. "There's only one reason you're along for this ride, Upham."

"Yes. To Translate."

"No. As food, in case we get lost, or get bored with K-rations."

"Amen," Jackson said, his sharpshooter's rifle held protectively to him, like a child he was sheltering.

"Nobody's eating the corporal," Miller interjected absently, eyes still slowly scanning the map. "Violation of the Geneva Convention."

"Even the Germans won't do that, Corporal," Sarge reassured Upham, taking his eyes off the road, despite his alarming speed. "Like the man said, they can kill you but they can't eat you. It's against the law."

"Besides," Miller said, "Upham here speaks French, and his German has a touch of the Bavarian."

The men in the backseat shrugged and looked away. Upham withdrew into himself, like a turtle into its shell. They jostled along, occasionally hitting a rut and bouncing. After a while Caparzo leaned forward.

"Captain, where's this Ryan come from, anyway?"

"Iowa, Private Caparzo. The great Middle West."

"Iowa?" Reiben echoed caustically. "Oh, well, that's different. Who wouldn't mind riskin' his ass to save some fuckin' farmer? The world couldn't get along with one less sod buster, it's not like it's rainin' fuckin' sodbusters back home or anything. Western civilization would cease."

"You know Gleason, in Baker Company?" Caparzo asked Reiben.

"Yeah, I know the asshole."

"Asshole is right. Always picking fights, when he isn't pickin' his nose."

"Gleason, who spits on the mess hall floor?" Mellish asked. "*That* Gleason?"

"Gleason," Jackson asked, "who don't go to chapel?"

"That's the shitbird," Caparzo confirmed. "I'm pretty fuckin' sure *he's* from Iowa."

"We're not saving Private Gleason," Miller said. He hesitated, as if caught up in a moment of soul-searching. "I'm going to tell you all something you're not supposed to know."

All eyes fell on Miller—even Sarge's, which was

disconcerting considering that they were flying along the rutted dirt road, which they seemed to have to themselves now. The thunder of explosions continued—not as distant.

"I got a look at Ryan's service record," Miller said, "which is exemplary."

"That changes everything," Reiben said.

"But," Miller continued, "it also included his high school report cards—he got an A-plus in civics and won the school's Good Citizenship Award . . . two years in a row. Now—isn't that worth risking your asses over?"

Upham clearly didn't know what to make of this dry sarcasm, but Reiben played along.

"Was he an Eagle Scout, sir?" the private asked.

"Youngest in the history of the state of Iowa. Forty-eight merit badges."

"Jack Armstrong, all-American boy," Reiben said. "That's who we're rescuing."

"Pretty much."

"Well, you're sacrificing Beethoven to do it."

Mellish couldn't follow that; neither could anyone else in the jeep, except Reiben himself, who explained, "See, it's like I'm Beethoven."

"You couldn't carry a tune in your helmet," Caparzo said.

Reiben gestured with one hand, as if directing an orchestra, clumsily. "Beethoven was the greatest composer who ever lived and then he goes deaf; some fuckin' irony, huh?"

"What the fuck's 'irony'?" Caparzo asked. "The next village over?"

"No, shit for brains. Irony is me, the Beethoven of ladies' foundation garments, footsteps away from Caen, the center of the lingerie universe, and instead I'm going to Neuville to save some fuckhead farmer who's probably already dead, is irony."

"Look at the bright side, Reiben," Miller said.

"What bright side is that? Sir, you know what Neuville is famous for?"

"No."

"Cheese."

"Really."

"Everybody and his duck is goin' to Caen, where the only way you won't get laid tonight is if your dick got blown off in the bad sense of the phrase, and we, the gallant survivors of Charlie Company, we're goin' to the goddamned cheese capital of France. There *is* no bright side. Sir."

"There's always a bright side, Reiben."

"I'm listening, sir."

"Well, I, for one, like cheese. When's the last time you had a decent piece? Of cheese?"

Reiben glowered, hugging his B.A.R.

Upham asked Miller, "Shouldn't we really have a tank for this mission, sir?"

Miller didn't get the chance to answer that—which

he wouldn't have, anyway—because the jeep was rounding a corner and Sarge was skidding to a stop, confronted suddenly by a bottleneck of backed-up American vehicles, tanks, dozers, jeeps. Through the dust cloud Sarge had stirred moved an M.P.—a first lieutenant—and three enlisted men, playing traffic cop along the roadside.

"Lieutenant!" Miller called.

The M.P. spotted the twin captain's bars on Miller's helmet and came quickly over, leaned against the jeep like a drive-in waitress taking an order.

"We gotta hold up here, sir. Eighty-eights are knocking hell out of our traffic."

"How's the road to Neuville?"

"Suicide run, sir."

Miller glanced at Sarge. They traded facial shrugs, knowing they had no choice. Orders from General Marshall were not to be ignored.

"Let us through, lieutenant," Miller said.

"Sir . . ."

"Let us through."

"Yes, sir."

The M.P. waved them through, and Sarge rode the side of the road and bridged the shoulder, passing the traffic jam, and soon they had the dirt road to themselves.

Or nearly so. The crater-pocked roadway was strewn with burning wreckage, the fog of dust and smoke creating an obstacle course that Sarge swerved through with set jaw and glittering eyes. Barreling along, Sarge veered without slowing around first one jeep, then another, both having taken direct hits and were now scorched, smoldering abstract sculptures. Then the jeep of GIs roared around an American troop truck, on its side, torn apart as if it were a paper bag, spilling flame. The truck had already spilled and strewn onto the roadside the charred bodies, the glowing human embers, of at least a dozen soldiers.

"It's something out of Bosch," Upham uttered, unable to look away from the nightmare vision. Nobody in the jeep knew what he was talking about, except Miller, though his expression gave no indication of that.

"Shhh," Miller said.

Upham said, "I told you, we coulda used a tank. . . ."

"Quiet, I said."

Calm green hills rose on either side of the road now, and Miller's eyes were slowly scanning them, searching for the source of the 88 shell that had destroyed that troop truck.

Sarge eyed the captain. "Got a line on it?"

"No. Step on it, will you?"

"Why didn't you say so?"

And Sarge floored it, hitting ruts, narrowly avoiding craters, bouncing the boys in back like rubber balls. They gripped the sides and each other and did whatever they could not to get themselves and their weapons and gear flung out.

"Hell," Caparzo yelled, "this beats Coney Island all to shit!"

Then they hit a crater, and the bump was huge, almost wrecking the vehicle, shaking its every nut and bolt and part, sending Reiben up in the air like a teeter-totter, and slamming him back down.

"Shit, fuck!" Reiben yowled. "I landed on my goddamn entrenching tool!"

"Just trying to make room for Private Ryan," Miller said, eyes still glued to those hills.

Reiben, who appreciated dark humor, grinned at that, and shifted his entrenching tool from under his bruised behind.

When they rounded the next bend, a long, straight stretch of road awaited; but half-a-dozen smoldering, smashed vehicles littered it, indicating the gauntlet they would have to run.

Sarge barreled down the road, as all eyes—except Corporal Upham's—nervously searched the surrounding hills.

"Captain," Mellish said with brittle, forced good humor, "something just occurred to me. . . ."

"What would that be, Private?"

"We're the front now. Point of the spear. Leading the charge. We go a foot, the front goes with us. Wouldn't that be correct, sir?"

"That would be correct. Everybody else is behind us."

Sarge was slowing now, trying to dodge the craters.

"And by everybody," Mellish picked up, "of course you mean, the other one hundred and fifty thousand GIs with the four thousand armored vehicles, all the ammo, the food. That's the everybody you're talking about, right, sir?"

"That's correct."

"Just checking, sir."

The unmistakable screech of an incoming 88 seemed headed right for them, then hit right in back of them, blasting a new crater in a shower of dirt and rock, greasy black fingers of smoke reaching out for the jeep.

"Sarge?" Miller prompted through a clench-toothed smile.

Sarge floored the jeep again, craters be damned. Everybody held on to whatever they could as the little vehicle rocketed along, swerving, jostling, but mostly flying. Then another shell screamed in and hit hard, and the earth seemed to quiver as they drove right toward the blossom of black smoke mingled with dust-dirt-rock debris.

Somehow Sarge skirted this new hellish pothole, and they came out of the smoke and dust like a plane through a cloud.

Sarge asked the captain, "You got him?"

Miller had caught the muzzle flash from the hills. But his eyes were fixed on another wooded hillside now, maybe three quarters of a mile from the road— possible cover, and out of the big gun's range. . . .

"Yeah," Miller said. "This road is zeroed . . . one big fuckin' target!" Miller nodded toward the left, where a farmer's field lay fallow. "Make a new road!"

Sarge yanked the wheel over, the jeep dropped off the cliff of the shoulder, nearly throwing everybody out. Somehow they held on, and stayed on the bucking bronco's back, settling in for the rough ride ahead, the jeep's gears gnashing as Sarge guided them up onto the fallow field, where the vehicle soon tore along the rutted terrain.

Behind them, like the footstep of a giant in pursuit, a screaming shell landed and ruptured the earth in a shower of dirt and rock. Smoke chased them as Sarge, not slowing a whit, did his best to avoid the biggest ruts, the nastiest bumps; occasionally he succeeded.

To their left, another shell hit, and dirt clods and stones cascaded down on them, hammering the jeep like hailstones, salt-and-peppering them with debris. They covered their faces, though not their eyes, from the dirt and smoke. Upham was coughing.

"Christ, they're pulling lead!" Sarge shouted. "Fuckers are *good*!"

Another explosion rocked the earth, lifted the jeep

onto its left side wheels, then set it back down, hard, as dirt and debris pummeled the jeep and its occupants.

"Try S-curves," Miller told the Sarge.

Horvath did as he was told, turning shallow curves without slowing, and the maneuver seemed to be working, until suddenly they had S-curved themselves toward a drainage ditch. Sarge tried to avoid it, jerking the wheel around, braking, but it was no good: the jeep took the fall and half its nose plowed into the dirt, in an abrupt stop that sent Reiben, Upham, and Wade flying out of the vehicle in various directions, depositing them rudely on the rutted earth, a child's scattered toys.

None of them were hurt, to speak of, and Jackson, Caparzo, Miller, and Sarge, who'd managed to stay in the vehicle, were more shaken than those who'd exited; battered by the sudden stop, they sat there stunned, jeep nosed in the ditch.

Miller, first to regain his bearings, leapt from the jeep and gave the vehicle a quick once-over.

"She's fine," he said. "This dirt is soft. . . ."

The banshee shriek of an 88 had everybody ducking. The boom was nearby, rupturing the earth perhaps thirty yards away, sending a mild shower of debris on them this time.

"Sarge," Miller said, scrambling into the shallow ditch, throwing his shoulder into the jeep. "Reverse!"

Sarge shook his head, clearing it, and threw the

jeep into reverse, its wheels spinning as Miller dug his heels in and pushed, at the exposed left of the vehicle.

"Come on, you shitbirds!" Miller yelled at the men in the jeep, and the others, who'd tumbled into the dirt, and were struggling to their feet, dusting themselves off. "You wanna ride or walk?"

Dazed, his squad—minus Sarge at the wheel—assembled themselves on either side of the jeep and did their best, putting their shoulders into it, trying to push that bastard out. But the wheels kept spinning, mocking them.

Then another 88 wailed toward them, and they ducked and covered as it blew another crater in the rutted field, with the expected debris and smoke pelting them, after.

This time, however, the big shell had landed to their right, again about thirty yards away.

Miller ignored that, and dug his heels back in, shoulder to the jeep.

"Captain," Sarge said, hands tight on the wheel, eyes anxious. "They got us bracketed. . . ."

"I know about bracketing," Upham said, stepping away from the jeep, turning in a fidgety circle, "I've read extensively on that subject. . . ."

The others were back at it, ignoring the corporal, working with their captain as he directed the sergeant to drive forward, then put it in reverse, getting a rocking motion going.

"Listen to me," Upham said. "The next shell is going to hit us!"

Miller kept at it, and everybody pitched in, even Upham, but the corporal's concern was catching, and all eyes were skyward but Miller's as they waited for that next shell to screech in.

"Captain . . ." Sarge began.

"Push!" Miller commanded, and his men did. They were making progress: the jeep was damn near out of the ditch.

"Uh, Captain," Sarge said, even as the scream of tires seemed to foreshadow that of the next shell. Wade, pushing along the side of the jeep, reached in and plucked his medic's pack out of the back, clutching it tight under one arm.

"Jesus Christ," Upham said near tears, "it's gonna hit any *second*. . . ."

This time when the jeep rocked, it lost ground, digging back in, deeper.

"Shit!" Miller screamed, and a shell screamed, too, coming right at them. Time was up. Snatching up his Thompson from the ground, the captain shouted, "Go! Go! Go!"

And then they were grabbing what they could from the jeep, weapons, gear, anything, scrambling, scattering, hauling ass and gaining precious yards.

"Hit the dirt!" Miller cried, and they did, tumbling to the rutted earth, sending small puffs of dust up as the shell howled in and hit and seemed to snatch the jeep in beastly tearing jaws and shake it, a direct hit, a stunning blast, the shredded vehicle cartwheeling thirty feet in the air, then slamming back down again in a flaming, flattened heap.

Barely outside the blast perimeter, the men felt the earth shudder and shake and held their helmets on tight as a deluge of rubble, dirt, rock, debris threatened to bury them. Slowly, they raised their heads, then themselves, their eyes traveling to the fiery, flat snarl of metal that had been their ride.

"Fucker's out of the ditch, at least," Caparzo observed.

A familiar, sinister coughing—so soft, compared to the 88's blare—sent Miller and his men to their feet, shaking off the detritus without trying.

"Here come the mortars!" Miller said, but the comment was redundant, as they all, except perhaps Upham, had recognized that harsh *poof poof poof poof,* and were taking off like sprinters toward those sheltering trees.

"Mama said there'd be days like this!" Reiben yelled as he ran.

The eight men dashed across the open field as small explosions went off around them, each man knowing that the exploding shells were throwing whistling fragments upward, outward, in a cone-like shower of death at worst and pain at best.

Upham stumbled, fell, and Miller plucked him from the ground like a flower and half dragged him to the edge of the field, where trees awaited, cover, shelter. At various intervals every one of them went crashing into the trees, breaking and snapping branches and twigs, collapsing to safety perhaps twenty yards in.

The cough of mortars soon stopped.

Miller's men were here and there, flopped onto the sloping ground, leaning against trees, heavily out of breath.

"Sound off if you're hit," Sarge said.

Nothing.

"Anybody?" Sarge asked, looking around him, not believing it. "Not even a shrapnel wound?"

Upham's hand was to his face. "My nose is bleeding, a little . . . but I'm kinda prone to that. . . ."

Everybody stumbled to their feet and looked around at each other, apparitions considering each other's existence. Amazement slowly dawned, as fear and adrenaline drained away.

"Nobody hit," Miller said matter-of-fact. "Good."

Panting, the men checked their body parts, found them present and accounted for. Everybody had their weapons, but some gear had been left behind or lost, in the jeep, on the run.

"It's a miracle," Wade said softly, still clutching his medic's pack.

If anybody else had said that but Wade, the squad might have laughed. Considering how much shrapnel had been flying out there, however, they all knew he was right.

"Yea, though I walk through the shadow of the valley of death," Jackson drawled softly, "I will fear no evil. Thank you, Lord. World without end, Amen."

"Maybe we got an angel on our shoulder," Wade said. "Maybe this Private Ryan's good luck."

Reiben looked back across the field at the smoldering, shattered carcass of the jeep.

"Let's not be too fuckin' grateful to that farmer," Reiben smirked, shaking his head. "He's makin' us *walk* the rest of the way, isn't he?"

8

Working their way through the wooded hillside, their captain led the squad to a pastoral vista as yet undisrupted by the war. No fresh sod thrown up by 88's or mortars, no ruptures in the pasture's grass to indicate land mines. That didn't mean the peaceful surface of the pasture, with its scattering of munching cows, didn't conceal mines; little of this countryside didn't secrete the Germans' deadly little welcome mats.

"Form a column and follow me," Miller instructed the men."Flankers out."

"Yes, sir!" Upham said, saluting.

Miller rolled his eyes, while the rest of the squad shook their heads. How had this idiot lasted this far into the afternoon?"

Miller began his slow, careful trudge across the cow field, stepping in cow pies as if they were stepping stones.

"Ah, hell's bells," Upham said as his boots sank in shit.

Behind the corporal, Reiben—following in the shitty path—uttered various obscenities, then called out to his captain, "Uh, sir—maybe you haven't noticed it, but we're up to our hips in yesterday's cow banquet here. There's trees edging the entire pasture—think maybe we should move over there?"

"No," Miller said. "Stick to the manure."

"Cap, it's sticking to me!"

"Follow my lead. All of you."

The men looked around at each other, realizing that their captain was intentionally walking in cow pies.

Caparzo's eyes narrowed as he tried to figure out this strategy, then he announced, "I get it—the cows know where the mines are. They got some kinda sixth sense or something."

"Yeah!" Mellish said from behind him, seeing the brilliance of that logic. "Nature builds in all kinds of defenses in helpless animals."

As the men gingerly stepped on manure piles, some of which were fresh enough to send ripe Bronx cheers back at them, Reiben, up ahead, said, "I don't get it. . . . If they got a sixth sense for recognizin' land mines, why do the dumb fucks walk right into the goddamn slaughterhouse?"

"Dumb fucks is right," Sarge's voice came from behind them. "You walk in the cow shit, you walk in the same path as the cows. None of these cows got blown to hamburger yet, so you 'helpless animals' won't, either. . . . Sixth sense my bleedin' ass."

Miller, hearing this, said, "Cows may not have a sixth sense, but they *are* naturally curious creatures. . . . Look at 'em."

The cows had all gradually turned to face the GIs crossing their field, brown and white statues, big eyes watching.

Miller, stepping in yet another squishy pie, grinned back at his men. "They're waitin' to be milked. Anybody thirsty?"

Having crossed the pasture, they came to a hedgerow, an example of Normandy's towering shrubs, so ubiquitous and potentially deadly; a mound of dirt half a dozen feet high topped by a lushly green jungle of vines, branches, roots, and trunks, the hedgerow was virtually impenetrable. They came upon a single gap in the row, where the farmer whose pasture this was could get his cows and equipment in and out. Through that doorway in the shrubs, a narrow, hard-dirt cart lane beckoned between this and a parallel hedgerow.

Sunken between hedgerows as it was, the road was a virtual trench, and should provide safe passage— as long as the Germans weren't covering that gap with machine-gun fire. Miller, when briefed by his C.O., had been informed of this threat, and decided to handle it himself, his own way.

"Hit the dirt," the captain told his men as they approached the opening in the shrub wall.

"You mean the grass," Reiben said. "Is it okay, sir, if we avoid the cow pies?"

"Stay low in case return fire comes flying through those bushes," Miller said.

"What does he mean, 'return fire'?" Mellish asked Reiben as they—and everyone else—had positioned themselves flat on the pasture floor.

Then their captain stepped out into the opening, blasting away with his Thompson, ejected shells flying, fanning the deadly gun around, muzzle belching flame and bullets, as he traced a wide C with the chopper that included chewing holes in the hedgerow opposite.

Ducking quickly back in, Miller threw himself to the ground. And waited.

Ten or fifteen seconds had passed when Miller got to his feet, "No return fire—should be okay—on your dogs."

And the squad, exchanging wild, wide-eyed expressions, the scent of cordite drifting, got up and followed their captain out into the shaded shelter of the hedgerow-lined lane.

"Sometimes I think the captain is tryin' to win the Wooden Cross," Reiben said.

"Bastard's charmed, I tell you," Caparzo said.

"The Lord's on that man's side," Jackson drawled solemnly.

As Miller—Thompson at the ready—walked point down the lane, his squad followed him warily in two groups of three, Sarge bringing up the rear. The shade helped, but in their heavy uniforms and gear, they were hot on this June afternoon, and worn-out. An utterly miserable Upham, who had been assigned the task of hauling Reiben's B.A.R. ammo, was loaded down like a packhorse; appropriately, he was slapping at horseflies.

The hedgerow gaps into fields were rare, but whenever they approached one, they slowed, eyes cautiously scanning. Between gaps, they talked quietly, killing the time, seeking to make their hazard less burdensome by losing themselves in the common human act of conversation.

"So, um," Upham said to Mellish, "where are you from?"

"Go fuck yourself."

Upham swallowed. So much for Mellish. Waving off a horsefly, he turned to Caparzo. "How about you? Where you from?"

"Shove it, shithead," Caparzo said, and spat. "And another thing, every time you salute the captain, you're pinnin' a big fat target on him. So knock it the hell off . . . 'specially when *I'm* standin' near him."

"Oh-okay," Upham said, and smiled feebly. "I mean, live and learn."

"Drop dead."

From behind him a more friendly voice—Wade's—

offered, "So I understand you're a writer. What's your book about, Corporal?"

Upham, loaded down as he was, still managed a shrug. "I don't know, now."

"Yeah?"

"It *was* gonna be about the bonds of brotherhood that develop between soldiers in combat."

Caparzo almost whispered as he said to Upham, "Why don't you ask the captain where he's from, Upchuck?"

"Why?" The men around Upham, as they walked the green-walled shady lane, were snickering. "Why not?"

"Private joke," Mellish said.

Upham managed to work up some indignation. "Hey, I'm part of this squad."

"Yeah," Caparzo said, "but you're not a private."

Upham decided to trudge along silently for a while.

Up at point Reiben was falling in alongside Miller.

"You know, Captain, this little expedition goes against everything the Army taught me."

"How so?"

"I mean, it doesn't make any sense."

"What doesn't make sense, Reiben?"

"The math, sir, the sheer fuckin' math of it. Maybe you could explain it to me."

"Sure," Miller said casually, though the way he held his machine gun as he walked was anything but casual. "That's what I'm here for. To make you boys feel everything we do is logical."

"Gimme a break, Cap."

"So what do you want to know?"

"Well, sir, strictly just talkin' arithmetic here, what's the sense, the strategy, in risking eight lives to save one? I mean, it's not like we're goin' in to save Eisenhower or Patton or something. The guy's a fuckin' private, sir."

"And we all know how worthless privates are."

Reiben grinned. "Hey, my privates are valuable to me. But how about it, Cap? How about an answer?"

Miller threw the briefest glance back, saying, "Anybody wanna take a crack at that?"

"Jesus, Reiben," Wade said immediately, "think of the poor bastard's mother."

"Nice, Wade," Miller said, pleased, as if responding to a star pupil. "Very good."

"Hey," Reiben threw back at Wade, "what about *my* mother? What about your mother? We all got mothers, you, me, Sarge, even Corporal Upchuck." Reiben, having to work a little to keep up with Miller, said, "Captain, I'll bet even you have a mother."

Miller smiled faintly, but his eyes never left the lane and the hedgerows on its either side.

"Well," Reiben said, reconsidering, "the rest of us got mothers."

" 'Theirs not to reason why,' " Upham recited softly, glumly. " 'Theirs but to do and die.' "

Miller glanced back at Upham, recognizing the reference, though no one else did.

"What's that supposed to mean?" Mellish asked crankily. "That we're all supposed to die?"

"Nothing," Upham said. "Never mind."

"He's talking about duty," Miller said, working his voice up a little. "He's saying that we've got orders. And these orders supersede everything . . . including your mommies."

"Even if you think a mission's *foobar*?" Reiben asked.

"Especially if you think a mission's *foobar*," Miller said. "That's the definition of duty."

Upham risked a question of Mellish. "What's the definition of '*foobar*'?"

Mellish glanced at Caparzo, and then replied with a straight face, "It's a German word. Surprised a smart translator like you don't know it."

"German? Well, I never heard it before."

Jackson suddenly entered the colloquy. "Sir, I have an opinion on this subject."

"Let's hear it," Miller said. "By all means."

"Seems to me, Cap'n," Jackson offered in his soothing drawl, "this mission is a serious misallocation of valuable military resources."

"Go on, Private."

"Well, sir, seems to me, God gave me a special

gift, namely I can shoot the eye out of needle. The Good Lord fashioned in me a fine instrument of warfare."

"Reiben," Miller said to the private trudging alongside him, "pay attention. . . . *This* is the way to bitch. Jackson! Continue."

"What I mean, sir, is if you was to put me with this here Springfield rifle anywhere up to and including one mile from Adolf Hitler, and give this country boy a nice clear line of sight . . . well, hell. War's over. Amen and good night."

Reiben was studying his captain. Finally he asked, "What's your opinion, Captain? You still haven't answered my question. I'd almost say you're duckin' it."

Miller's expression was good-humoredly disgusted. "Reiben, what the hell's the matter with you? I don't bitch to you. I'm a captain. There's a chain of fuckin' command. Bitchin' only goes one way—up. Only up, never down."

"I was just askin' your opinion, sir. . . ."

"Here's how it works—you gripe to me, I gripe to my superior officers. Shit goes upstream, got it? I don't gripe to you, I don't gripe in front of you. How long have you been in this man's Army?"

"You're right," Reiben admitted. "I'm sorry." Then, slyly, he went on: "But, Captain, if you *weren't* a captain, or if I were, say, a *major* . . . then what would you say?"

Miller thought about that even as his eyes searched the green barriers of the hedgerows. "In that case, I would say this is an excellent mission, sir, with an extremely valuable objective, sir, worthy of my best efforts, a privilege to serve my country in this way . . . sir."

Reiben rolled his eyes, shook his head, smirked, nearly laughed.

"Moreover," Miller said, quietly, almost solemnly, "I feel heartfelt sorrow for the mother of Private James Ryan, and I am more than willing to lay down my life, and the lives of my men . . . especially yours, Reiben . . . to help relieve her suffering."

Behind him the men had thoroughly enjoyed this performance, laughing, even clapping a little, including—perhaps especially—Upham. But Reiben, the master of sarcasm, was confused, not sure whether to take his captain at face value, or admit to himself that Miller had beaten him at his own game.

9

To the north of Ste.-Mère-Eglise—the surrounding hills humming with medium artillery, the late afternoon punctuated by occasional small-arms fire and mortar and grenade explosions—the little village of Neuville-au-Plain had been reduced from a picturesque tourist's dream to a rudely distributed pile of rubble. One- and two-story stone cottages and buildings, having withstood centuries of weather abuse and human use, had crumbled like stale cake. Other structures were architectural amputees, half standing, a wall sheared away here, a roof caved in there.

Wood and stone and debris littered the cobblestone street as Captain Miller led his squad toward the sound of a sporadic firefight, which seemed just around the corner of a half-shot-away wall where Miller, hand in the air, gestured to his men to follow his lead and flatten against the brick. They did, closing ranks behind him.

He poked his head out, just as a handful of villagers dashed across the detritus-cluttered street. A family apparently, father, wife, perhaps an aunt, several children, wore the dazed expression of earthquake survivors. Miller couldn't help being touched by this poignant reminder of real life, these civilians in the attire of daily living interrupting his olive-drab world—a man in a dark suit, two women in gay print dresses, a girl in a short skirt, a boy in white shirt and shorts—and was relieved the little family made it safely across into a half-demolished building. Was it their home, or what was left of it? Had enemy shells killed this town, or friendly artillery?

He pulled back, just as a bullet carved a chunk out of the brick near his head, only after he'd taken a mental snapshot of a virtual sniper's alley, where American paratroopers—one of the 101st, no doubt—crouched in doorways, hunkered behind wreckage, exchanging gunfire with an unseen enemy.

"Thunder!" Miller yelled.

A moment later came the response: "Flash! Come on across!"

Miller looked back at his men. "When I call for you, make the run, one at a time. Broken field running, girls."

His men nodded, and Miller sucked in a breath and took off, quick, unpredictable in his zigs and zags as German bullets seemed to trail him, landing just behind him, never finding where he was, only where he'd been. Within seconds he had taken cover in doorway across the way.

Upham, whose admiration for Miller was about all that was keeping him going, had gone pale white.

Jackson, noting this, said, "Don't worry, kid. They can't kill the captain."

Sarge said, "Like hell they can't."

"Jackson's right, Sarge," Reiben put in. "It's some kinda supernatural or maybe scientific thing. I can't explain it, but I've seen it. It's like he's magnetized and the bullets get repelled."

"We've all seen it," Caparzo said, grinning, shaking his head. "He's got nine lives or somethin'. Like he's bulletproof, or some damn thing."

"Nobody's bulletproof," Sarge said, his disgust at this combination of jocularity and admiration apparent. "Don't kid yourself—*nobody* is."

Across the sniper's alley, Miller ducked out of his doorway, staying low as he charged down the block, Thompson in his hands seeming to pull him along, slipping into the alleyway where a cluster of paratroopers awaited.

Just out of the line of fire—and under it, the alley wall's top half shot away, a jagged sawtooth smile of brick above them—sat ten dirty, battered, exhausted paratroopers with their backs to the wall and weapons at the ready; four of them were wounded, nothing that looked fatal, blood-splotched legs and arms, accompanied by smudged in-shock faces.

Crouching before them, Miller called back down the block. "Wade! Wounded!"

"Private Goldman, sir," a round-faced kid said by way of introduction.

"Miller."

Small-arms fire popped. Wade was making his run.

"Are you a sight for sore fuckin' eyes!" Goldman, twenty-three, Chicago, Illinois, called out to his sergeant: "Sarge! Our relief showed up!"

And Sergeant William Hill, twenty-nine, Pensicola, Florida, scurried down the line to where Miller knelt, leaning on his Thompson.

"How many are you?" Sergeant Hill asked, desperation leaking into his voice.

Wade ducked into the alley, and Miller directed him to the wounded, who Wade quickly began attending.

"Sorry to disappoint you," Miller said, "but we're not your relief. There's just eight of us."

Gunfire popped—another man made the run.

"No? What the hell . . . ?" Then catching himself, the sergeant asked, "What do you mean, sir?"

"We're on a special assignment, looking for a Private James Ryan."

"Who?" Goldman asked, more confused than disappointed.

"Private James Ryan," Miller repeated patiently.

"What for?" the sergeant asked, bewildered and mildly pissed.

Reiben scrambled into the alleyway, B.A.R. in hand.

Miller nodded to him, then asked Sergeant Hill, "Is he here?"

Hill rolled his eyes, shook his head in frustration, forced himself to be civil to this officer, saying, "Maybe in a mixed unit on the other side of town. Hard to get to . . . Germans punched a hole in our center a few hours ago, cut us in two. What was his name again?"

More popping of small-arms fire, another of his men taking the deadly run.

"Ryan," Miller said. "James. Private. Dropped in with you guys, 101st."

They waited for the rest of Miller's men to arrive, one by one, even milky-faced Upham, all of them successfully dodging the small-arms fire that welcomed them.

Only then did Hill yell back over his shoulder: "Runner! Get that runner up here now!"

Private Harold Nelson, twenty-one, Omaha, Nebraska, scurried forward, a wiry-looking, freckle-faced kid, unencumbered by gear. The better to run a gauntlet.

"Locate Captain Hamill," the sergeant told his runner. "There's a patrol here looking for a Private Ryan, James. Probable mis-drop from the One-oh-One."

The kid nodded, then stole a look up over the wall, picking his pathway, then skirted the corner and took off in a sprint that would have landed him a spot in any college's backfield. Small college, anyway.

Miller and the others leaned out, just enough to get a decent position to watch the runner, who was ducking behind walls, dipping into doorways, quickly scampering across streets.

With Miller's squad interspersed with the paratroopers, Sergeant Hill explained his situation.

"We got stopped here by intense rifle action from the eastward," he told them. "Jerries been reinforcing two regiments all day long. Streets have been pretty quiet for"—he checked his wristwatch—"damn near forty-five minutes. Jerries are concentrating most of their fire westward now."

"It didn't seem quiet to me," Reiben said, "when those bullets were making me dance."

As if making his point, small-arms fire kicked in, sounding surprisingly innocuous, like theater popcorn popping, alerting them to the runner's peril.

Miller leaned out, seeing the hard-packed dirt of the street puffing around the runner as bullets struck. Then one clipped the runner, in the leg, and the kid went down on his good knee.

"Suppressing fire!" Hill yelled, and his men, and Miller's, stood at the half wall of the alley and threw bullets everywhere but at the fallen kid.

"Where the fuck do we shoot?" Reiben asked, between volleys from his B.A.R. "Where are those shots coming from?"

"Around that blind corner," Miller said. "We're wasting ammo, but we are making noise."

Hill finally said, glumly, "Hold your fire. . . . Give him room."

The poor wounded kid wasn't a runner, anymore—just a crawler, that popcorn popping sound all around him, little puffs of dust bursting about him as he snaked on his stomach, seeming to try to swim to safety, crawling for cover.

Then, at last, he lay very still. And the sound of popping corn stopped.

"Poor bastard," Reiben said.

"Our father, who art in heaven," Jackson began, then kept the rest of it to himself.

Then, startling the GIs, it was like another batch of theater popcorn had started popping. Bullets were riddling the obviously dead body, shaking it like a disobedient child. Puffs of dust, puffs of blood mist.

"Fucking animals!" Caparzo screamed, eyes huge, veins and cords in his neck sticking out. "You sadistic fucking cocksuckers!"

The unnecessary desecration of the runner's corpse continued; dozens of rounds gave quivering false life to the dead body.

Quietly, Sergeant Hill said, "They know we're not in direct contact. They're gonna single out the runners. Discourage us from sendin' others."

"Jesus Christ!" Caparzo yelled. "Why do they keep shooting him up like that?"

"As long as there's any chance there's a breath in him," Miller said, "the message he carries is alive."

Rage and fear were mingled on the faces of the men before him, hunkered under that half-wall clutching their weapons, and Miller commented flatly, "We'd do the same thing."

That sobered the men, erasing the rage, and even the fear, but leaving an emptiness.

Miller told his medic to get the wounded ready to travel, which Wade did, as Sergeant Hill called a private over, saying, "Boyd, try again. See if you can raise Captain Hamill, and let him know we're comin'."

Private Jerry Boyd, twenty-two, Cleveland, Ohio, nodded and began trying to get something other than static out of his SCR-536 walkie-talkie.

Miller stepped to the mouth of the alley, where the half-wall was at its highest, and eyeballed the street. Sergeant Hill came to his side.

"Next block is two-story buildings, both sides of the street," the sergeant said. "Lots of windows, then a wide-open square."

"Another shooting gallery?"

"Not necessarily. Pretty good cover on the left."

"Okay," Miller said, thinking quickly. "We'll backtrack two blocks, then cut over right, and get those buildings between us and wherever that fucking enfilading fire is coming from."

Sergeant Hill was studying the captain, clearly sizing him up.

Miller said, "Four men up. Two of mine, two of yours."

Hill's expression indicated to Miller that the sergeant believed this captain knew what he was doing.

"Yes, sir," Hill nodded. "Hastings! Goldman! Up front."

"Reiben," Miller called. "Caparzo."

Private Boyd, nearby, was shaking his head no. "Still jamming us, Sarge."

The four men summoned moved up in position, while the rest got ready, helping the wounded, bandaged by Wade, to their feet.

"Fundamentals," Miller said calmly. "Short runs, double up at the corners, one man close, one man wide."

Nods all around.

Miller added: "Prepare for close contact."

More nods, from all but Upham, who was peering over the wall, at the fallen, shot-to-shit runner. Upham's expression was blank, but the corporal was shaking. Of course, so was Miller's hand, but no one had noticed. Except Miller.

"Upham," Miller said, not unkindly. "The pointed part of the bayonet blade faces out."

Upham swallowed, muttered, "Yes, sir," and corrected his mistake.

Soon, bathed in the light of the dying sun, throwing long shadows, they took off, scurrying, crouching, darting through the rubbish pile that had been a village—bricks, stones, chunks of cement, portions of walls, scatterings of wooden plank, as if a lumber wagon had upended and spilled and scattered itself. Miller led the way through the obstacle course of rubble as those at the rear helped the wounded along. Wade kept a watchful eye on them. Quickly they made their way up the street, leapfrogging positions, hugging the recessions of doorways for cover, eyes searching windows and rooftops for that glint of gunmetal that signaled a sniper.

Upham and Reiben shared a doorway, along the way, Upham whispering, "So where's the captain from, anyway?"

Reiben whispered back: "Figure that one out, Upchuck, you win the big cee-gar."

Jackson had just ducked in a nearby doorway, and had overheard this whispered discussion. Clutching his precious sharpshooter rifle, he added his two cents: "Over three hundred smackers, last I heard."

Mellish was moving quickly past, heading for a rubble pile to duck behind. Along the way he offered this information to Upham: "Company's got a pool goin'! Five bucks gets ya in."

Moments later the entire group was edging along a stone wall. Miller, up ahead, wasn't hearing himself discussed.

Upham asked whoever might care to answer,

"Doesn't anybody know where he's from, or what he did for a living?"

Sarge yanked Upham and dragged him along, backs to the wall. "Been with him since Kasserine Pass," Horvath said, "and I ain't got the foggiest."

Reiben was coming up behind them, also with his back to the wall. "It's easy. They assembled the cap at O.C.S., from spare body parts offa dead GI joes."

From up ahead Caparzo said, "Hey, I know all about the captain. I sneaked a look inside his pack one time."

"Bullshit, Caparzo!" Jackson said in a rare outburst of profanity, though significantly not one that took the Lord's name in vain. "You don't know nothin', boy."

"Call it bullshit if you want, ya dumb hillbilly," Caparzo said cockily. "I'm just bidin' my time for the pool to get big enough to make it worth my while. Then I'll pass it on to the rest of you bums, and you can read it and weep."

"Shhhh!" Sarge said from up ahead.

After that no more talk ensued as the screws of tension seemed to tighten, the squad getting closer to their precarious destination, where snipers waited. Their boots scuffing over cobblestones, Miller's men darted this way and that, like figures from one bedroom to another in a French farce, though despite the French trappings, there was nothing farcical about it, moving from position to position, trading looks and acknowledgments, Miller motioning them forward, his expression saying, *Let's go, keep moving, you next. . . .*

Soon they were edged along a three-story house where the wall had collapsed, baring three stories of rooms, intact but for the missing wall, furniture still in place, like an exhibit in a museum showing middle-class life in a French village.

Something above them creaked, and the squad dropped into a crouch, weapons tilted, ready to open fire upward.

Sergeant Hill called out the code word: "Thunder!"

Long seconds passed with no response.

"Thunder, goddamn it, thunder! Or we open up on you. . . ."

A man's voice drifted down to them: *"Ne tirez pas! On est francais!"*

"Hold it, hold it!" Upham called. "They're civilians!"

"Yeah?" Horvath said. "Let's see the color of their duds!"

The male voice again: *"Montrez-vous!"*

A man stepped into view from the second story, clearly a local resident, slender, perhaps thirty, brown suit, yellow tie, distraught expression on a narrow face. His hands were raised.

"Ne tirez pas!" he said, a peculiar mix of hope and despair coloring his voice.

A woman in a floral-print dress stepped into view,

pretty, perhaps twenty-five, with an infant bundled in her arms; her expression asked for pity, for understanding.

"On est pas des soldats et on est pas arnes," she said, while at the same time her husband said, *"Baissez vos fusils, nous sommes vos amis!"*

To the Americans, this would have sounded like gibberish even if the apparent husband and wife weren't talking on top of each other.

"Stop jabbering!" Miller commanded, holding up a palm in the universal gesture of "stop." "One at a time!"

The captain motioned for Upham, who scurried up as Miller said, "Ask them where the Germans are."

Upham nodded, looked up at the couple and child and asked, *"Où sont les allemands?"*

The man nodded frantically, the words streaming out of him: *"Ca va pas! Ils sont partout, vous devez emmener les enfants!"*

"What about infants?" Miller asked, frowning. "What the hell's he saying?"

"I don't know exactly," Upham said, frustrated. "He's talking so quickly . . . something about taking the children. . . ."

The couple stepped from view for a few moments, then returned with the father holding the hand of a girl who couldn't have been older than four; holding on to the mother's skirts was a frightened boy of maybe five. The father escorted the daughter to the edge of what appeared to be their living room, grasped her by the wrists and suddenly dangled her off into the air, lowering her toward the soldiers. The girl began crying, her legs kicking under the short blue skirt with petticoats.

"Je vois la passe!" the father said, suspending his daughter over them, as if offering her to firemen from a burning building.

"Shit!" Miller said.

"I think that's *merde* around here," Reiben said, using up about a third of his vocabulary in the language of the village.

"They want us to take their kids," Upham said meekly.

"I figured that out," Miller said as the girl swung over them. "You tell him we can't take children. . . ."

"Don't cry, sweetie," Caparzo was saying to the little girl, smiling up at her. He made faces, and she began to laugh; now it was as if they were playing, father swinging the child, the funny men below.

Upham was saying, *". . . Nous ne pouvons les predre avec nous!"*

But Caparzo was reaching up for her, arms out, and she squealed with delight as her father let loose of her and she leapt into the American soldier's arms.

Smiling, taking this as a real seal of approval, the father pulled his son away from the mother, and clutched him by the wrists as well, lowering him. The boy didn't cry—he was scared, confused—but then so were Mellish and Jackson, who together received the boy, setting him gently down.

The mother above was quietly weeping; her infant was crying, too, but not at all quietly.

Miller sucked in air, tried not to get completely pissed off, even though suddenly two French kids were in the middle of his world.

"Je veuz pas y aller!" the little girl said aglow.

Joyfully teary, the mother above called, *"Tu dois! Vous serz en securite avec les americains!"*

Upham said to Miller, "They figure the kids'll be safe with us."

"It's not safe with us," Miller snarled. He sighed, and more kindly said, "Tell 'em it's not safe anywhere, but it's particularly not safe with us. Tell them."

Upham nodded. *"Ils ne seront pas en securite avec nous, vous ne comprenez pas, on ne peut pas les emmener!"*

Caparzo and the little girl were playing, the boy from Chicago, Illinois, swinging in his arms the girl from Neuville-au-Plain. "Reminds me of my little niece," Caparzo said. "Sofie."

"Caparzo," Miller said, refusing to lose control of the situation. "Put that kid down."

But the child was having fun in Caparzo's arms, and Caparzo seemed pretty damn content holding on to her.

"Captain," he said. "Let's do the decent thing."

"The decent thing."

"The decent thing." And the tone in Caparzo's voice was one none of his combat buddies had ever heard before; it held a softness, a tenderness, that had been part of the hard-boiled Italian's civilian life. "Let's at least take these kids down the road to the next town."

Miller was not untouched by this, but the hardness of his tone did not betray that. He snapped, "We're not here to do the decent thing. We're here to follow orders. You're here to follow orders."

"Captain . . ."

"Now, hand that fucking kid back to her fucking parents."

Around him Miller's squad blinked in surprise. Their captain was a decent man, and hard-nosed military though he might be at times, this seemed unduly harsh. Even Sergeant Hill's battle-worn paratroopers were taken aback.

Caparzo looked at the child in his arms, and she giggled and snuggled to him. He swallowed. His eyes were wet.

"Hand her back up, Caparzo," Miller said, his voice gentle but not soft. "Do it. Now."

"But, sir," Caparzo said. "I don't think—"

They never knew what he thought, because a bullet whined in, a sniper's bullet from a high-powered rifle not unlike Jackson's, and blew right through the private, through his chest, in a spray of blood that spattered the family furniture in the sitting room exposed by the missing wall. The impact took Caparzo off his feet and slammed him to the cobblestones. Only then did the sound of the gunshot catch up with the bullet, ringing through the street.

The private from Chicago had finally let loose of the little girl from Neuville. She fell, but landed on her feet, unhurt, though terrified and confused.

Like everyone around her.

10

Screams of surprise and shouted obscenities mingled with the distressed babble of the children's parents, who hovered at the edge of their exposed living room. Rising above it all were howls of pain from Private Caparzo, a bug on its back, yelling, "I'm shot! I'm shot!" and spilling blood like a sieve.

Just across the way, heaped in the street, rose a hillock of rubble that Miller and most of his squad scrambled behind, planks and pebbles, slabs of cement, chunks of brick wall, topped off by a decorative wrought-iron tangle that had been a balcony railing. Sergeant Hill and his paratroopers sought the same refuge, though a few found recessions of doorways to flatten into.

But two of the captain's squad lingered in the kill zone: the medic, Wade, was heading to his fallen comrade's side, and Upham was going after the two kids. The girl and boy stood paralyzed, eyes huge, hands frozen in midair, like tiny statues in a park.

"Caparzo!" Mellish cried from behind the rubble pile.

"I'm shot!" Caparzo screamed, thrashing, bleeding. "Oh, God have mercy, I'm shot!"

"You're gonna be fine, buddy," Wade said a moment before Sarge grabbed the medic and hauled him bodily to cover. Miller had bolted out in the open, too, to snatch Upham by the collar. Miller yanked him back so roughly, the corporal began to choke, to gag, as his captain hauled him away from the petrified children.

Another shot zinged by, slamming into a stone wall—traveling through the space Upham had just occupied—and its resounding report followed a second or so after. The children, standing fear-frozen but crying now, were unharmed. They were not targets. But as long as any of his men tried to help them, Miller knew, the kids would serve as bait.

Miller's men kept craning up above the rubbish mound to view Caparzo, on his back, writhing in pain, screaming to his friends and his God for help, blood spreading in a widening pool. Caparzo's torture was their torture.

"Stay down!" Sarge snapped at them, and they reluctantly obeyed.

"Goddamn it!" Sergeant Hill had his back to the rubble pile, rifle in hand; he was next to Miller. "Where the fuck did that shot come from?"

Miller said nothing, but glanced at the man next

to him—his own sharpshooter, Jackson—for an expert opinion.

"Weren't close," Jackson said. "Bullet laid 'im on the ground, 'fore we even heard the shot."

Caparzo's wailing agony was tearing the squad apart. The cries and shrieks of fear of the father and mother for their children, stranded weeping below them, frozen in the line of fire, weren't helping, either.

Wade scooted up next to his captain; the medic's face was contorted with frustration and concern. "We gotta get Caparzo the hell outa there!"

"Stay put, Wade," Miller said. "That's an order."

Suddenly Caparzo stopped screaming, as if that had become too difficult to maintain, and poked and prodded at himself with his left hand, examining his wound at the right of his chest. The entry point wasn't bleeding so bad, but the exit wound was a faucet, the puddle of red enlarging around him, putting the private in a crimson spotlight. He seemed to be trying to move his right arm, which he couldn't; it lay inert, human debris.

Then Caparzo's left hand found its way under his jacket and into a blouse pocket, from which he withdrew an envelope, a V-mail letter, red and damp with the life he was leaking. He seemed to try to sit up, not getting very far, but able to view the puddle of blood as it expanded into a rippling pool.

"Oh, God . . . oh . . . oh, God," Caparzo said,

watching survival seeping out of him, streaming away from him. "God . . . God . . ."

Prayer? Curse? Was there a difference in this war? Miller was dying inside, witnessing this, but he didn't show his men—couldn't show his men.

He told Jackson, "Give me an estimate."

Reiben was peering out from behind the rubble heap, desperately wanting to pull Caparzo to cover and to hell with the captain, when a chunk of cement on the pile at his left seemed to suddenly explode, cement shrapnel flying.

This prompted Miller to dash out, snatch the kids in his arms, and he was dragging them to cover, even as the gunshot's report arrived and reverberated. He deposited the children in a doorway behind him, motioning for them to stay low, which they did.

"Fuck," Reiben was saying, somewhat stunned; he was back behind the pile of debris again, blood trickling down his left cheek; a sharp fragment of cement had caught him.

Miller was standing, Jackson at his side. "Private?"

"Four hundred fifty yards, Cap'n. Give or take."

Upham, who was seated, his back to the rubble pile, looked up, bewildered, somewhat in shock. "Is that a long shot?"

In the house with the missing wall, across the way, the parents were huddling, infant in the mother's arms, and they were sobbing with relief, their children in sight and safe.

"I'd say *that's* where the eagle's roosting," Miller said, pointing, eyes gazing way down the street toward the green hillside beyond the village, where a quarter mile away a chateau nestled, with a chapel bell tower, quaint, scenic, strategic.

"That's where I'd perch," Jackson agreed. The narrow eyes in his narrow face might have been an Indian's.

"One man's vantage point,' Miller said, "is another man's target."

Jackson nodded. "Reckon that's what they pay me sixty bucks a month for, sir."

And Jackson withdrew form his pack a long leather case that might have shielded a pool shark's favorite cue. He unsnapped it to reveal a gleaming, elongated telescopic sight.

Caparzo was fading. He held up the blood-soaked letter in his left hand, as if offering it to anyone who might be willing to take it. He might have been floating on a lake of his blood.

"Help me . . . somebody . . . I'm losing my blood . . . blood's goin' out of me . . . help . . ."

Mellish, trying to hold back tears, fists clenched, yelled, "Hang on, pal! You hang on, buddy!"

Jackson was crouched down, attaching the telescopic sight to his Springfield sniper rifle. Upham hunkered next to him, asking, "What is that thing?"

"Unertl special scope for my thirty-ought-six," he

said. "Made the mounts myself. Not bad for a hick, huh?"

Jackson worked the bolt, inserted a single, oversize shell that might have been a dame's lipstick tube if she had a generous mouth.

Upham swallowed. "You must be a hell of a shot."

"Back where I come from," he said," 'bout middlin'."

That precious letter Caparzo was holding was suddenly forgotten as the wounded man wadded it in a fist; the pain must have intensified. Miller kept his face blank while inside he shared the private's torment, and that of his men, watching their brother bleed.

"Help me," Caparzo whimpered.

"Don't talk!" Wade called from behind the rubble pile. "Save your energy."

Mellish, next to Wade, and like the medic, dying to rush to their friend's aid, called out, "We'll be with you in a sec, buddy! Just hold on!"

"No . . ." Caparzo was trying to sit up again. His eyes fixed upon them, dull and yet filled with urgency. ". . . This letter . . . important . . . it's to my pop . . . but it's all bloody . . ."

"You be quiet, now," Wade said, almost scolding. Then the medic turned to Miller and pleaded, "You got to let me get out there."

"Stay put, Wade."

"Captain, please . . ."

"The order stands. Jackson! Today?"

" 'Bout there, sir."

Jackson's sniper rifle was fully assembled now, and he stood behind the rubble hill and sighted something on the hillside—clearly not the chateau or its bell tower—and squeezed the trigger. On the hill, five-hundred-some yards away, a branch snapped off a tree, shattering into twigs.

"Checkin' for drift," Jackson said casually.

The lanky private reloaded and raised his rifle, which he held tenderly, his touch light, bracing with his shoulder, his body one with the rifle. Jackson's namesake, Daniel Boone, had drawn a bead like this—Davy Crockett, too. Bears and Indians and Mexicans had fallen under the cool considerate aim of backwoods Americans like Jackson. Now it was the Germans' turn.

Caparzo was unaware that he was about to be avenged. His only concern was to use all the strength his drained body could muster—which wasn't much—to toss the balled-up bloody letter toward his friends, to Wade and Mellish.

"All bloody . . . copy it . . . don't want Papa, Mama . . . see the blood. . . . Copy it over. . . ."

"You shut up, now," Wade said, "you're gonna be okay, I'm gonna see to it. . . ." Then to Miller, Wade whispered desperately: "Captain . . . he may still have a chance. . . ."

"Stay put," Miller said. "Jackson?"

"O my God, I trust in thee," Jackson said quietly,

solemnly. His eye at the scope. Waiting. Waiting for his shot. "Let me be not afraid. . . ."

In the chateau bell tower, on his stomach in the shadows, perfectly but rather precariously positioned beside a gaping hole in the floor near his window on the village, Corporal Wolfgang Gottberg, twenty-three, Cologne, was attempting to fix another target in his crosshairs. His first hit was still alive, but not worth another bullet, thrashing in his own blood as he was. Panning his sniperscope toward the rubble pile, behind which the other Americans had scurried, Gottberg focused in on a helmeted head that had poked up above the detritus. Something glinted in the late afternoon sunlight.

Something metallic.

Hair prickled on the back of the German's neck. The barrel of a rifle, in fact, the long barrel of a sniper's rifle. . . .

Aiming that rifle, Private Daniel Boone Jackson said, "O my God, I trust in thee; let me not be ashamed. . . ."

And Wolfgang Gottberg suddenly realized another sniper was aiming right back at him. He quickly fixed the man in his crosshairs, knowing he was already locked in his opposite's sights. His finger moved frantically to the trigger, but it never squeezed. The American's bullet had entered through the German's rifle scope, then through Gottberg's blue right eye, popping it like a grape, traveling through his cerebrum and blowing out the back of his helmeted head in an eruption of shattered glass and blossoming blood and brain matter.

Gottberg's rifle tumbled from fingers and hands to which signals had ceased, pitching through the collapsed floor to *clunk* below, followed by Gottberg himself, who was dead before the American's gunshot echoed through the countryside and the chateau courtyard—his death far more merciful than the one in progress, which Gottberg's final victim was yet suffering.

Jackson lowered his rifle, nodded to Miller and the rest, and said, "Amen. Lord have mercy on a soldier's soul."

It was unclear whether he was referring to himself or the German.

"Go," Miller said to Wade.

The medic rushed toward Caparzo, Mellish scampering after, and then they stopped at the edge of the sea of blood, as if to go farther would somehow be disrespectful to their now obviously dead comrade. Caparzo's head was tilted toward that expanse of shimmering red, eyes wide open and unblinking, his glazed stare seeming to assess the liquid that represented the life he had lost.

"Aw, shit," Mellish said, voice tremulous.

Stepping out from behind the hillock of refuse, Reiben muttered, "Goddamn it . . . goddamn it . . ."

Miller approached, and Wade shot him a glare. The captain didn't avoid the medic's accusing eyes.

"And that," Miller said brusquely, with a nod to the village children behind him, "is why we don't baby-sit."

This jarred his squad, even Sarge. With shaking heads, intakes of breath, humorless laughs, they looked numbly at their captain. The smile Reiben sent Miller's way was nearly a sneer.

"What do you expect?" Miller asked. "You want me to lead you in a few hymns? Or shall we just stand around and pout and wait for the next god-damn sniper?"

The captain waded through the blood of the dead private and crouched, yanking off one of Caparzo's dog tags, pocketing it. Then he stood and nodded in the direction they'd been heading.

"Jackson," Miller said with a sideways glance, "take Mellish. Check that chateau. Make sure it's secure."

"Yes, sir," Jackson said, and Mellish fell in with him, moving past Reiben, whose gash on the side of his forehead was being cleaned by Wade.

Reiben snorted a dark laugh and said, "So the angel on our shoulder was a sniper."

"Oh, no, we still got *our* angel," Mellish said, tromping by, rifle cradled in both hands. "Can't you feel him shittin' down our shirts?"

"Well, I say fuck Private James Ryan," Reiben said,

"fuck him sideways, fuck him six ways to Sunday, just so you fuck the goddamned son of a bitch."

"Lord A'mighty, Reiben," Jackson said as he and Mellish headed off, "give it a rest. You're killin' me, boy."

"It's not me killin' you, Li'l Abner. Caparzo's just the first of us to pay for Private Ryan's ticket home. Just you wait and see."

Warily, as he pressed Reiben's bandage in place, Wade said, "Private Ryan didn't kill Caparzo. A German sniper did."

As Jackson and Mellish trudged toward the hillside where the chateau awaited, Miller told Horvath to take point. While his men resumed their journey to the town square, Miller eyed Caparzo's bloody, wadded-up letter. He was about to pick it up when he realized Wade was standing there; the medic's gaze was shifting from the letter to the captain. Like western gunfighters, each waiting for the other to draw, the two hesitated. Finally Wade bent down, plucked the letter from the hard dirt street and stuffed it in a pocket. Then the medic fell in behind the other men as they hugged walls, ducked into doorways, leapfrogging, darting here, there.

Miller glanced up at the man and his wife enfolding their youngest child in their arms; their dismayed expression told him they at last understood that the Americans would not be taking their two older children along to a safer haven. He flicked a smile at the two kids in the doorway behind him; they waved good-bye. So did he, a little.

Then he fell in behind his men, carefully scrutinizing the street, the surrounding buildings, doing his best to keep his men safe. To not lose another man . . .

Within the chateau's simple, deserted chapel, dying sun filtered through stained-glass windows that had survived an onslaught that cluttered the church with its own remains, including floorboards from above. Pebbles of plaster, paint chips, and chunks of building materials sat in the pews, a congregation of ruin.

Long-barreled rifle in his bony hands, Jackson entered silently, not out of respect for his Lord, but for any Germans that might be lurking. Mellish followed him in, then stayed downstairs while Jackson took the tower stairs to a small landing, where he faced a closed door.

Jackson kicked the damn thing in, rifle ready—and found an empty bell chamber, the rope of the bell dangling from above and arched open windows looking out on the green countryside and Neuville-au-Plain . . . but no sniper, alive or dead.

"Jackson!" Mellish called from below, voice echoing up. "Found something you left behind!"

The lanky sharpshooter ignored that, creeping into the small chamber, knowing there was no place an enemy could hide, fanning around cautiously just the same. Then he spotted the collapsed area in the floor, off to the side near the window facing the village. He edged closer to the jagged hole, until the opening in the floorboards revealed the twisted sprawl of his dead German counterpart a story below.

And Mellish standing near the corpse, looking up. "Come on, Jackson," Mellish said irritably. "Let's get the hell outa here—joint's empty, and this bastard's shot his last round."

Jackson lowered himself through the hole in the floor, and dropped down beside the dead German, debris crunching under his boots.

"Gimme a second," Jackson told the other private.

The tall Tennesseean crouched over his late counterpart.

"Dear God," Jackson said softly.

"Christ," Mellish said, "you ain't gonna pray for him or anything are ya? How can you feel sorry for a—"

"Will ya look at that shootin' iron." He began to inspect the German's rifle, its shattered sniperscope loose and hanging, holding the weapon up, working the bolt, letting out a low whistle. "Lord have mercy. . . ."

"If you're through checkin' out the competition, Jackson, there's a war on. Fuck this guy! Let's go!"

"Comin', Mother," Jackson said, but he lingered. When Mellish was out of the room, Jackson lifted the soldier's lapel and saw the dead German's sniper badge pinned there.

"Bingo," Jackson said, undid and pocketed it, and hustled after his pal.

Soon Jackson and Mellish had caught up with Miller and the squad, and Sergeant Hill and his men, in the town square, flattened into the recessions of doorways of two-story houses. The rattle of small-arms fire tinged the air, not close, not far, but near enough to keep these men tense and cautious, fingers poised on triggers. Across the open if debris-strewn square, a brick three-story structure identified by Hill as the town hall, vines crawling its brick walls, perhaps the grandest building in the village, seemed battered but unbowed.

Miller and Hill were sharing a doorway. The captain nudged the sergeant, then nodded and pointed toward a window where a machine-gun muzzle poked between third-floor shutters. Time to move, and quickly. . . .

But a voice from that window called out: "Thunder!"

A very American voice.

Relief flooded through the men, as Sergeant Hill called back, "Flash!"

The machine-gun muzzle withdrew, and Hill and Miller traded tiny smiles and let out some air.

Then Miller stepped out, Thompson ready, and motioned *Let's go*, and he and all the men broke cover and hustled across the wide square, drawing no fire, using a pair of huge crumbled holes in the town hall brick walls that served as doorways. Hill and his men went in one of the impromptu entrances, on one side of the building, while Miller and his squad used another, around behind.

Miller's group found themselves in a back room, moving past sections of caved-in ceiling, into a central lobby, two floors of banistered landings above, overseen by a fairly fancy cut-glass chandelier that had somehow survived the war thus far. The place was otherwise a claustrophobic disarray of overturned, broken-up furnishings, fallen beams and scattered bricks and brick wall chunks—a dusty, gloomy area the GIs' eyes had trouble adapting to.

A handful of men in the lobby shadows were huddled and whispering, but Miller thought nothing of it, the town hall having been identified as American held. Their boots crunching on fallen plaster, Miller's squad skirted an ungainly stack of fallen beams, just as these men—five of them—turned to face the newcomers.

The five soldiers wore gray uniforms, not olive drab, which was appropriate, because they were Germans.

The briefest moment of shock on both sides elapsed into screaming pandemonium as in both groups, men shouted in their native language for the other sons of bitches to surrender. Weapons jerked up into position, fingers grew taut on triggers.

And as quickly as it had erupted, the shouting stopped. In both languages. The Americans and the Germans were in a Mexican standoff, and both sides knew it. For what seemed a very long time—and was, in fact, fifteen seconds—no one spoke, no one moved.

Then a young German wielding a Luger panicked, squeezing the trigger but producing only the click of a hammer falling on an empty chamber. But as clicks went, this was a loud one, announcing to Miller and his men the German's intention to shoot them. . . .

And before Miller could sort through his options, knowing that to open fire could only initiate a mutual slaughter, machine-gun fire rained down from above. Muzzle flashes lighted the gloom like the flames of wind-tossed matches, metal snouts poked through banister posts, spitting fire and lead and smoke. The quintet of German soldiers did a grotesque marionette's dance as the gunfire chewed through them (and as Miller and his men hit the deck), tossing them, tangling them in each other. Clouds of blood mist mingled with the sour cordite fumes and the stirred-up dust of debris, and the gray uniforms had scarlet polka-dots now. Hitting the floor, a dying German returned fire. Finally, his Schmeisser, belching bullets and flames at the ceiling, succeeded only in bringing down the chandelier, on the floor and on himself, throwing glass shards that had Miller and his men protecting their faces with forearms.

The silence was as abrupt as the barrage of gunfire it followed. Banister fragments fluttered down and settled. Cordite smoke drifted like fog.

Sergeant Hill and his men entered the lobby through a wall and appraised the carnage. Weapons were lifted into firing position—eyebrows were lifted as well.

From above came a voice: "Clear, up!"

"Clear, down!" Sergeant Hill returned.

On the floor Horvath and Miller exchanged blankly stunned expressions.

"Enough to make an old man out of ya," Sarge said.

"Let's hope," Miller said.

The captain rose and then so did his men, debris powder on them like ungodly dandruff. They moved deeper into the lobby so they could look up at their saviors.

All along the banister, or what was left of it after catching some of that machine-gun fire, were airborne paratroopers, a dozen of them, gazing down at their grisly handiwork, nodding to the men whose lives they'd just saved.

Their leader, Captain DeWayne Hamill, thirty-one, San Diego, California, blond, jut-jawed, peered down through the haze of dust and gunpowder at Miller and his squad of Rangers, his expression thoroughly puzzled.

"We've come for Private Ryan," Miller explained.

11

With the aid of heaped rubble and freshly dug fox-holes, paratroopers of the 101st Airborne Division had established a defensive perimeter along the northern edge of the city. Despite the occasional sound of small-arms fire, this section of Neuville was relatively secure. The sight of American tanks poised in the perimeter's machine-gun-protected half-circle was a comfort to Miller. He and his squad, mingled with Sergeant Hill and his men, trooped along with Captain Hamill and his paratroopers as they crossed the train tracks.

"How was the road in?" Hamill asked.

"Scenic," Miller said. "Lost a jeep, some gear, some ammo."

"And a man," Sarge put in dryly, trudging along next to Miller.

Miller pretended to ignore that, though in truth it bothered him that Horvath felt compelled to play Jiminy Cricket. He expected boys fresh off the base to question his seeming heartlessness; but the battle-savvy Sarge should know better.

Hamill angled over to a scrawny, thirty-day-wonder lieutenant who stood halfway across the tracks, directing some tanks into position. Miller and his squad paused while the Airborne captain approached the man.

"Get Private Ryan up here," Hamill ordered.

"Ryan!" the lieutenant called out to the paratroopers lining the perimeter. "Front and center!"

A helmeted head popped out of a foxhole, and the soldier under the helmet came running, almost dropping his rifle, finally tripping on the train tracks. As he neared them, his looks proved no less goofy than his gangly gait: close-set eyes, lingering acne, a beaver overbite, and Andy Gump's chin, or lack of one.

"Sir," Ryan squawked, saluting the two captains with absurd, intense formality. "Private James Ryan reporting as ordered, sir!"

Reiben, leaning on his B.A.R., rolled his eyes and said to Mellish, "Told ya he'd be an asshole."

"At ease," Hamill was saying. "Captain Miller here wants a word with you."

Ryan frowned, as if this concept were beyond him, as if Hamill had just proposed an arcane calculus problem. "Sir?"

"Private," Miller said, businesslike but gentle, "I'm afraid I have some bad news for you."

The close-set eyes narrowed, the pimply forehead clenching like a fist. "Sir?"

Miller felt like he was getting ready to kick a stray puppy dog. "There's no easy way to say this, son, so I'll just spit it out. Your brothers are dead."

"What?" The color drained from the boy's face; he had the expression of a man struck a blow in the pit of his stomach. His flabby stomach.

"Your brothers are gone . . . son?"

Ryan sat, almost collapsing, as if the steel switching box his behind found was purely coincidental. "Dead . . . dead, sir? All dead?"

Miller nodded somberly down at him. "We've been sent to take you home, son. You're going home."

"Oh, my God," the boy said, and his rifle clunked to the tracks, his hands flying to his face to catch the tears that were bursting from him, as if this were a sorrow he'd been holding in. Of course, any man in this war was holding back those kind of feelings. . . .

"My brothers . . . oh, my God, my sweet little brothers . . ."

Reiben whispered to Mellish, "Really takin' it like a man, ain't he?"

Hamill squeezed the boy's shoulder. "We're sorry for your loss, James. Can't tell you how much."

"My piles bleed for him," Mellish whispered to Reiben, but Mellish actually did feel sorry for the goofy kid; he had brothers of his own.

Face streaked with tears, Ryan sobbed and hiccuped but managed to get out, "How . . . how did they . . . die?"

"They were killed in action," Miller said.

The boy frowned, puzzled. "What . . . what kind of action?"

"Well . . . I don't know the details. I'm truly sorry."

"This *can't* be . . ."

"It's always hard to accept something like this."

The boy's tears had eased. "No, I mean it just can't be. Ned and Richie, they're both in grammar school."

Now Miller was the one who felt he'd been struck a blow.

"Is that it?" Ryan asked. "A school yard accident? Like a slide collapsed, or maybe a teeter-totter went haywire?"

Miller studied the boy as if he were a germ under a microscope. "You are James Ryan?"

"Sure." He was sniffling.

"James F.?"

"That's right. So they *are* dead?" And the tears began anew.

Reiben, amused now, whispered to Mellish: "Maybe a land mine went off under the jungle gym. Maybe the Japs sabotaged a swing set."

Miller tried again. "You're James Francis Ryan?"

He shook his head, tears flying, spattering Miller like raindrops. "James Frederick Ryan."

Could be a typo on the middle name, a screwup. Miller asked, "Iowa?"

"Minnesota. Brainerd." And still the tears came. "Does . . . does this mean my brothers are all right?"

"Uh, I'm sure they are," Miller said. "We're looking for another James Ryan."

Ryan, James Frederick, was still sobbing. "Are you sure my brothers are okay? How do you *know* they are?"

"This is just a foul-up, son. I'm sorry."

"Maybe the foul-up is *his* brothers are okay, and mine are . . . oh, God . . ."

"No. I don't think so."

He blinked, tears pearling his eyelashes. "So you're not takin' me home?"

"No. We're not."

Now the tears *really* flew, and Hamill motioned some of Ryan's comrades over to comfort and settle him down as he squatted on the switching box. Paratroopers along the perimeter had heard enough of this to be amused, and derisive laughter at the squad's expanse kept Reiben from laughing himself.

Feeling like a jackass, Miller buttonholed Captain Hamill, saying, "Jesus, sorry for the mix-up."

"Military intelligence strikes again," Hamill said.

They moved off the train tracks, Hamill staying with them, Sarge moving up to Miller to ask, "So where the hell is *our* Ryan?"

"You got me by the short ones," Miller said. He turned to Hamill. "You in contact with your C.O.?"

"Not unless you got a spare Ouija board."

Miller grunted. "That's what I figured."

But Hamill was thinking, wanting to help. "What unit is your Ryan in?"

"Baker Company, five-oh-sixth."

That tightened Hamill's eyes. He called over to Sergeant Hill, who was having a smoke with his men, "That guy who busted his foot, he's five-oh-sixth isn't he?"

"Yeah—Charlie Company, I think."

Hamill looked at Miller. "It's not Baker Company, but it's a start."

"Beats anything I got. Where to?"

"Follow me. . . ."

Soon Hamill and Miller were visiting the bombed-out grocery store where the wounded of the 101st were huddled. One of them, Lou Oliver, twenty-four, Phoenix, Arizona, sat with his broken foot bandaged to the size of a loaf of bread, looking up at the two captains, saying, "Ryan? Sorry, don't know him."

"What was your drop zone?" Miller asked.

"Near Vierville."

Miller blinked. "Well, how the hell did you wind up way up here?"

Oliver let out something that was half a laugh, half a sigh. "Just lucky I guess. Sir, our C-47 drew heavy fire, and our pilot was just doing his best to dodge that heavy shit . . . sir. Turning every which way, and we took even more fire during the drop . . . got pretty messy."

Miller nodded.

"Anyway, I ended up here, glad to be anywhere. And I haven't seen a single guy from my stick. God knows where they are."

"Did any blowhard in Baker Company let slip where their primary drop zone was? Any loose lips?"

"No, sir . . . but I know Baker Company had the same rally point as us."

Miller sighed with satisfaction; finally, a real lead. He withdrew a map and began unfolding it.

"Good," Miller said. "Show me."

Within minutes Miller and Hamill were rejoining the squad and Sergeant Hill and his men, who were loitering outside the gutted grocery.

"We got someplace to go?" Sarge asked Miller.

"Yup," Miller said. "We'll wait till dark before we head out."

"What's that . . . three hours?"

"Three hours." Miller swiveled to Hamill. "Can you recommend a good hotel? Clean sheets, soft beds, room service?"

"Hot and cold running French maids," Reiben put in. "Except not runnin' *fast*, sir."

Everybody laughed at that.

"I think we can fix you fellas up," Hamill said. "Sergeant Hill, take 'em to church."

"Yes, sir," Hill said, and the men followed the sergeant, boots scuffing cobblestones, leaving the two captains by themselves in the ruined street.

"So," Hamill said, lighting up a K-ration Lucky Strike, finding a cement chunk to sit down on, "what do you hear? How's it all falling together?"

"Beachhead's secure, but it's slow goin'." Miller found his own concrete chair. "Montgomery's takin' his time getting to Caen, and we're treadin' water till he's ready."

"Monty," Hamill snorted, smoke trailing from his nostrils, dragon-style. "That Brit twit's overrated."

"No shit," Miller grunted.

They were strangers, these two captains, yet they spoke like old friends, as if they were picking up on a conversation that had left off only yesterday. It was a small club they belonged to—that brotherhood of combat captains—and when members ran into each other, they took advantage of finding someone they could talk to.

"We gotta take Caen to take St. Lo," Hamill observed.

"And we gotta take St. Lo," Miller added, "to take Valognes."

Hamill nodded. "Gotta take Valognes to take Cherbourg."

"Gotta take Cherbourg to take Paris."

"Gotta take Paris to take Berlin."

"Gotta take Berlin," Miller finished, "to take that boat home."

They allowed each other a few moments to think of their respective homes, then Hamill shook his head and said, "We sure as hell could use your help here."

"I sure as hell would like to pitch in. But orders are orders."

"I know. Anyway, I understand what you're doing."

"Really? Well, maybe you can tell me, so I'll know."

Hamill sucked on the cigarette, let it pull on his lungs. "That business with the Sullivans, it was tough on the moms and dads back home. Bad headlines . . . plus, I got brothers myself."

Miller nodded. "You're comin' in loud and clear."

"Good luck with this mission, buddy."

"Thank you, Captain."

"Find that lucky bastard, and ship him home."

They spoke for perhaps another hour, watching the sun turn the devastated village beautiful with hot orange light and cool blue shadows. Then Miller got directions to the church, and with nightfall to deceive him, he could almost tell what this village had looked like before the Germans and Americans had come.

At the church he found Jackson on guard duty not at the front door of the church, which was buried in rubble, but at the wall a mortar had made a sloping pile of stones.

"Thunder," he said.

"Flash," Jackson drawled, Springfield draped lovingly in his arms. "Welcome to the Ritz, Cap'n."

"Jackson," Miller said, taking a moment, "why is it you're the only one in the squad that doesn't think I'm a heartless bastard?"

"No, sir, I think you're a heartless bastard myself," he said. "That's your job right now, and thank God you're doin' it. And well, sir."

He smiled at Jackson, nodded, edged inside and poked his way through the piled stone and building materials and debris. Nothing much remained to say this was a church: a single stained-glass window depicting young Jesus teaching his teachers, a broken-winged angel watching down in a halo of moonlight filtering in, the occasional pew. Wade was in one of them, writing something.

Miller knew instinctively what Wade was doing: copying Caparzo's letter, moving the words from the bloody crumpled sheet to clean, fresh V-mail.

"We move out in two hours," Miller announced. "Try to catch some sleep."

Wade glanced up, almost glared at Miller, and returned to his copying. Miller moved down the aisle, noticing Upham on his back in a pew, glasses off, staring at the crumbly ceiling, shaking as if he were suffering a mild case of St. Vitus' dance.

The captain paused. Very quietly he asked, "How you holding up, Corporal?"

Upham smiled; it was a pretty ghastly smile, but a smile. "This is good for me, sir. All of it."

"How's that, son?"

He sat up and recited, clinging to the words like a life raft: " 'War educates the senses, calls into action the will, perfects the physical constitution, brings men into such swift and close collision in critical moments that man measures man.' "

Miller chuckled softly. "I guess that's Emerson's way of lookin' at the brighter side."

Upham blinked, then stared at his captain. "You, uh . . . you're familiar with the work of Emerson, sir?"

"Ralph Waldo and me, we're friendly acquaintances."

Upham was interested now, and his shaking had stopped, though he hadn't noticed. "Captain . . . where are you from, anyway?"

"Why?"

"You know, just wondering . . . what you did for a living in the real world . . . that kinda thing."

"What's the pool up to?"

Caught, Upham grinned. "Uh, it's up over three hundred."

Miller considered that, said, "Not bad. . . . Tell ya what, when it hits five c's, I'll pass you the answer and we'll go fifty-fifty."

Eyes narrowing, Upham whispered conspiratorially, "If that's how you feel, why don't we wait till it's up to a grand?"

Miller shook his head. "I might not live that long."

Upham's grin faded as he realized his captain was not kidding.

"Okay," Upham said. "Five hundred, then."

"It's a deal, kid."

Miller winked at him, and moved to one side of the church, found a clear spot on the floor to sit, and began to spread out his maps, using a flashlight to study them, occasionally marking them. Before long, his men asleep around him, their snoring rumbling gently through the little sanctuary, Miller began having trouble steadying the hand holding the flashlight; damn thing was shaking again.

"How long has this been goin' on?"

The voice was Sarge's; it was neither loud nor unkind. Horvath crouched next to his captain, who said, "Started in Portsmouth, when they brought us down for loading . . . comes and goes."

"Maybe you should think about gettin' in a new line of work. This one doesn't seem to be agreein' with you anymore."

Miller laughed gently. "Yeah. This current occupation *is* losin' its charm."

Sarge sat next to him; Miller took it as the gesture of reconciliation it was.

"What was the name of that kid at Anzio?" Miller asked.

"There were a lot of kids at Anzio. Too many fuckin' kids at Anzio."

"The one that walked on his hands, singin' that filthy song?"

Sarge laughed. "The man on the flyin' trapeze, with the 'unexpurgated' lyrics?"

Miller laughed, too. "That's the one."

"Vecchio."

"Yeah, yeah—Vecchio." Miller shook his head. "Goofy fuckin' kid . . . Vecchio. Caparzo. Jesus . . ."

"Jesus?" Sarge gave him the needle: "You mean, you got *him* killed, too? I had no idea. You're at the right place to make amends."

Miller smiled at that, shaking his head; he was working to keep the tears inside—he understood how that other Private Ryan had come so unglued.

"Every time you get one of your boys killed," Miller said softly, almost prayerfully, "you tell yourself you just saved the lives of two, three, ten, maybe a hundred other men and boys."

"Not a bad way to look at it."

"You know how many men I've lost under my command?"

"Not offhand."

"Caparzo made ninety-four. So, hell, that means I probably saved the lines of ten times that many. Maybe twenty times. See, it's simple. Just do the math—it lets you choose the mission over the men, every time."

"Except this time," Sarge said, "the mission is a man."

Miller laughed again, but it was bitter. "Suppose it had been that goofy kid today—suppose he had been our Private Ryan. Would he have been worth Caparzo?"

"Maybe to his mother."

"I got a mother, you got a mother, Caparzo had a mother. Jesus fuckin' Christ . . ." And he was staring at the stained-glass window as if daring God to do something about his blasphemy. ". . . This Private James Francis Ryan better be pretty goddamn special. He better get his ass home and cure cancer or invent a lightbulb that never fuckin' burns out, or a car that runs on water. Because the truth is, I wouldn't trade ten Ryans for one Vecchio or one Caparzo."

Horvath thought about that, then said, "You know, Ryan doesn't just have a mother . . . he has a captain, too, who probably feels the same about him as you do about these kids."

Miller's mouth twitched with something that wasn't a smile. "Well, then, let *him* get his precious Ryan's ass home. Shit . . . there it goes again."

His hand was shaking, the way Upham had trembled. He focused on it, willing it stop. Finally, it did.

He got onto his feet, checked his watch, barked

out: "On your dogs, girls! Rise and shine. Beauty sleep's over. Let's go. Go! Go!"

And, grumbling, bones creaking, leaving dreams of home and mothers and naked girlfriends behind, they crawled off the floor and out of pews and shouldered their gear, following their heartless captain, trading the shelter of the church for the waiting night.

And the waiting war.

12

Moonlight washed the countryside, and Miller and his men, in a soothing ivory. The quiet of the night was broken only by the song of crickets, an occasional questioning owl, and the footsteps of the seven soldiers themselves, as they moved cautiously along the edge of a field, parallel to the grooves of a cart path.

Miller was proud of his boys, his men. They were a small group, relatively new to fighting, but Omaha Beach had been one hell of a crash course. They were seasoned combat vets now, and with their heavy weaponry and in their full-battle gear, his little squad looked formidable.

He noticed Jackson and Wade drifting too close to each other, and snapped his fingers. All eyes went to him, and he motioned curtly for the pair to open it up a bit. He'd warned them about bunching up.

A sudden flash of light in the sky might have been lightning, but wasn't; rumbling shook both the sky

and the earth. The horizon began to strobe an orang-
ish white, the ground quivering beneath their boots,
with the tremors of shells bursting in the distance.

Then the sky behind them lighted up as well, and
soon opposite ends of the sky seemed on fire. The
tidal wave of sound kept rolling over and under
them, and they could see the mighty shells streaking,
hear them whizzing, overhead. For a few moments
the squad stood frozen in the neutral zone of a massive artillery battle, in the quiet of the eye of a man-
made hurricane.

This battle would not touch them, Miller knew,
unless by freak chance an American 88 collided in
midair with a German one and showered death
down on them. He tried to catch the attention of his
men, but their faces were turned toward one end or
the other of the burning sky. They were transfixed
by the otherworldly beauty of warfare at a distance,
and shaken by the magnitude of its fury, the orange
and white lights playing on their faces like kids at a
Fourth of July fireworks show.

He snapped his fingers again, and the tiny sound
stood out against the battle thunder. His men blinked
out of their spell and trudged on.

They walked through the night, the sound of artillery growing ever distant, the sky lightening again,
this time with the threat of dawn, not conflict. At a
crossroads Miller paused to check his map while
Sarge shone a red-filtered flashlight onto an array of

directional signs, giving them plenty of options to unpronounceable French villages.

The captain refolded and tucked away his map. "Be light soon. Let's pick up the pace."

Avoiding the hedgerow-lined lanes, they stayed on flat farmland, pastures, and fields, and soon—Sarge taking point, Miller tail end—they were walking in dewy grass with the chirp of waking birds and the pleasant gray-blue sky to lull them—and the weapons in their hands to remind them why they were taking this pleasant morning jaunt.

Reiben, who'd been uncharacteristically quiet for some time, burdened with both the B.A.R. and its heavy ammo, posed a question: "You know what the best thing could happen is?"

"How 'bout," Jackson offered, "Private Reiben steps on a rusty nail, comes down with lockjaw, and never says another word, long as he lives?"

Miller laughed at that, loud enough for the men to hear, not because he thought it was particularly funny, but to keep his squad's spirits up.

"I'll bite, Reiben," Miller said as they moved along at a pretty good clip. "What's the best thing that could happen?"

"Best thing," Reiben said, "is we find Ryan, croaked."

"And why's that?"

"Sir, consider the possibilities. A: Ryan is alive, and we have to haul his sorry ass back to the beach.

Knowing you, Cap, you don't let him help carry our gear, even though he should pitch in like any other dogface, and we carry him back on a pillow so him and his mom get reunited like the brass wants, and us? We all get killed trying to keep the son of a bitch alive."

In the distance a dog barked, not very urgently.

"Okay," Miller said, as if he agreed with all of that, which made the men smile.

Reiben went on: "Or, 2: Ryan is dead and—"

"Wait a minute," Mellish said. "You said 'A.' Now you're sayin' '2' . . ."

"Yeah, yeah," Reiben said, "or B: Ryan's dead, blown to shit, millions of pieces floating in some creek bumping into himself. And you, sir, you make us fish him out a piece at a time and we're trying to put Humpty-Dumpty back together, you know, to make sure we got the right Private Ryan this time, while the Krauts pick us off, one by one."

"That one I don't much care for," Miller said.

They were at a hedgerow, but one of the lower-standing ones, not impenetrable. They were able to squeeze through onto the next field, where Reiben resumed his discourse.

"I don't like that one myself, either, sir. So let's look at C: we find Ryan and he's wounded."

"Not good," Mellish said.

"The worst," Reiben agreed. "Not only does he not carry *our* gear, we gotta carry *his* gear. Not to mention Private Ryan himself and his sorry, wounded ass."

"Could happen," Miller said.

"That's what I'm saying, sir. Best possible situation is, D: he's dead, as a mackerel, more or less intact. We grab one of his dog tags, and hotfoot it back to the beach."

"Do we take his body?" Mellish asked.

"Hell no! Leave him to some lucky burial squad."

"I got a better idea."

Reiben smirked. "I'm sure, Mellish."

Mellish looked around at his fellow ground pounders and asked, "Anybody besides me ever notice how close the name 'Reiben' is to 'Ryan'? Reiben, Ryan . . . Wry-*ben*, Wry-*yan*."

The squad was nodding, grinning—except for Reiben.

Mellish continued: "I vote we shoot Reiben, leave him for the burial squad, and scratch over his dog tags, passing him off as Ryan.'"

"Mighty temptin'," Jackson said. "But what if somebody catches on?"

"Mistakes happen," Mellish shrugged. "It's a sloppy war . . . worst thing is, we have to keep lookin' . . . few days from now, when things are gettin' quieter."

"Interesting," Miller said, keeping a straight face. "A real possibility."

"No offense, sir," Reiben said, beaten at his own game, "but I like my idea better."

Wade, who had not been playing along with the black comedy, said, "I don't think Ryan's mother would."

"Ryan's mother!" Reiben shook his head. "Jesus Christ, let's not start with Ryan's mother again. What did Ryan's mother ever do for you? Did she ever tuck you in, or haul your ashes or anything? Ever occur to you, maybe she doesn't even *like* her god-damn kid? Maybe he was a pain in the ass down on the farm? A bad apple!"

"She loves him," Upham said.

"How do you know?"

"She's his mother."

"So? Maybe she didn't even want him. Maybe the rubber broke. Maybe it was the other three kids she loved, and she woulda just as soon sent little Jimmy back for a nickel refund."

"Or how 'bout this?" Jackson asked, getting into the swing of it. "How about he accidentally killed ol' Bessie, the prize-winnin' Hereford?"

"How'd he kill her?" Mellish asked.

Jackson was ready: "Burned down the barn by accident playin' with matches."

Mellish's eyes glittered. "Maybe it wasn't an accident!"

"Yeah," Reiben said, having fun, back on top of his game, "maybe he's one of those sadistic farm boys you hear about, likes to torture chickens, and rub the blood on his overalls. . . ."

"No," Upham said, "you're wrong—he's not sadistic."

Everybody looked at the corporal.

"He's amoral," Upham said, "unprincipled and thoroughly corrupt. He's depraved, dishonest, and tricky. He's a slippery, fibbing, unreliable, utterly useless bovine-fornicating farm boy . . . that's a cow fucker, in case anybody's interested . . . but sadistic? No."

The men around him were grinning, nodding, viewing the new meat with sudden respect. Mellish whistled appreciatively, and Reiben was eyeing the corporal with a new regard, wondering if he had a rival now, in the bullshit-slinging arena.

Miller was pleased, even relieved, to see Upham assert himself and the group finally accept the four-eyed corporal into its fold. But the griping sure had taken a weird turn. . . .

Walking through the night, it had been as if the squad were exploring an otherwise unpopulated planet. The morning began the same way, then perhaps an hour into sunshine, after moving across fields and pastures, encountering occasional cows but no people, Miller and his men exchanged wary glances as a murmuring of activity beckoned them through a hedgerow.

Pushing through the hedge, which was more forgiving than many of its ilk, the squad was confronted by (as Reiben immediately put it) "Grand Central Station in a bean field."

American troops, paratroopers mostly, had set up a circular defensive perimeter—freshly dug foxholes, machine-gun positions guarding the flanks—within which, like performers in the center ring of a circus, clusters of GIs wandered aimlessly, and French refugees milled and squatted. Hedgerows hemmed the field on three sides, a dirt road on the fourth.

The soldiers, smoking and swapping stories, were clearly a ragtag assortment cut off from their companies. The civilians were old and young, women and children outnumbering men and the elderly, clutching salvaged possessions that ranged from absolutely essential to poignantly personal. One camped-out family was having a sort of picnic from the food carted here in an elegant suitcase, while an old lady clasped framed family photographs to her bosom, and a little girl pushed her doll in a tiny stroller. Other kids, eyes wide with hero worship, were watching the soldiers who guarded the perimeter.

The soldiers and refugees were navigating a graveyard of gliders. Flung about the flatness of the field were half a dozen of the low-slung, wide-winged ships, with American markings, scattered like huge discarded toys. Their plywood husks yawned open at the rear, where men and gear had departed.

Five were intact, but a sixth glider had crashed

into the hedgerow on the far side of the field, and a score or more of wounded American soldiers were clustered there, some using a broken wing for shade. Other wounded were being shuttled to the holding area, in commandeered civilian vehicles, including a battered old farm truck and a horse-drawn milk wagon. Still others were making their way under their own steam.

As the squad tramped onto the field, a ragged group from the 506th wearing the blue and red double-A patch of the 101st Airborne was escorting a handful of German prisoners to a holding area.

Miller realized this was the first close-up look most of his squad had ever had at the enemy, living examples anyway, and knew his boys would be shocked, as he had been, by how normal they looked and how young many of them were. They bore the unmistakable odor of sweat and leather and unwashed uniforms so typical of the German combat soldier. And they seemed dazed, amazed, that they'd been captured.

"Master race my ass," Reiben muttered.

As they passed, Mellish identified himself as a Jew. "Juden," he said to them again and again, "Juden," pointing to himself and his gun. Just letting them know. . . .

Over by the wrecked glider, where the wounded were gathered, a young American Air Corps pilot was motioning them over, calling to Miller, "Captain! Captain!"

As they trooped over, Miller turned to tell Wade to tend to the wounded, but Wade was already half-way there.

Miller stopped in front of the pilot. "Want to fill me in here, Lieutenant?"

"Dewindt, sir," the pilot said. William Dewindt was slim, blond, twenty-five, from Scottsdale, Arizona. "Ninety-ninth Troop Carrier Squadron, carrying the 325th glider infantry. This wrecked baby was mine. . . . Twenty-two dead."

Miller's mouth flinched in sympathy.

"I got tossed ass over teakettle," Dewindt said, pointing into the field, "windin' up over there. Not a scratch. My copilot lost his head."

"What did he do?" Miller asked. "Panic?"

"No, no! I guess I didn't make myself clear. He was decapitated."

There wasn't much to say to that. So Miller stayed businesslike, asking, "Where's the unit? Who the hell are all these people?"

"The guys we brought in, sir, they went off, first night, and we haven't seen 'em since. Meantime, guys keep showin' up, one, two, half a dozen at a time. Sooner or later some officer'll come along, patch together a mixed unit, and head off to make noise. You must have had heavy losses yourself, sir."

That was a natural assumption to make, a small group like his headed up by a captain.

"No," Miller said, "we're on a special patrol, Lieutenant. Looking for a Private James Ryan. Baker Company of the five-oh-sixth. Seen him?"

Dewindt shrugged. "Wouldn't know if I had, sir. Lot of guys have been through here, in and out."

"Yeah." He glanced over at his medic. "Anything?"

Wade looked up from the man he was bandaging to say, "He's not among these joes."

"Jesus," somebody said.

It was Sarge.

"Take a look at this," Horvath said, and Miller went over to where the sergeant was standing.

A corpse of an officer was wedged between what remained of the glider's bulkhead and a jeep that had been sent smashing forward, on impact.

"Couldn't pry him out of there," Dewindt said, then wryly added, "You wouldn't happen to have a spare winch on you?"

"Not hardly," Miller said. "Are those stars on his helmet?"

"Sure are," Sarge said.

"That's General Amend, Deputy Commander, 101st," Dewindt said.

"No shit," Sarge breathed. "How did he manage to die like that?"

Dewindt smirked. "Some fucking genius had the brilliant idea of welding steel plates onto our deck to keep the general safe from ground fire. Unfortunately, nobody bothered to tell me about this little precaution till we were just getting airborne."

"Sounds like fun," Miller said.

"Fun, like trying to fly a freight train. Gross overload, trim characteristics shot to hell. I almost broke my damn arms tryin' to keep 'er level."

The squad had gathered around; this was worth hearing.

"When we released," Dewindt continued, "I cut as hard as I could, tried to gain some altitude, keep 'er from stallin'. We came down like a safe somebody dropped out a high window. And you can see how we ended up." He pointed out to the other gliders. "Everybody else stopped on a dime . . . we were just too damn heavy. Wet grass, downward slope . . . twenty-two men dead. . . . Guess it was real important to keep General Amend alive." He grunted a humorless laugh. "One man."

"Lot of that goin' around," Reiben nodded.

Miller shot a glare at Reiben, but Reiben just stared calmly back at his captain. And finally Miller shrugged, nodded; how could he argue?

Reiben sighed, said, "Another typical *foobar*."

"Fuckin' A," Mellish said.

"Hey," Upham said, "how do you spell that, anyway?"

"F-U," Reiben grinned, then patted his B.A.R.

"That's how I thought you spelled it," Upham

said. "I looked it up in my German dictionary. No such word."

"Upham," Miller said.

"Sir?"

"Talk to every one of these paratroopers, on the perimeter, inside the circle. Look for Ryan or word of him."

"Yes, sir."

And Upham hustled off.

Dewindt shook a little pouch tied on his belt. "Might want to check these out, too."

"Yeah?" Miller said, not understanding.

The pilot untied the pouch and handed it to the captain. "That's my dog-tag collection," he said wearily. "More of 'em than I care to count. Those cover a lot of bodies, sir. Your man could be in there."

Miller took the sack from the pilot, then handed it to Jackson, saying, "See if you can find Private Ryan."

"Yes, sir."

"I'll help," Reiben chimed.

They sat on the grass, and Mellish joined them, like kids playing jacks or marbles. They passed the bag, each taking a handful, checking, then tossing tags in a pile on the empty pouch at their center.

"Think he's in here?" Reiben asked.

"Bet ya he is," Jackson said. "Bet that barn-burnin', cow-lovin' bastard's just waitin' for us. . . ."

"Bet ya I find him," Mellish said.

"Five bucks says I find him," Reiben said.

"You're on," Mellish said.

"I'm in," Jackson said.

Now it was more like a back of the barracks craps game. A good-natured gambling fever gripped them as they searched faster and faster through the metal tags.

"Come on, baby, come on, I know you're in here," Mellish said.

"Screw you, buddy," Reiben said to Mellish, "he's mine!"

"No use hidin', Ryan," Jackson said. "Cain't hide from this ol' hound dog. . . ."

"Olly olly oxen free," Mellish said.

Reiben, laughing, said, "Let's make it really interesting . . . make it ten bucks. . . ."

"Ten's fine with me," Mellish said, then announced, "I got him!" He held up the tag like it was the winning ticket stub on free dish night at the movies. "Here he is—Ryan! I got him!"

Miller, from the sidelines, asked, "James Francis?"

"Uh . . . no . . . shit. It's not Ryan, it's Reyes . . . R-E-Y-E-S. Hell, that's close."

"This ain't horseshoes," Jackson said.

"Piss on it," Mellish said, tossing the tag on the pile and digging back in.

"Close my ass," Reiben laughed.

Miller smiled, too, then he glanced at Sarge and saw disgust. Dewindt had a similar sickened expression.

Then Wade, hands bloody from tending wounds, strode over to the little game circle, his face tight with fury, but his voice was a whisper, a steady one, as he said, "What the hell do you think you're doin'? Those guys over there can hear you."

Wade nodded toward the huddled, ashen-faced wounded under the broken wing.

"Every one of those dog tags is a *dead* man, you dumb fucks," Wade said, almost spitting the words.

Like scolded children—children who knew they'd done wrong—the trio whitened and went silent as they continued to check the names on the dog tags, slowly now, somberly.

Miller's hand was shaking. He clutched it with his other hand, while his mind swam with doubt and guilt: *how could he have gone along with that?* He had been telling himself the hardened surface he showed his men was a facade, for their benefit; but had he gone hard underneath the facade now?

Or was there nothing left behind it? Had this fucking war killed his humanity like it killed Vecchio and Caparzo and the rest?

Reiben, Mellish, and Jackson were getting to their feet now, finished with their search.

"He's not here, sir," Jackson said, handing the refilled pouch respectfully back to Dewindt. "Sorry, sir. Guess we're all a little battle-wacky."

The pilot said nothing.

Miller nodded to Dewindt and, seeing Upham

moving his way, walked toward the corporal, moving toward the middle of the field. The squad followed along.

"No Ryan." Upham shrugged with a nod back at the cluster of men he'd just spoken with.

Miller kept walking, joining the jumbled chaos of civilians and GIs, and his men followed.

"Now what, sir?" Sarge asked him.

Miller just shot him a dirty look—thanks for asking, drop dead—and stalked off toward the road, where more refugees and wounded were coming along to join the circus.

"Goddamn radios don't work," Miller muttered. "Chain of command nonexistent . . ."

As his men tagged after him, they exchanged glances of concern.

"Is he bitching," Reiben whispered to Mellish, "or cracking up?"

Miller stopped suddenly and so did everybody else, piling on top of each other like bowling pins struggling not to be a strike.

"Here's an idea," he said. "Let's split up into two groups and wander the fucking countryside. Like town criers, you know? Calling his name? Sooner or later, he's bound to hear us."

"Good thought, sir," Sarge said, clearly not sure whether Miller was kidding or not, "but that could take a while."

"I *hope* he's just bitching," Mellish whispered back to Reiben.

"Okay, let's ask the locals," Miller said, "maybe they've seen him."

An old couple moving down off the road into the field recoiled as the captain moved quickly toward them, saying, *"Parlez vous Ryan? Oui? Non?"*

Speaking to each other in frantic French, the old couple moved quickly away from Miller, as if he'd been about to assault them.

Upham whispered to Reiben and Mellish: *"They* think he's cracking up."

Another group of German prisoners was being paraded from the road onto the field, escorted by more paratroopers wearing the blue and red insignia of the 101st. The prisoners looked fresher than their paratrooper guards, who had obviously seen heavy action; many were walking wounded.

"Hey!" Miller called to them. "One hundred first! Any of you fellas know a guy named Ryan?"

The men passing by shook their heads, no.

But as the ragged column continued on, Miller kept asking, his desperation showing, his men behind him shaking their heads with worry. The paratroopers were shaking their heads, too—no.

"Anybody know James Ryan?" the captain persisted.

Then a voice from down the line called out, not to Miller but to someone even farther back: "Hey, Joe—

isn't Ryan that guy Michaelson pals around with? The one from Company C?"

"I think so, yeah!" a voice returned.

"Well, get his ass up here," the paratrooper hollered back, "would ya?"

Pretty soon a pair of paratroopers had separated from the prisoner escort group and planted themselves before Miller and his squad.

"Either of you know a guy named Ryan?" Miller asked.

"Michaelson here knows a Ryan, Captain," the paratrooper on the left said. He was Private Joe D'Amato, twenty-two, Elizabeth, New Jersey. "But you'll have to speak up, sir, his hearing's not so good."

"My hearing's messed up, sir!" Private Roger Michaelson said, twenty-three, Rock Island, Illinois. *"You'll have to speak up!"*

"German grenade went off next to him," D'Amato said. "His hearing comes and goes."

"Grenade went off next to me!" Michaelson began to explain.

"Yeah, yeah, I get it!" Miller said, weary of this Abbott and Costello routine already. *"You know Ryan?"*

"Who?"

"Ryan! Do you know Ryan?"

"Jimmy Ryan?"

Behind him, Miller's men perked up at this.

Reiben whispered to Mellish, "He ain't cracking up, he's a human devinin' rod."

Miller was grinning, nodding. *"James Francis Ryan?"*

Michaelson winced. *"Jimmy Ryan? What?"*

Miller turned to his squad. "Who's got a pencil?" The men started patting their pockets.

"A pencil, anybody! Come on!"

"Sir . . ."

It was Upham, holding out a stubby pencil.

". . . Just this small one, sir."

The captain and corporal exchanged stony dead-pan expressions, but their eyes shared a smile and a private moment.

Then Miller asked, "Paper, Upham?"

"Yes, sir," he said, and held up a small notebook.

"Good. Now, write this down: 'Do you know James Francis Ryan?' "

Upham nodded, jotted that down, and held up the little notebook like a flash card for Michaelson to read.

"Of course I know him!" Michaelson exploded. *"He's my best pal!"*

"Ask him if he knows where Ryan is," Miller said to Upham, who jotted that, and held up the note-book page.

Michaelson nodded and said, *"Yeah. We missed our drop zone by about twenty miles, ended up way over by Bum-ville or some damn place! Jimmy, me, and a couple other guys were headin' here, to our rally point! Ran into a colonel who was gatherin' men to go to Ramelle. . . . That's the last I seen of him!"*

The men of Miller's squad were energized by this news, trading smiles, shaking fists in triumph; their fishing expedition had turned into a real mission.

Miller patted Michaelson's shoulder and began, *"Thank you!"*

"What?"

The captain sighed, told the other paratrooper, "Just thank him for me, will ya? When his hearing comes back."

A minute later Miller had spread a map out on the grass with his men gathering around him as he pointed, saying, "We're here—Ramelle is there. On the Merderet River, about fifteen miles west by northwest."

Sarge was squinting in thought. "Why Ramelle?"

Miller unfolded the map farther, and pointed as he spoke. He didn't notice that his hand was shaking, but his men did—they were staring not at the locations he was singling out, but at his trembling fingers.

"The target has always been Cherbourg," Miller said. "We can't push on to Paris unless we take a major port. Rommel knows that, of course, and'll come across the Merderet and hit us in the flank when we make that right turn for Cherbourg. . . . That makes any village on the river with a bridge valuable fucking real estate."

And the captain dimpled the map with a fingertip. Right at Ramelle, its bridge indicated boldly on the map.

"That's where we'll find Private Ryan," he said.

And he looked up at the hovering faces, to see how well they'd taken in this lesson, and realized at last that their focus was on his hand. His trembling hand.

But he did not acknowledge that this was any big deal; he just folded up the map.

"Let's get moving," he said.

He did, and they did.

13

Morning had turned into afternoon, and the shadows the squad threw across the French countryside had changed direction. Reiben hadn't: he was still bitching.

"I'm just saying," he said, loaded down with his B.A.R. and its ammo, as they trudged through yet another hedgerow-lined field, "the guys in the Pacific got it easier."

"I don't know," Mellish said, "they gotta catch malaria before they start raving—with you it comes natural."

"I'm tellin' ya, shootin' Japs is easier, on account of Nips don't look as much like people as Krauts do."

Miller, walking point, smiled knowingly to himself; seeing those Germans up close had gotten to his boys, some.

"I don't have any trouble shootin' Krauts," Mellish said.

"Killing a man is killing a man," Wade said, "no matter what he looks like."

"Not that there ever was a German worth a flying fuck," Reiben observed. "They're all cocksuckers and pricks. Always have been. It's in the blood."

Miller glanced back. "What about Beethoven? Remember him?"

Everybody recalled Reiben's rant about the irony and tragedy of the great composer going deaf.

"A prick," Reiben said.

Miller tried again. "Martin Luther."

"Cocksucker."

"Hey," Sarge growled from tail end, "I'm a Lutheran!"

"What about Immanuel Kant?" Upham asked.

"Who?"

"He was a great philosopher."

"Prick."

"Yeah?" Mellish said. "What about Marlene Dietrich?"

"Cocksucker," Reiben said. Then he grinned. "But that could just be wishful thinkin'. . . ."

Everybody laughed, even Wade. Their footsteps padded over the grass, their gear clinked and clanked along. In the distance, small-arms fire chattered, so common a sound walking through this otherwise quiet countryside, it might have been birds chirping or a horse braying.

"Still," Upham said, "they can't *all* be pricks and cocksuckers."

"Sure they can," Reiben said.

Wade, serious again, snapped, "Are you listening to yourself?"

"Would you," Mellish posed, "if you were him?"

Wade, taking this entirely too seriously, continued: "Just so I got this straight, Reiben . . . there isn't a decent man, woman, and child in their entire country."

"Hey, you're bein' too generous," Reiben said, shifting, trying to find some way he didn't feel like a pack mule with all the gear he was burdened with. "I'd include every dog, cat, squirrel, horse, cow . . . any sauerkraut-snapping, schnitzel-munching, son-of-a-bitchin', Hitler-lovin' thing that breathes. All pricks."

"And cocksuckers," Mellish reminded him.

"That, too," Reiben nodded.

"Reiben," Wade said, with no humor at all, "you have to be the most backward, bigoted, ignorant excuse for a human being I've ever met."

"Maybe," Reiben said. "But I'm not a prick or a cocksucker."

"Let's take a vote," Mellish said.

"Yeah, yeah, all right—name me one decent German. Go ahead . . . just one. . . ."

Nobody said anything.

Reiben grinned. "Ain't so easy, is it?"

"Not when Martin Luther's a prick," Mellish said, "it isn't."

"Cocksucker," Reiben corrected.

"Albert Schweitzer," Wade said.

"Who?"

"Albert Schweitzer. He's a German."

Reiben had the expression of a man sniffing sour milk. "Who the hell is that? Not that it matters. He already sounds like a prick."

Wade was shaking his head, frustrated. "Albert Schweitzer's' only the most famous fucking doctor in history! Spent the last thirty years in Africa, helping natives. . . ."

"Why'd he do that?" Reiben asked.

Wade exploded: "Because he was trying to help his fellow man! Because he isn't a selfish asshole like you, Reiben!"

"Hey, you think I came to France for the cheese?"

The usually low-key Wade was getting worked up. "Look, shithead . . . Albert Schweitzer is the reason I became a doctor in the first place. So the next time you step on a land mine, you better hope I feel like slappin' a bandage on an asshole like you!"

Reiben smirked and shook his head.

"What?" Wade demanded.

"Nothin'."

"*What?*"

Reiben shrugged. "It's just, I thought you said, one time, both your parents are doctors."

"That's right, Reiben. What about it?"

Reiben reared back in mock shock. "And it takes

some fuckin' prick Kraut to convince you to go into the family business?"

"Somebody hand me a weapon," Wade said.

Miller, weary of this discourse, called back, "Reiben, lose an argument, for once, okay? Albert Schweitzer was not a prick and not a cocksucker. You, however, are an asshole."

Laughter rippled over the squad, except for Reiben, who said, "Okay, okay," shrugged again and shut up.

"Take point, Sarge," Miller said, and as he and Horvath traded places, the captain fell briefly in alongside Wade and, making sure Reiben was out of earshot, whispered, "Albert Schweitzer was born in Alsace."

Wade looked in sharp surprise at Miller.

"He's of German descent, all right," Miller whispered, "but he's officially French."

Wade processed that.

"It'll be our secret," Miller assured him.

Then Wade gave Miller the slightest smile. But that smile felt very good to the captain, who valued his medic's friendship, and was glad to have worked his way off Wade's shit list.

This time, woods bordered the far end of the field, rather than the thickness of those ubiquitous hedgerows, and the seven soldiers worked their way carefully through the trees, Miller halting them at the thick, waist-high brush at the edge of the adjacent field, not allowing his men to emerge until he'd completely scanned the landscape.

Atop a rise overlooking a vast pasture were the concrete pickup sticks of a destroyed German radar station and its pillbox support bunkers, blasted to slabs and chunks and pebbles, probably by the massive air strike that had flashed over the heads of the squad last night. The surrounding pasture was pitted with bomb craters; it looked like the moon's surface with grass. All around the pasture, cows seemed to be on their sides, sleeping. But they were all dead, legs sticking out in rigor mortis, making them look like discarded toy animals, a distant fence hemming them in, though they weren't going anywhere.

Miller motioned his men to stay back and stay down. He moved, keeping low, into thinning trees and high brush, peering at the grassy rise and the concrete rubble ruins, like relics of some ancient Grecian temple, the torn radar panel silhouetted starkly against the sky.

He waved at Horvath and Jackson to join him in the weeds, and something nearby caught Sarge's eye.

"Good Christ," Sarge whispered. "Look at this, Cap. . . ."

Miller turned and saw nearby trees, smaller ones at the woods' edge, that had been pockmarked with bullets, in some cases shattered, splintered, shot to shit.

"When did that happen?" Miller asked.

Sarge was taking a close look. "Recently."

"You mean, after that station and bunkers got hit?"

"I'd say."

From the thicker trees came Wade's quiet but urgent call: "Captain! Y'gotta see this. . . ."

Keeping low, Miller and the sergeant and the sharpshooter scurried through the whispery brush. An ashen Wade was crouching, pointing to a trail of blood spatter—fresh enough to still look red, not black—which led to grass that was flattened with a scattering of fresh bodies, sprawled in the weeds, paratroopers, bullet-chewed. At Wade's prompting, Miller and Sarge rose just enough to see more corpses littering the brush—a patrol like theirs, a little larger, a lot deader.

Miller gazed over the top of the weeds, studying the rise and its apparently out-of-commision installations. "Below that bunker, Sarge—y'see that hole? At one-thirty?"

"Yeah," Sarge nodded, hunkered next to him. "That'd be my guess, too."

"Look hard—you can see the sandbags."

The rest of the squad had gathered around now. Upham, eyes wide and bright behind the glasses, looked out at the torn bodies and asked, "What do you think did this? A machine gun?"

Jackson spat, nodded. "Yep. . . . I'd say a MG-42."

"Jesus, *one* gun did that?"

Mellish, also gazing at the corpses, said,

"Paratroopers . . . maybe one of them's Private Ryan."

"Check out the 82nd patches, you birdbrain," Miller said irritably. "You guys aren't getting off that easy."

"Sir," Reiben said, and he pointed off to the left. "Why don't we just head over that way, stay in the woods, hustle around, quick and quiet. They'll never know we were here."

Miller was slamming a full magazine into his Thompson.

"I mean, sir," Reiben went on, "what I'm saying is, why borrow trouble when we can just go around it?"

"We're not going around it," Miller said, "we're going to take it."

"Maybe Reiben's right, sir," Jackson said. "I mean, we left them eighty-eights behind. . . ."

"For the Air Force to take out," Miller said. "But the flyboys aren't gonna expend their ordinance on one little machine gun, are they? That's what they pay the infantry for."

"I'd like to wait to see if my latest check clears, sir," Reiben said.

"Sir, don't take this wrong," Mellish said, "but we can skip this step, and still accomplish our mission. . . . Actually, get right down to it, this *isn't* our mission. . . ."

"So we should just leave this machine-gun nest for the next company that stumbles along?" Miller said, looking pointedly at Mellish. "A company that might not notice these dead bodies in the high grass?"

"That's not what I meant, sir. It just seems . . . like an unnecessary risk, given our objective."

"Our objective's to win the war, Private."

"I thought we were here to save Ryan."

"Yeah," Reiben said, brightening, "I mean, it'd be great to wipe these Jerries out, but think of Private Ryan. Think of his poor mom."

"Reiben . . ." Miller began ominously.

"It's just that I got a bad feeling about this one, sir."

"Yeah?" Miller asked, slipping off his pack, fishing out two grenades. "And when did you ever have a good feeling about anything?"

Reiben didn't have an answer to that one.

"Okay," Miller said, "three runners with suppressing fire, take off one at a time—one, two, three. Mellish, you hook right. I'll head up the middle. We need somebody to handle the third baseline. . . . Who wants to go left?" He was clipping the grenades onto the webbing of his gear, not aware the hand he was using was trembling like a drunk checking an empty glass.

When he got no volunteers, Miller frowned and snarled, "Who's goin' fucking left?"

"Uh, I'll take it, sir," Jackson said.

"Good. Jackson goes left." He looked from Mellish

to Jackson and back again, saying, "Shoot and scoot, till we're within grenade range."

"How 'bout if I go up the middle, sir?" Sarge asked. "We really shouldn't be risking our—"

"My grandmother runs faster than you, and she's dead."

"I'll go left, then," Sarge said.

"You'll shut up," Miller snapped. "That *would* be a stupid risk, sending us both . . . Reiben, base of fire."

Reiben nodded, businesslike now.

"Keep those clips and mags where you can reach 'em," Miller continued. "You'll sound the starting gun. . . . When your B.A.R. goes, we go."

Reiben nodded again, so did Mellish and Jackson, to whom Miller added, "Extra grenades for the runners."

Reiben and Upham handed their grenades over.

The trio of runners positioned themselves, waiting. Miller gave Reiben a curt nod, and the B.A.R. opened up, shattering the afternoon with its thunder.

Keeping low, under Reiben's covering fire, Mellish sprinted toward the hill, cutting right, then Miller took off right down its throat, and Jackson headed left, each of them finding a crater to roll into for cover, before the machine-gun nest even came awake.

But once they had found cover, it roused, big time, spitting flame, spitting bullets, and Miller had caught a glimpse of the crew in the nest, just before he ducked into the shell hole: three flat-helmeted Krauts in camouflage, one firing, one feeding, one spotting.

From the high weeds, Reiben was pouring it on with the B.A.R., and Sarge and Upham were pounding return fire, too, bullets cracking by, over and above and around them.

Miller looked toward Jackson, who was in his own crater. "You were right," the captain told the private. "MG-42."

On the other side of him, from where he hid behind a ridge of artillery-plowed dirt, Mellish said, "Figures. Who are those guys?"

"Falshirmjager," Miller said, almost yelling to be heard over the firefight raging above their heads. "Elite paratroopers. Fuckin' fanatics."

"I was hopin' for the Hitler youth," Mellish said, hugging his carbine like his best girl.

"If we press 'em," Miller said, "they'll have to change barrels." He nodded toward the grenades hanging off his webbing. "Then we can throw the ball to home."

"What do you mean, 'press 'em'?" Mellish asked.

"Shoot and scoot!" Miller said. "Move out!"

"That's what I was afraid you meant. . . ."

Mellish scrambled toward the next dip in the defilade, blasting up at the machine-gun nest, then burrowing in and banging away, emptying a full clip up at the nest, attracting the fire-and-lead-spitting snout of the MG-42.

And as the machine gun swung in Mellish's direction, Jackson dashed to a twisted steel section blown from the destroyed radar tower. He took cover there even as the machine gun again swung, this time in his direction, slugs spattering dirt, clanging off metal.

This prompted Miller, temporarily under the arc of fire, to run straight up toward a zigzag trench near the bottom of the hill. The machine gun dropped to try to get at him, but the angle was wrong, so it swung instead toward Mellish, who was blasting away as he cut back to another, smaller shell hole, bullets dancing in the dirt. Miller rolled into the trench, then scurried down its zigs and zags, looking up to see Jackson as the sharpshooter and his Springfield moved along that long twisted tower wreckage, the nest raining lead down on his position, bullets whining and whanging off metal.

Miller smiled tightly. That machine-gun barrel had to be overheating about now—they'd attracted a hell of a lot of fire, without getting a scratch.

He glanced back at Mellish, signaling him to follow, and the captain scooted out of the trench toward another shell crater, with the private tagging along, machine-gun fire arcing overhead. Then both men went sliding into the shell hole, and found they weren't alone.

Two American paratroopers were already there. Dead ones, eyes wide and empty, khaki splotched red.

"Where the hell did they come from?" Mellish asked, drawing away from the dead men as if what they had were catching.

"Something's wrong," Miller said, whitening. "That MG-42 couldn't have hit these boys, at this angle. . . ."

As if proving Miller's point, the machine-gun nest sent a short burst slamming their way, but arcing over, falling short of its target.

Then silence.

Miller waited—were they switching barrels?

Jackson lunged from behind the twisted steel debris, firing up at the nest as he went, heading for a trench. The machine gun let a short burst out, and spun him to the ground.

"Jackson!" Mellish cried.

"Shit," Miller said.

Silence again.

A more lingering silence. . . .

They were changing barrels!

"Grenades," Miller instructed.

Miller pulled a pin, Mellish the same, rose, reared back, lobbed, and ducked back down.

"We were high," Miller said, knowing the grenades had landed on the slope above the hole that housed the nest.

More silence.

"Go again!" Miller yelled. "Get that runner out at third base!"

He pulled a pin, and threw. He could hear the grenade thud against a sandbag. First one, then another explosion—the first two grenades they'd thrown, doing the nest no damage. Mellish tossed his next grenade—and it was a perfect lob, only one of the Germans managed to hurl both grenades back out and they exploded one, two, like ugly fireworks over the pasture—none of their nasty fragments finding Miller or Mellish.

Someone was yelling: "Christ!"

It was Wade's voice, from the weeds, where the medic had been moving quick and low, heading toward the fallen Jackson.

"Another gun!" The medic was standing up, yelling, waving his arms, signaling, Red Cross armband apparent. "Sir, another gun!"

Miller whirled and saw, just over at the left, another flat-helmeted, camouflaged Kraut. Lifting from where he'd been concealed by grass and dirt, his hands held an FG-42 machine gun. With a magazine like that, sticking out at the side, he could lay flat on the ground and wait for his prey to move into his kill zone. . . .

But one of his previous victims, a dead paratrooper, had been blocking his shot at Miller and Mellish, and so he had raised up. . . .

Almost simultaneously, three things happened.

The machine-gun nest, a fresh barrel on their MG-42, resumed their firing and took advantage of a new target—Wade—and Miller caught a terrible glimpse of the medic crumpling, his startled expression disappearing into the weeds.

Jackson, his forearm bloody, managed to lean on his rifle and fire it at the same time, catching the camouflaged second machine gunner with a hole through the front of the helmet. Pitching his handheld machine gun, the sniper slumped, spasmed, and died.

And finally Mellish peppered another grenade in the nest, hard, the kind of fastball that burns a catcher's mitt. The trio of Germans were fumbling around, trying to retrieve it before it went off.

And then it went off.

In the weeds Sarge was saying, "All right . . . *now* we're in business. . . ."

Upham had noticed Wade, sitting in the grass, looking embarrassed, exhaling slowly, looking up at the hill and the hole exuding smoke beneath the defunct bunkers.

"All right," Wade said softly. "All right . . ."

"Wade," Upham said, alarmed. "Wade!"

"Wade?" Sarge asked, coming over. "You get hit, buddy?"

Miller and Mellish were already running over, dodging craters. Reiben, too, followed, leaving the B.A.R. behind, and Jackson scrambled over, clutching his grazed arm. Everyone put on the brakes when their eyes met the same appalling sight: their medic was sitting in the weeds, looking down, astounded, at the five blood-leaching bullet wounds in his torso.

14

Miller heard somebody say, "Oh, Wade, oh, Jesus Christ," then realized it was himself, looking down at the four bullets stitched across the medic's abdomen and the other in the lower right chest. Wade was having trouble breathing. Upham, stunned, said, "They're not supposed to shoot medics, they're not supposed to shoot medics."

Then multiple hands, Miller's among them, were grabbing and ripping through Wade's medical pack in a flurry. Other hands, Sarge's among them, were tearing the medic's shirt open, baring the terrible wounds, and everybody was talking and shouting all at once.

"Sulfa," Miller said to Jackson, who was rummaging through the medical pack with him, "gimme the sulfa . . ."

"He was helpin' *me*, goddamn it," Jackson said. "Comin' after *me*. . . ."

"Shit," Sarge said, hunkered over the bleeding medic, "get some pressure on it. . . ."

"Help me out, Upchuck!" Mellish yelled, hands red with Wade's blood, "shit, help me out here, use your hands!"

Upham got in and helped, while Jackson, fumbling with medical supplies, his own arm bleeding, was not his usual cool country self. "Oh, God, oh, Jesus," he was saying.

Prayer? Curse?

"Sulfa, where's the goddamn sulfa," Miller said.

"Fuck sulfa, he needs morphine," Sarge called back, wild-eyed. "Morphine!"

Then they were injecting the morphine, pouring sulfa, blood everywhere, a blur of help and panic and adrenaline.

Miller, hovering over the medic, said, "Wade? Wade? Can you hear me?"

Wade's body was shaking, as if he were piloting a crashing plane that was coming apart. In a way he was, he was riding the pain, looking at them with distant eyes and a feeble smile.

"How's it look?" he asked, voice calm, body shivering.

"You're fine," Miller said. "You'll be okay. . . ."

Wade reached out and gripped Miller's left wrist with surprising strength. "Don't lie to the doctor. . . ."

Miller swallowed. "Hell, I don't know, Wade. Doesn't look so good, I guess."

The shaking eased; the morphine was taking effect.

Wade tried to raise his head to see his wounds, but couldn't, gasping with the effort.

"Am I . . . am I shot in the . . . spine?"

"I don't know," Miller admitted. Then said to Sarge, "Here . . . lift him up a little. . . ."

Sarge and Miller lifted the medic gently, slightly onto one side, carefully, so carefully, as Upham and Mellish kept pressure on the wounds.

"What . . . what do you see?" the medic asked.

Miller was sliding a hand underneath Wade, touching the man's back gently, searching, probing with delicate care, fingertips finding gaping exit wounds, blood drizzling through his fingers like melting ice cream, only much warmer.

"Exit wound right on the spine," Miller reported. "Small of the back."

Wade, craning to watch Miller, gulped air. "How . . . how big's . . . the hole?"

"Size of an acorn."

Wade gulped air again, but it was more of a sob. Miller withdrew his bloody hand and eased Wade back to the grassy ground, the others keeping the pressure on; the gushing wound beneath Wade's right nipple was the nastiest, and took both Mellish and Upham's efforts to minimize the bleeding.

"I . . . can't move," Wade said. His voice was thinning, fading like an old photograph.

"You're not dead, Wade, goddamn it!" Mellish insisted, even as he worked to keep the man's blood inside his chest cavity. "This doesn't mean you're dead!"

"Let me . . . let me feel. . . ."

Wade was trying to find his stomach wounds, but his hand missed, his coordination off.

"Help me . . ."

Miller took the medic's wrist and guided his hand, allowing him to slide it under where Sarge and Jackson were covering the wounds, staving off the bleeding. The groggy wounded doctor tried to determine the severity of his wounds by feel.

"Any . . . anything . . . bleeding worse than others . . . ?"

"Yeah," Mellish said, "me and Upham are pressing on it. . . . I don't think we oughta move our hands. . . ."

"Show me . . . gotta feel . . ."

Exchanging tortured expressions as they hunkered over their shot-up comrade, various hands guided the medic's hand as Upham's and Mellish's lifted off the nasty wound, below the right nipple. Wade inserted his fingers down into the wound, and blood burbled up past his knuckles. The squad, who had seen terrible things in recent days, watched in unsurpassed horror.

Then Wade's expression was not one of pain, but of a sad child, a child holding back tears to be brave. "Oh, God . . . it's my liver . . . my liver. . . ."

Upham, trying not to panic, not doing very well,

blurted, "What do we do about it? You're a doctor! Tell us how to fix you!"

Wade looked at Miller, and the medic's eyes tightened, sending his friend an unmistakable message: *it's over; nothing you can do. . . .*

The medic's hand withdrew from his wound, and Mellish and Upham pressed down on it again.

Wade's voice was suddenly calm; resignation softened his tone. "I could use . . . little extra morphine . . . really could. . . ."

The eyes of the captain and the medic were still locked; Miller knew exactly what his friend was asking him to do.

"More morphine," Miller said to Sarge.

Sarge complied, handing him the ampoule. Miller injected Wade, who immediately said, "Another one."

"One more," Miller said to Sarge.

"Sir, I . . ."

The squad's eyes were on Miller. And on Sarge.

"Do I have to repeat every goddamn order? I said another one."

"Yes, sir," Sarge said, handing it over.

Miller injected Wade a third time.

"Jackson . . ." Wade muttered.

"Right here, Wade."

"Lord's . . . Lord's prayer. . . ."

Jackson nodded and began. "Our Father . . ."

They kept the pressure on the medic's wounds,

frustrated faith healers in a futile laying on of hands. They waited, Jackson prayed aloud, and Wade smiled, his eyes hooded, as he drifted in and out.

Woozy with morphine now, Wade managed to lift his right arm and direct Miller's attention to something: on the ground, near the spilled contents of the medical pack, was a V-mail.

The letter Wade had recopied for Caparzo.

Miller's eyes went back to Wade's, and he nodded, moved away from the bleeding medic and retrieved the letter. Then he made sure Wade saw him put the letter into his breast pocket.

"I'll see it gets where it needs to," Miller assured Wade.

And Wade, drifting on the drug, eyes glazing, smiled faintly at his friend, Captain John H. Miller, Addley, Pennsylvania. Then he was looking upward, as if seeing someone, greeting someone, when he said, "Mama . . . Mama . . ."

The men could feel the life beneath their bloody hands leaving; more than just air had escaped this body. Wade was gone, leaving the torn bloody husk behind.

For a long time they didn't move; just sat there and stared at their dead friend. No one offered words of faith or anger, either. No recriminations to Miller, whose insistence on taking that machine-gun nest had cost this life—none were necessary, because Miller considered this his fault. Stealing looks at their captain, each man knew his sleepy-eyed expression conveyed as much.

Only Upham was crying, sobbing, weeping openly. He had known Wade two days, and felt a depth of sorrow that could not have been greater had a sibling been taken from him.

"Kamerad!"

All heads whipped toward the crater-pocked pasture, across which came stumbling a German soldier, in camouflage uniform, staggering toward them from the direction of the hill, arms raised, blood trickling down his china-blue-eyed face from under his flat helmet.

"Kamerad! Ich ergebe mich! Nicht schiessen!"

"That tears it," Reiben snarled, and grabbed the nearest M-1 from the ground and lurched to his feet and charged to the German who was backing up in terror as the private was on top of him, slamming him in the face with the rifle butt.

The German dropped in an untidy pile as Reiben began kicking him, driving his right boot into the bastard's body; then that Christian country boy Jackson was there, kicking along, and Mellish, too, joining in the beating.

"You prick!" Reiben was saying. "You cocksucker!"

"Was it you, Heinie?" Mellish was saying. "Did you kill Wade? You don't kill fuckin' medics, you garbage bag!"

Miller stood on the sidelines, in the grass, watching. His boys might have been kicking a tin can around the pasture, for all the emotion he showed. Or felt. At his side, Sarge said and did nothing, either.

"Aw, hell," Jackson said, "let's quit beatin' 'round the bush and git it over with. . . ."

Mellish pointed his carbine in the German's wide-eyed face. "Any last words, Kraut? Before we send you off to meet Moses and my Grandpa Max?"

Reiben was yanking the German to his feet, the others readying their weapons for an impromptu firing squad, when Miller finally called out, "First make him cover up Wade for the burial squad."

Their eyes went to Miller; they didn't like having their moment taken from them, but he was their captain.

"Those poor bastards, too," Miller said, motioning toward the dead paratroopers, sprawled in the grass nearby.

The terrified German was on his feet now, eyes wild and wide and white in a bloody red mess of a face; his hands were in the air. Reiben was just staring at the enemy soldier, blankly; suddenly the wise-cracking private didn't seem to have anything to say.

"Check him for weapons," Miller advised.

Staring at his prisoner, Reiben stood frozen—whether with rage or shame, Miller couldn't say; maybe it was both.

"I'll handle it, sir," Jackson said.

The sharpshooter patted down the German, whose legs were shaking as he kept his arms raised high.

"Ask him one thing for me, Upchuck," Mellish said bitterly. "Ask him if he's the one that killed Wade."

From the weeds Sarge called out, "Fuck that. It don't matter. Wade's dead either way."

Miller was approaching his sharpshooter, whose arm was still trailing blood. "Jackson, are you okay?"

"Bullet took a little bite outa me," Jackson said. "I'll be all right."

"Get it cleaned and dressed. We're our own medics now."

"Yes, sir."

"Then you and me'll stand watch. You're south perimeter, I'll take north."

"Nicht schiessen!"

Miller wheeled casually and looked at the battered, bloody German.

"Ich will mich ergeben!" He seemed on the verge of tears. He continued, his voice small, pitiful: *". . . bitte . . . totet mich nicht . . . Ich will mich ergeben. . . ."*

"Sir," Upham said, "he says—"

"I don't give a shit what he says," Miller replied, walking past the German, out into the crater-ruptured pasture. "Reiben, come with me. . . ."

Reiben fell in with Miller, while Upham, behind

them, said, "Sir, you're not gonna let them just kill this guy?"

Miller said nothing.

"Sir—this isn't right, sir. There are rules . . ."

Miller didn't stop, but looked over his shoulder and said, "Help the fucker with the bodies."

They climbed the hill, the captain and private, and entered the machine-gun nest, where the lingering smell of singed hair and seared flesh mingled with acrid cordite smoke. Two charred, bloody bodies, torn like paper by metal fragments, lay slumped over their big machine gun and their split-open, sand-bleeding sandbags. In one corner a soldier's pack, tossed and ripped apart by the blast, lay open, its contents strewn.

"Check for maps," Miller said. "Any kind of intelligence."

Reiben said nothing; he seemed to be sleepwalking.

"You hear me, Private?"

The boy nodded, staring vacantly at the corpses. Then numbly Reiben began poking through debris with Miller, crouching over the contents of a ripped-open pack. German rations—cans of rice leaching thick yellow chicken gravy, a change of uniform, a wallet.

The captain checked inside the latter, found some German currency, ticket stubs from a concert in Munich, a foil-wrapped condom, a ribboned lock of hair presumably from some girl, several photographs, including a snapshot of a young man holding a soccer ball, another of the same boy in uniform posing with his proud, beaming parents.

The grinning young soldier in the photo was their prisoner.

Near the sprawl of bodies, Reiben found a shopping bag with the image of the Eiffel Tower on it and a Paris address. A smile broke through his dour mood, and he reached inside, checking the contents, his bloodstained fingers bringing back a beautiful red silk teddy.

His smile faded. He tossed the lingerie near the corpses and stalked out of the nest.

Miller, watching him go, said nothing. The photograph of their prisoner and his parents was still in his hand. He stared at it for several long moments.

Then he ripped it into pieces, flung them fluttering to the debris-strewn ground, and went out.

15

In a smaller, adjacent, hedgerow-hemmed field, Upham was supervising, mostly, as the German prisoner covered bodies with rocks gathered from the remains of a stone fence that had been dismantled by an artillery shell. The corporal and the prisoner had potato-sack hauled the nine bodies here—the ambushed paratrooper patrol and Wade—and it was a hard, grisly, thankless task.

Upham had seen to it that Wade was taken care of first, and now all but two of the paratroopers had been covered with the stones, the German's breath heaving with toil and fear, his boyish face blood-streaked, his hands stained red. The corporal was marking each temporary, aboveground grave with a rifle, alerting the burial squads to these American bodies. Now and then the German's eyes would meet Upham's cold gaze, and the prisoner would work harder, even more industriously covering up the carnage he'd helped create.

Finally Upham told the prisoner to take a break, and they both sat on the ground. Upham lighted up a K-ration cigarette, and the German watched hungrily. Upham gave him one, matched it.

"American cigarette," the German said, puffing, grinning crazily, desperately. "I like American. . . . Steamboat Willie! Oompah! Oooompah!"

Upham nodded, said grimly, "Yeah, yeah. Mickey Mouse. Steamboat Willie."

"Yah! Mickey Mouse!"

They were still smoking when Miller came tromping into the field, followed by Sergeant Horvath and the rest of the squad, what was left of it anyway: Reiben, Mellish, Jackson.

"Get him off his Aryan ass," Mellish snarled.

Upham rose, pitched his cigarette; the German mimicked him.

Miller went from grave to grave, removing ammunition from the rifles Upham had set there, deactivating the weapons. Sarge followed, as if he were tidying up after the captain, gathering the extra ammo. Rifles in hand, Reiben and Mellish and Jackson moved slowly, ominously toward the prisoner, forming a loose semicircle around him. The prisoner took anxious notice of this, and went back to stacking rocks atop the next body, as if getting the corpses covered would make his problem go away.

"*Ich brauche mehr Steiner*," he said, and nodded to the rock-pile graves, still working feverishly, proving his obedience, his worth. *"Sie sind nicht hoch genug. Ich bin nicht fertig . . ."*

"He's says he's not finished," Upham said.

"That's what he thinks," Mellish said. Then to the prisoner, Mellish said, "You're finished, all right, Adolf!"

Mellish grabbed the prisoner by his camouflage shirt, and Jackson joined in. They dragged him from the stony grave, the latest rock slipping from his fingers, his face contorted with fear, as he cried, *"Nein! Ich bin nicht fertig!"*

And the German pulled away from his captors, scooping up the rock he dropped, and hastily returned to covering the latest corpse. The sound of the bolt on Reiben's rifle racking froze the prisoner, and he carefully got to his feet and turned to face them.

"Please," he said. "I like America." His accent was thick, almost precious, his teeth bared in a miserable, desperate excuse for a smile. "What a cinch! Go fly a kite! Cat got your tongue?"

Jackson racked the bolt on his rifle.

The German began to laugh, softly, hysterically. Tears were welling as he said, "Betty Boop! What a dish! Betty Grable? Nice gams!"

And the prisoner lifted his trouser legs to the knees, laughing.

Mellish racked the bolt on his rifle.

The prisoner stood straight now, his legs still exposed. He sang, "Oh, say can you see . . ." That was all he knew; he kept singing it again, and again: "Can you see? . . . Oh, say can you see?"

The three privates were standing in firing-squad fashion now, facing the prisoner. Sickened, Upham looked away. Miller was still dismantling rifles, Sarge gathering ammo, as if completely unaware, or anyway unconcerned, about what was happening.

The young prisoner played his trump card: "Fuck Hitler!"

"Fuck you," Reiben said.

The prisoner lurched for Upham, grabbed his arm, and spewed a terrified stream of German at the corporal: *"Tut mir leid fur den Mann, den ihr verioren habt. Den Sanitater. Das ist halt Krieg, nicht wahr?"*

Upham called to Miller, "Sir, he says he's sorry about Wade. I don't think he was the gunner, sir."

"Tell him 'sorry' don't cut the mustard," Jackson said, that big Springfield loose and deadly in his hands. "Tell him my piles bleed for him."

"Tell him," Miller said, "the war's over for him."

The squad members were nodding, Mellish saying, "Fuckin' A," and Miller was dropping the last of the disarmed rifles down and striding over to the German.

A handkerchief came from one of the captain's pockets, and he swiftly tied it around the German's head, in blindfold fashion.

"Sir," Upham said softly but urgently, "this isn't right."

"Just tell him, Corporal. Tell him what I said."

Upham did.

Miller spun the German around, so that his back was to the squad. Resigned to whatever Miller's order might be, Horvath reluctantly fell in line with the others and racked the bolt on his rifle. The prisoner jumped. Miller looked at his squad—Mellish's eyes were glittering, Jackson's were hooded with a hunter's nonchalance, Reiben's were dead as the stones covering the corpses.

Then Miller said to Upham, "Tell him to march two hundred paces and wait until he can't hear us anymore. Then he's to surrender himself to the first Allied patrol he runs into."

"What?" Reiben said, shaking his head as if his ears were lying to him. "Wait a goddamn minute—"

"Yes, sir," Upham said, relieved, not quite smiling. And to the young German he said, *"Wir werden dir die Augen verbinden. Lauf' zwei hundert Schritte, dann kannst du die Binde abnehmen."*

Miller checked the blindfold, snugging the knot tight, then whopped the German twice on the shoulder, signaling him to take off, which he did.

"Close shave," the German said. "Lucky Strikes! *Ich danke Euch. Ich gehe jetzt. Bitte mir nicht im Rucken Schiessen."*

"You're letting him go?" Reiben asked Miller. The private was reeling in disbelief.

The German was singing now, voice receding: "Take me out to the ball game! Take me out to the crowd! Buy me some peanuts . . . *Ich wed-nicht halt-machen. Ich werd'nicht zuruck schauen. Ich versprech'es.*"

"All right," Miller said. "Everybody gear up."

But nobody moved. Everyone was staring at him, or watching the shrinking figure of the German, heading for the far hedgerow.

Miller sighed. "We can't take him with us. He'll impede our mission. Direction I sent him, he'll get picked up by our troops."

"If he doesn't get picked up by his own *Wehrmacht* first," Reiben said bitterly, "and get back into circulation. Maybe to shoot another of us. . . . You just let the enemy go, sir. Just let him walk off."

Mellish was watching the shrinking figure. "It ain't right," he said.

"Right?" Upham exploded. "Jesus! We don't execute prisoners! We're not goddamn butchers! It's against the goddamn rules!"

"This isn't fucking cribbage," Reiben snapped. "Upchuck, the rules just walked off with Heinie, over there!"

"Reiben," Miller said flatly, "gear up and shut up."

Reiben didn't move. He heaved a breath, his face

twitched with insolence, and he said, "No, sir. I don't think so . . . sir."

All eyes were on Miller and Reiben, now—except for the German, who had disappeared into the hedges.

"That's not a suggestion, Reiben. It's an order."

"Yeah? Like the one you gave to take that machine-gun nest? 'Cause that order was a real corker, sir. Fuckin' doozy."

Miller said nothing, but Horvath's face contorted with outrage. "Soldier, you are way the hell out of line!"

Reiben ignored the sergeant, saying to Miller, "Yes, sir, Cap, that was one hell of a call. We took out that nest all right, and only lost one man doing it. Just our medic . . . course, with you leadin' the charge, who needs a fuckin' medic? We'll all be dead by sundown."

"Reiben . . ." Sarge said, moving toward the private.

But Reiben ignored this considerable threat, saying to his captain, "The more men we lose, the more it's gonna make Mama Ryan's day, to think her little boy's life was so valuable. Only, we ain't found her son of a bitchin' baby boy yet, but that's just a minor fucking detail. . . ."

Sarge was on top of Reiben now, almost shouting, "Fall in, Private, and shut up!"

Reiben snorted a contemptuous, dismissive laugh,

and turned and walked away from them both, captain and sergeant.

Miller was just standing there, motionless, lifeless, but Horvath was white with rage, shaking as he yelled, "Don't you walk away from your captain!"

"Aw, hell," Jackson said. He was staring at the rifle in his hands, perhaps reconsidering what he and his buddies had almost done. "Let the loudmouth go. . . . We don't need 'im."

Feeling detached from all of this, Miller was watching Reiben stalking off when suddenly Mellish was in his face, the private's expression, his voice, tinged with desperation.

"Listen, Captain, never mind Reiben, he's an asshole. I'm with you all the way. But listen, my sense of things, sir? Ryan's dead. Dead in the grass someplace just like those paratroopers. I'm positive. We oughta just head back. Sir."

Miller said nothing, backing away from the private. He saw a nearby stump and went to it, using it as a stool, where he sat and contemplated how it had come to this, his squad falling apart in front of him. . . .

"Reiben!" Sarge yelled to the departing figure, walking away in the same direction the German had gone, whether to desert, or track the prisoner down, was unclear. "Get back in line—now!"

His back to them, Reiben called, "No, sir. I'll spend

the rest of my life in Leavenworth, if I have to. But I won't be part of this shit detail no more."

"I'm not going to say it again," Sarge said, and the menace in his voice startled all of them. The .45 came scraping out of its holster. *"Fall in, soldier!"*

The sound of Sarge racking the slide on the automatic froze Reiben, and it caught Miller's attention, too; but the captain remained seated—he, too, was frozen, couldn't seem to make himself move from this spot.

Reiben turned and walked back toward the Sarge; his eyes were wide with fear and amazement and anger as he said, "You'd shoot me over fucking Ryan? Somebody we never fucking met?"

"Just fall in, soldier," Sarge repeated, softer now, but that .45 was leveled at the returning Reiben.

"Well, fine! Swell! Good, do it, shoot me in the leg, would you please? The million-dollar wound that sends me home? Blow me a fuckin' kiss, Sarge!"

"On your lips, shithead," Sarge snarled, still pointing the weapon as Reiben neared, "and shut you up!"

Reiben threw his hands up, taunted, "Do it, Sarge! Do it!"

Jackson said, "This is gettin' interesting. . . ."

"Jesus Christ, Sarge," Mellish said. He seemed almost on the verge of tears. "Put the gun away, will ya!"

But Sarge was boiling with rage as the contemptuous Reiben walked right toward him, daring, "No, no, don't listen to 'em . . . shoot me, Sarge! Save the Germans some fuckin' ammo!"

Sarge's hand was shaking; he was clearly tempted, and tortured, by Reiben's taunting.

Upham scrambled over to where Miller sat on his stump, on the sidelines. The corporal urged, "Sir, *do* something!"

Miller just looked at Upham.

Reiben's jeering cries continued; he was closing the gap between himself and the Sarge and the pointed .45.

"What's the pool up to?" Miller asked Upham, casually.

"Huh? What?"

"You know, the Miller pool. What's it up to?"

The corporal's stare was incredulous. "Uh . . . I have no idea."

Sarge was yelling, "Just stop right there!"

"Come on, Sarge! Put one in my leg! Send me home!"

"You coward . . . you yellow son of a bitch . . ."

Reiben planted himself right in front of Horvath, looking right down the barrel of the big automatic. "You're the coward! *Shoot* me! Make Mama Ryan happy!"

Upham, stealing looks back at the bizarre confrontation, stood before his seated captain and said, "Uh, sir, I *really* think you need to do something about this—"

"I'm a high school teacher," Miller said. Casual, but in a firm voice.

Mellish heard him, and looked over.

"I teach English," Miller said, straightening, "at Thomas Alva Edison High School."

Now Jackson looked over at the captain. So did the Sarge.

And Reiben.

"Addley, Pennsylvania," Miller went on. "Back home, somebody asks me what I do, and I tell 'em, they take one look at me and say, 'It figures,' or some such. But here . . . I guess it's not so obvious. . . ." They were all staring at him. ". . . by the looks on *your* faces, anyway."

They moved toward him, slowly, gathering around him.

"Maybe I've changed," he said softly. Then he laughed, just a little. "Sometimes I wonder if my wife would even recognize me."

Mellish turned to Jackson and mouthed, *Wife?*, and Jackson, eyes wide with this new knowledge, shrugged.

Slowly, bones creaking, gear clinking, Miller rose and let out a huge sigh. Then he said, "Look . . . I don't know anything about Private James Ryan, and I don't give a fuck about him. The man's nothing to me. I just want to go home and see my kids."

Mellish looked at Jackson and mouthed, *Kids?*, and got another amazed shrug.

"And if going on to Ramelle and picking up Ryan gets me closer to goin' home," Miller continued, "then that's what I'm gonna do." And he looked from face to face. "If any of you want to go back and fight the war from some other direction, I won't stop you. I won't report you, either, should I happen to survive this shit. We just got separated, that's all. Fucked-up things happen in a war. . . . I don't know anything anymore, except that the more killing I do, the farther away from home I feel."

Wind was whispering melodically through the hedgerows, the high grass, the weeds, the leaves of trees, and these men stood silently listening to that music for a long time, considering each other. Sarge had long since lowered and holstered his .45.

Finally Jackson said, "A goddamn *school*teacher?"

"That's right," Miller said.

"Caparzo knew," Upham said. "He told me he knew. . . . I say, send the money in the pool to his folks."

"Good call, Upchuck," Mellish said.

Reiben was studying the captain. "Schoolteacher. You know, I enlisted to get away from shitheads like you."

And Reiben grinned.

So did Miller.

"Otherwise, how's the war workin' out for you?" Mellish asked Reiben.

"I also coach the baseball team," Miller admitted.

Everybody was smiling now. They weren't happy, not in these circumstances, but they were pleased to be a squad again. Miller directed Upham and Mellish to finish covering the last two paratrooper bodies with stones as the rest geared up.

"We in business?" Sarge asked, looking the men over.

"We're in business, sir," Jackson said.

"All right, then," Sarge said. "Fall in."

And they did, moving out.

"Next stop," Reiben said, "Ramelle."

16

Under a warm but not sweltering afternoon sun, Miller and his men trudged wearily through the tall grass, the terrain beginning its gentle drop to the valley where Ramelle nestled along the Merderet River. The slope was too gradual to allow them a view of the river and the bridge that made Ramelle so strategically important. But they could see, perhaps half a mile away, the glorified rubble pile the village had been reduced to, by the Allied bombing. Neuville-au-Plain was untouched compared to these ruins, though some buildings remained standing and a church bell tower had survived, as if God had left a scolding finger.

"Looks pretty quiet down there," Sarge observed, walking point. "No civilians in sight—and I don't see any sign of the one-oh-one."

Miller, walking tail end, said, "You will when we get to that bridge. But, yeah . . . I'd say the good citizens of Ramelle long since turned refugee. Just don't count on it staying quiet long."

As if proving the captain's point, the sound of an engine behind them turned their heads, a sound that didn't alarm them because it was not unlike that of the occasional farmer's tractor they'd heard on their jaunt (though the whinnying of horses pulling plows had been more common).

But the vehicle suddenly bearing down on them was not a tractor, though it had tractor treads on its rear and front wheels. The vehicle suddenly bearing down on them was an armored one, a German half-track, barreling across the field, with a trio of support infantry tagging along on its either side, running full throttle to keep up, rifles held high above the tall grass.

The German gunner atop the half-track opened fire with his mounted machine-gun as the squad took off running toward the town, legs churning through the high grass, bullets whining all around. No time to even return fire, just run like hell. Then a drainage ditch was in their path, a wonderful obstacle that could put them under the line of fire, and they leapt into it, some sliding down, as bullets tore up sod along the lip of the ditch, rifles cracking, machine-gun chugging.

On the other side of the ditch were railroad tracks, and probably another ditch, and then the town. If Miller and his squad could just clamber over the tracks, they'd have good cover and a fighting chance. They splashed across the trickle of muddy water at the bottom of the ditch, and began scrambling up the other side, toward those waiting railroad tracks, when a barrage of machine-gun fire whittled the wooden railroad ties to matchsticks, driving the squad back down into the muddy ditch.

"Shit!" Sarge said.

The half-track engine wasn't sounding much like a farmer's ride now; it was growling toward them, the machine gun silent but anxious to talk again. And those half dozen infantryman would be on top of them, any second. . . .

"Dig in!" Miller yelled. "Let 'em have it!"

Using the ditch as an oversize foxhole, they positioned themselves at its lip and returned fire. But lead was raining on them, driving them back down to where all they could do was fire up blindly over the edge. The rumbling clanking of the half-track let them know the armored vehicle was drawing closer, and closer. . . .

"Heads down!" somebody yelled.

Miller and his men obeyed, even as they looked around at each other, wondering which of them had said it. Then realizing that none of them had, that it had come from behind them, up on the railroad tracks, they could see the tubular snout of a bazooka above them, pointing toward the field. They saw the flame and smoke flash as a projectile hurtled over them.

· The boom of a direct hit encouraged the squad to

peer up over the lip of the ditch, and the half-track was streaming black smoke from its engine compartment, staggering to a halt. The machine gunner was blown out of his perch, and pieces of him were tossed here and there.

The German foot soldiers were staggering, too, from surprise, from the tremor of the earth, waving smoke from their faces. They were still in this awkward state when four Airborne paratroopers rose like phantoms from the tall grass to the left of where Miller and his squad were in the ditch. Immediate, unrelenting American submachine-gun fire raked the Germans, and they disappeared beneath the sea of weeds, screaming, bleeding, dying.

Then even the screams stopped; nothing remained but silence and black drifting smoke.

Shaken and relieved, the squad gazed up behind them at a tall, athletically trim paratrooper, kneeling on the train tracks with his bazooka leaned across a thigh, gazing back at them. He was a good-looking kid, blond, with pug nose, apple cheeks, and cleft chin, blue eyes laughing, cute as a cartoon, though the expression on the oval face was serious, even respectful.

"Everybody okay?" he asked, his voice husky. "Anybody missin' any spare parts?"

"We're in one piece," Miller said. "Thanks for saving our ass. Who the hell are you, son?"

"Private First Class Ryan, sir . . . sir? Is there something wrong?"

The five GIs in the muddy ditch were staring up at their savior with stunned expressions. Then they began shaking their heads and laughing as thinning smoke rolled over them. Private James F. Ryan, twenty, Peyton, Iowa, wondered if these unshaven, disheveled ground pounders, whose lives he'd just saved, had gone completely battle wacky.

By the time the squad had climbed from the ditch up onto the railroad tracks, their laughter was over. The terrible familiar fragrance of singed hair and charred flesh wafted on a breeze riffling the high grass, a sobering reminder of their purpose. This bright-eyed, farm-fed kid who had rescued them was not aware of their purpose here—part of which was to inform him he had lost his brothers to this war.

Leaving his bazooka behind, Private Ryan and several of the paratroopers who'd aided in the rescue escorted Captain Miller and his squad through the ruins of Ramelle. From within the shambles of buildings, an occasional paratrooper watched as the little group passed. No civilians at all in this dead village, and the paratroopers, Miller noted, looked at least as scruffy as he and his men did: haggard, unshaven, occasionally wounded.

They said nothing to Ryan, as yet. Miller and the men of his squad stole looks at him, his clean-cut, bumpkinish features living up to his Iowa heritage. But saving their lives had bought Ryan some respect.

The Ramelle bridge over the Merderet was narrow but impressive enough, a brick-paved steel structure on a stone-pie base. Below, the Merderet lay wide and glistening blue, looking more like a lake than a river—the Germans had opened wide the locks at the mouth of the river, by Carentan, creating minor flooding to drown invading paratroopers.

Either end of the bridge was blocked, heavily sand-bagged machine-gun emplacements barring the way. From behind the first of these, nearer the town, emerged Corporal Fred Henderson, twenty-four, St. Louis, Missouri, brawny, blond, shovel-jawed. A world-weary smile formed as he got a good look at the small, bedraggled patrol coming his way.

"Sir," Henderson said as Miller and his group trooped toward him, "if you're our relief, I just may file a complaint."

"Can't blame you, Corporal," Miller said. "I need to report to your commanding officer."

"That would have been Colonel Jennings, sir." And the corporal nodded toward the nearest riverbank, where two dozen corpses lay under mattress covers, waiting for a burial squad.

"I'm afraid," the corporal said, "I'm the highest-ranking officer we can muster. Henderson, sir."

"I'm Captain Miller."

"What brings you to this former town, Captain?"

"Him," Miller said, thumb indicating Ryan, whose surprise was immediate and wide-eyed. "We came looking for Private Ryan."

"Me?" Ryan squinted in amazement. "Why in hell . . . ?"

Now in the presence of the closet thing to a commanding officer as Ryan had, Miller was ready to get this over with. "James Francis Ryan? Iowa?"

"Yes, sir," Ryan said, bewildered, a little worried, "Peyton, Iowa, sir. . . . What's this about?"

"There's no easy way to say this, soldier," Miller said. "James, your brothers have all been killed in action."

Ryan swallowed; he had the tough veneer any man who'd lived through combat acquires. But his voice sounded frail, as he asked, "All of them? Not all of them . . . must be some mistake . . ."

"No mistake, Private. Thomas died on Omaha Beach; Peter on Utah. Daniel died over a week ago, in New Guinea. . . . I'm sorry, son."

The tough paratrooper who'd been standing before them melted away, and in his place was a kid barely out of his teens. His face, his eyes, flickering with the dire news that the boys he'd grown up with, brothers he'd fought with and laughed with and sometimes loathed and always loved, were gone. They may have died by bullets or artillery fire or a land mine, but to James Ryan, words had taken them from him—words that seemed unreal, without substance. Yet he knew they were as real as a bullet or artillery fire or a land mine. He knew his brothers were gone. He would never see them again, not even in a casket. They had vaporized with Captain Miller's words.

Removing his helmet, running a hand through a shock of dark blond hair, Ryan stumbled toward a bridge girder and leaned there. Miller and his squad looked at their feet, studied the bricks beneath their boots, not watching as tears rolled down the apple cheeks. Ryan's paratrooper pals looked away, gazing out at the shimmering river, letting him get it out.

Soon the private wiped the tears from his eyes, dried his hand on his trousers, and looked toward Miller. Then he asked, "How far did you come to deliver this message?"

"From Omaha Beach."

His eyes tightened. "All that way, just to tell me this? Why? What's this really about, sir?"

Miller walked over to where Ryan was still bracing himself against the girder. "They're sending you back home, son. We have orders to bring you back."

Now his eyes popped wide. "What do you mean, bring me back?"

"Just that. You're from Iowa. I don't have to tell you about the Sullivans."

A faint smirk passed across his somber features, and he said, "I'm bad publicity, dead."

"Your mother's suffered enough of a loss. . . . You

can take ten minutes to get your gear, say your good-byes."

Ryan was reeling with all this, understandably. Miller turned to Henderson and asked, "Any chance of reinforcements reaching you out here?"

"Never can tell, sir."

"Radios working yet?"

"Jammed or broken. We got no idea what's happening south of us."

Then Ryan said, "I have orders, too, sir." The private wasn't leaning against a girder now—he was right at Miller's side, spine straight, voice firm. "And they don't include deserting my post."

Miller swallowed, sighed, said, "I understand how you feel. I'd feel the same way, if I were you. But I'm afraid my orders supersede yours."

"I don't look at it like that, sir."

It had already been a long, hard, costly day, and despite the sympathy he had for this kid, Miller was getting irked. "Private, these orders come directly from General Marshall, Chief of Staff of the United States Army."

"With all due respect, sir," Henderson chimed in boldly, "Private Ryan has a point. General Marshall isn't here to judge the situation as it now stands."

Miller's mouth tightened. "In town five minutes, and challenged by both a private *and* a corporal—you must do things differently in the one-oh-one than we do in the Rangers."

"Sir," Henderson said, "our orders are to hold this bridge—at all costs. Our planes and the 82nd have blown up every bridge across the Merderet, except for two—one at Valognes and this one. If the Germans take them, we'll lose our foothold and have to retreat."

"I didn't come to pull you and your men off this bridge, Corporal, or out of this town. And I don't envy you your job, or doubt its importance. But you're going to have to manage with one less man."

Ryan was shaking his head, no. "I can't leave them, sir. At least not until reinforcements arrive."

Miller's smile had little to do with smiling. "Apparently while my squad and I were on our way here, skipping through the French countryside, picking daisies, having picnics, and laying farmer's daughters, the Army must have turned into a democracy."

"Sir," Ryan said, "there's barely enough of us as it is. . . ."

"Private, forget about that ten minutes I offered you. You've got five to grab your gear and report back to me."

Ryan was still shaking his head, no. "Captain, if I go, what are they gonna—"

"Hey, asshole!" Reiben exploded. "Two of us died, buyin' you this ticket home! Fuckin' *take* it! I would."

It was as if Ryan had been hit by a bullet; blood drained from his face. He looked at Miller for confirmation, and Miller nodded. Then again Ryan stumbled, this time over to the sandbags of the machine-gun emplacement, where he sat.

He mumbled a question.

Miller asked, "What was that, son?"

"What . . . what were their names?"

With just a hint of accusation in his voice, Mellish said, "Wade and Caparzo."

Ryan repeated: "Wade . . . and . . ."

"Caparzo," Mellish finished.

The private repeated the names quietly, to himself, several times, memorizing them, and trying to turn these words into dead men.

Finally Ryan said to Miller, "Sir, this doesn't make any sense. What have I done to deserve special treatment?"

"Give that man a cigar," Reiben said.

Miller shot Reiben a glare, then said to Ryan, "This isn't about you. It's about politics . . . and your mother."

But Ryan didn't seem to hear that. "I mean, for Christ's sake, my life isn't worth the lives of two others."

The men in Miller's squad were looking at each other, confused, and a little ashamed, at hearing their preconceived opinions about Ryan thrown back at them by Ryan himself.

The private gestured to his comrades around him, the paratroopers who'd accompanied the squad here, and the pair manning the machine-gun nest, Corporal Henderson, too.

"Hell," Ryan said, "these guys deserve to go home as much as I do, as much as anybody. They've fought just as long, just as hard."

"Should I tell your mother that?" Miller asked. "That she can look forward to another flag in her window?"

Ryan's expression went suddenly cold. "My mother didn't raise any of us to be cowards."

The captain stared at the private. "She didn't raise you to lose you."

"Well, then, you just tell her when you found me, I was with the only brothers I had left. Tell her that there was no way I was going to desert those brothers. You tell her that . . . and she'll understand."

And the private stared at the captain.

Miller said nothing.

"I'm not leaving this bridge, sir," Ryan said. "If you'd care to shoot me for not deserting my post, go right ahead . . . though I'm not sure how you'll explain that to my mother."

Ryan moved past Miller and his men and got behind the sandbags in the machine-gun emplacement, hunkering in.

Miller stood staring out at the sun-dappled river hugged by trees. The world seemed peaceful now. Perhaps coming all this way was worth it, with a view like this. . . .

"What are your orders, sir?" Sarge was at his side now. His expression was blank, but his eyes seemed strangely alive.

Horvath had spoken softly, and Miller's response was that way, too—their conversation was a private one, and no one even attempted to eavesdrop.

"Sergeant," Miller said, "we have crossed over some invisible boundary. Stumbled over a booby trap and tumbled down a rabbit's hole."

" 'Curiouser and curiouser,' sir."

And Miller smiled at this literary reference coming from this rough-hewn man, who added, "But the question stands, sir: what are your orders? Arrest, perhaps shoot this man, who General Marshall wants delivered to his Iowa mother? We could wound him and cart him back the way we came; it'd only slow us down by half, and who knows? Maybe we've met all the Germans in Normandy already."

"What are you thinking, Sarge?"

Sarge flinched a smile. "I'm not sure you really want to know, sir."

"Mike, I really do."

Horvath hesitated, but Miller's eyes tightened and signaled that he meant what he said.

"Hell, I don't know," Horvath sighed. "Part of me thinks the kid's right—he doesn't deserve special treatment, and he doesn't deserve getting pulled off his post, leavin' his buddies in the lurch, either. He wants to stay here, fine—let's fucking leave him and go home."

"Part of you thinks that."

"Yeah. The other part thinks . . . what if we stay and give these poor bastards a little of the reinforcement they need? And what if then we actually make it out of here, with Private Ryan willingly in tow?"

"Yeah?"

Sarge shrugged. "We did that, someday we might look back on this and figure savin' Private Ryan was the one decent thing we were able to pull out of this goddamn shithole of a war."

Miller thought about that.

Sarge continued: "You said it yourself, Cap—maybe if we do that, we all earn the right to go home."

The captain sighed, smiled. "You know, for a minute there . . . I thought I was listening to Wade."

"I, uh, appreciate the compliment, sir. . . . Anyway, those are just my thoughts, sir."

And Horvath stepped away, rejoining the squad, allowing Miller a few moments of privacy, of reflection, while they waited for his decision.

Then, casually, Miller ambled to Corporal Henderson, who stood near the sandbagged emplacement, and asked him, "What's your plan, Corporal?"

"My plan, sir?"

"Just how do you propose preventing the Krauts from crossing this bridge?"

Henderson gestured. "Well, uh . . . we've got machine guns at either end, as you can see . . . plus we mined the road through town. . . ."

Miller nodded, considering that. "Machine guns and mines'll slow 'em down for thirty seconds, maybe a minute. Anything else?"

Henderson seemed embarrassed. "No, sir. Just that and the dozen of us left, sir."

"What, you think they're gonna come at you with donkey carts? So far they've been picking on you like a little scab, pecking at you with a little infantry, maybe an armored vehicle. But when they come to town to cross this bridge, they'll be coming with tanks."

"I'm aware of that, sir."

"Maybe your new commanding officer can come up with something better."

Henderson frowned in confusion. "Who, sir?"

"Your new commanding officer," Miller said. "Me."

17

On the ground near the mouth of the bridge, with the ruins of Ramelle looking on, an array of weapons awaited Captain Miller's inspection: a pair of thirty-caliber machine guns, seventeen grenades, eleven Hawkins mines, two bazookas with eight rounds, a flamethrower, and assorted small arms.

"Is this everything?" Miller asked. Sarge was at his side, taking the same tour, and the boys of the squad were gathered behind them, like judges at a beauty contest who'd been hoping for prettier girls. Ryan was tagging along, too.

The two paratroopers who'd been manning the nearby sandbagged machine-gun nest with Corporal Henderson were making this presentation of their unit's meager arsenal. Bill Trask, twenty-three, Dallas, Texas, was dark and lanky like Jackson, while fair-haired Ray Rice, twenty-two, Tulsa, Oklahoma, had the compact frame of a halfback.

"Except for carbines and side arms, sir, yes," Trask

said. Apologetically he added, "We had a sixty mortar, but an artillery round took 'er out."

"We might as well be shootin' spitballs at 'em," Rice said glumly, "if they roll on us with tanks."

"*When* they roll on us with tanks," Miller corrected.

Sarge was gazing down at the handful of weapons, knowing Rice was right; but Miller's eyes had raised to the cobblestone road that curved from sight through the devastated village.

"What are you thinkin', Cap?" the sergeant asked.

"I'm thinkin'," Miller said, "the Jerries are gonna whip around the flanks and squeeze us."

"Yeah," Sarge nodded. "And pop us like a pimple."

Miller was pointing. "But what if we can suck some of 'em into the main road . . . between those buildings? There's enough rubble to create a bottleneck."

Ryan said, "Not enough to stop a tank . . . unless you disabled one of 'em. . . ."

"Yeah!" Miller said, grinning. "We turn one of their tanks into a fuckin' sixty-ton roadblock. We do that, we got a fightin' chance on the flanks."

Nobody was grinning back him. Much as they would like to have shared his enthusiasm, these soldiers knew what Miller was suggesting would have been a tall order, even if they had a tank or two, themselves. Which they definitely didn't.

But Corporal Henderson was nodding, seeing the

potential. "Yeah . . . that would split 'em up. Don't let 'em mass anywhere."

"Right," Miller said. "Then we could hit 'em hard, one on one, not one big battle, little battles we win one at time, and as we do, we keep fallin' back toward the bridge, and take on what's left of 'em."

Sarge was nodding now and pointing along the roadway. "We can have a machine gun on the move down here. . . ." His pointing finger moved up to indicate the bell tower. "Number two machine gun up there, nice and high, where we can piss some lead on their heads."

"Good, good," Miller said, approving both notions. He turned back to Jackson, "You want to keep that machine-gun company in that bell tower?"

"Kind of a waste, Cap'n, makin' me a spotter," Jackson drawled, leaning on his Springfield.

"Well, I was thinking maybe, long as you were up there, you might pin the tail on a few German officers."

Jackson flexed his wounded arm, saying, "Always glad for a chance for a little time in church."

Miller slowly scanned the faces of his men. "Opinions?"

"You're askin' us, sir?" Reiben said.

"I appear to be."

"Well . . . this is not the worst idea I ever heard."

Mellish said, "Yeah—that would be Omaha Beach."

Grim laughs and nods followed; even Miller smiled.

"It's just that everything depends on gettin' a tank to roll down main street," Reiben said.

"Yeah," Miller said. "That, and takin' him out."

"Well, uh . . . how exactly do we do that?"

Sarge twitched a humorless smirk. "Much as I hate to admit it, Reiben's right for once." He nodded toward the display of weapons. "Who are we to argue with the Airborne? They're right: we're shootin' spitballs. How do we stop a tank with pea-shooters? Better yet, how do we make a tank go where we want it to?"

"Give him a rabbit to chase," Miller said. "Then we hit the tracks."

"Bait I understand," Reiben said. "But what do we hit the bastard with?"

"Sticky bombs."

And now his squad, the paratroopers, even the Sarge, were looking at Miller like he had finally gone Section Eight on them.

"Uh," Reiben said, "sticky bombs, sir?"

"You're making that up," Henderson said.

"It's in the field manual," Miller said casually. "Look it up."

"We would, sir," Ryan said politely, sarcasm barely discernible, "if we had a field manual handy. Lacking one, perhaps you could enlighten us."

"Glad to. You got demo handy?"

"Sure," Henderson said.

"Composition B or TNT?"

"Wanna speak to that, Private Toynbe?" Henderson asked another of the paratroopers who'd accompanied Ryan here with Miller's squad. "Toynbe's our demo expert."

"Plenty of both," said Alan Toynbe, twenty-five, Malden, Massachusetts. "Explosives are one thing we got plenty of. That bridge is wired with enough TNT to blow up twice."

"Then pull some offa there," Miller said, "and settle for blowin' it up once."

"Okay," Henderson said. "Why?"

"To make a sticky bomb. Here's how it's done, boys: take one standard issue GI sock, cram as much TNT inside as you can, rig a simple fuse, coat the baby with axle grease so it sticks when you throw . . . presto, one sticky bomb. Only we're gonna make a lot more than just one."

They were still looking at him like he was nuts.

"Where'd you get that recipe?" Reiben asked. "Off the back of a Bisquick box? Or in a comic book?"

"Can you think of another way to knock the treads off a tank, smart-ass?"

"No . . . but keep this in mind, Cap. Next time you tell us to drop our cocks and grab our socks, we're gonna be missin' the latter."

"At least," Miller said over the laughter.

Soon Toynbe, rigged in a rope harness, was dangling under the bridge, pulling down TNT charges. He handed them over to Trask and Rice, also dangling, who relayed them up to Mellish and Upham on the bridge. Mellish and Upham delivered them to Miller, Ryan, Sarge, and several paratroopers, who had formed an assembly line of sticky bomb manufacture.

Sarge stuffed a sock with TNT and handed it to the next man down, saying, "I feel like fuckin' Santa Claus."

"And you thought getting coal in your stocking was punishment," Miller said.

In the church midway through the village, more battle preparations were under way. Jackson pushed up through a trapdoor into the bell tower, and his Springfield was handed up to him, followed by the much heavier .30-caliber machine gun. On the ladder below, a pair of paratroopers—privates Ron Parker, twenty-one, Sommersville, Vermont, and Steve Weller, twenty-two, Omaha, Nebraska, two of the four who'd stood from the high grass to rescue Miller's squad—were relaying the weapons up to Jackson, followed by ammo belts and satchels of supplies.

Corporal Upham, loaded down with four ammo belts, hiked down the debris-strewn street, the husks of buildings staring at him. At a rubble pile over to the left, two paratroopers—privates Bud Lyle, twenty-three, Baltimore, Maryland, and Bill Fallon, twenty, Myrtle Beach, South Carolina—were settling in, sighting their machine gun. Upham delivered two of the four ammo belts to them, and moved on.

Within the shell of a collapsed building, Private Mellish and Corporal Henderson were setting up the second machine-gun position, angling the muzzle through what had once been a window. As Upham approached to drop off the other two ammo belts, Mellish was oiling the bolt of the big gun, working it back and forth.

"Upchuck," Mellish said, "listen to me. You listening? This little perch is just the starting point."

"I know."

"We're gonna be fallin' back like crazy sons of bitches, findin' a new temporary home, and then movin' on again. Got that?"

"Got it."

"So you're gonna be Johnny-on-the-spot with the ammo."

Upham took a deep breath, nodded.

"You okay, Upchuck?"

"I'm okay. . . . Just wondering how the hell I got here, is all."

Mellish grinned. "That's the question of the hour, ain't it? Ever see anything like this?"

"No. Unbelievable."

"Fucked up beyond all recognition."

Upham removed his helmet, massaged his scalp. "Yeah . . . hey. *Foobar!*"

Mellish grinned, and ruffled the corporal's hair.

"Yeah. F-o-o-b-a-r. . . . Look at it this way, Upham. Wherever we are, you're close behind . . . which means, wherever you are, you got a front seat on one hell of a show."

At the mouth of the bridge, the sticky bombs ready, Miller was on his way into the town, to check angles of fire and general battle prep. The group tagging after him included the demo man, Toynbe, Sarge, and Private Ryan. Miller paused at the sandbagged machine-gun emplacement just past the bridge entrance.

"Not bad for a forward position," Miller said. He turned and looked back at the similar sandbagged nest at the far end of the bridge. "That position back there? That's the Alamo."

Nobody liked the sound of that; but they understood it. Miller clarified, anyway.

"They push us back that far," Miller said, "the last man alive's got to blow the son of a bitchin' bridge."

"We have a thirty-second delay on the fuse," Toynbe said. "Last man alive won't be for long, unless he hightails it off that bridge like Jesse Owens."

Miller nodded grimly; Sarge, too.

To the captain, Private Ryan quietly asked, "What's my position?"

"Never more than two feet away from me. That's an order, Private. You do still, on occasion, obey orders?"

With an embarrassed, almost shy smile, Ryan mumbled, "Yes, sir."

Miller's inspection indicated things were going well. Demo teams were concealing Hawkins mines along walls, behind shutters, in window boxes, angling the nasty devices to blow their death outward, into the street, horizontally, to take down infantry. Paratroopers were picking positions in rubble piles, hunkering in the ruins, finding lines of sight onto the street.

Within the bell tower, Jackson had aided Parker in setting up a machine-gun nest, muzzle of the gun aiming down through the balusters. Jackson had found his own perch, where he could sweep up and over the balustrade, aiming and bracing his Springfield over that railing, targeting one end of the street to the other, eye pressed to the scope, checking his freedom of movement, which was good.

"Thank you, Lord," he said.

Then he did it again, practicing the move.

From below came Miller's voice: "Everything all right up there, Private Jackson?"

"Yes, sir, Cap'n! God's in His heaven, all's right with the world . . . or it will be when we finish with these bastards."

"Amen, Private," Miller said, and moved on.

When he had finished his inspection, satisfied that the welcoming committee was well positioned, Miller—with Private Ryan tagging along—chose as his own post the roofless remains of the building nearest the bridge, apparently a former café. With the private's help, the captain cleared enough wreckage aside to create a position at a window whose panes and frame and glass were rubble under their feet. Exploring the former café, Miller salvaged a windup Victrola and several disks; he sorted through them, smiling at a familiar name on a label.

Soon, courtesy of the scratchy seventy-eight, the melancholy voice of Edith Piaf was wafting from the window out into the hot, motionless air of midafternoon. It carried to the bridge, where near the forward sandbagged machine-gun emplacement, the rest of Miller's squad was taking a smoke break.

"What's that broad singin' about, Upchuck?" Mellish said. "The Army pays you to translate . . . translate, already."

Upham, as he sat lounged against the sandbags, had a distant look. " 'Even life itself represents only you. Sometimes I dream that I am in your arms.' "

Listening to the repetitious, haunting melody, Sarge said, "What's she sayin' now? She said that before."

"That's the chorus," Upham said. " 'You are . . . speaking softly in my ear. You say things that make my eyes close, and I find that . . . marvelous.' "

Mellish grinned. "I'm findin' myself curiously attracted to you, suddenly, Upham."

"Cut it out," he said. "Don't you get it? It's a sad song. Tragic, even."

"Tragic my achin' ass!" Mellish said, between puffs of Lucky Strike. "She's happy, can't you hear it?"

"No," Upham insisted gently. "Very first thing she said was, 'Then one day you left me. I've been desperate ever since . . . I see you all over the sky. I see you all over the earth.' "

"Why, did her lover boy step on a land mine?" Reiben asked.

The voice, sounding so eloquent in a language only Upham understood (and to him it was eloquent, too), seemed to throb with sadness now; even Mellish sensed it.

"Shit," Sarge said, tossing his cigarette in a high arc into the river. "One more song from that depressin' skirt, and the Krauts won't have to shoot me. I'll just slit my own wrists."

Horvath rose and wandered off toward the village. The rest of the squad stood or sat and smoked and thought. Reiben laughed to himself, a light little private laugh, but Upham caught it.

"What's so funny?"

"Nothin'," Reiben said.

"Come on. I could use a laugh about now."

"It's just Rachel Troubowitz, is all."

"Rachel who?"

"Troubowitz. I was thinkin' about what she said to me, 'fore I left for Basic."

"What, I have to beg for this story?"

"She's our super's wife. Came into my mom's shop, the day I hadda leave for Basic. Tried on a few things. Ever see Carole Landis?"

"Isn't she that babe in the dinosaur movie?"

"Yeah! Well, Mrs. Troubowitz makes Carole Landis look flat-chested."

"Wow . . ."

"She's a forty-four double E, easy. I'm sitting there, and she's in the dressing room, with the curtain back just enough for me to see . . . maybe she did that on purpose, maybe it was a patriotic gesture. But she asks me to hand her this side-stay, silk-ribboned, three-panel girdle with a shelf-lift brassiere. So I hand her a 38 D cup, and she says, isn't this a little small, and I say naw, that oughta be perfect. . . ."

"Nice," Mellish said. "Now, this is a story. . . ."

"So there she is with the curtain half open, and I'm watching her try to squeeze into that thing, and she looks at me, and sees me looking at her with the eyes poppin' outa my skull, and she kinda smiles and says, 'Robert—this is one of those moments.' And I says, 'Moments, ma'am?' And she says, 'One of those moments when you're over there, and you're scared or see somethin' terrible, you just close your eyes and see me instead. Would you do that for me, Robert?' And I says, 'Yes, ma'am!' "

The music was still going, but the French song-stress' voice seemed less sad now, and every man had his eyes closed, picturing Mrs. Troubowitz in his own special way.

Within the remains of the building nearest the bridge, Miller was in position at the window. Ryan, seated in a corner on a salvaged chair, sipping from his canteen, asked the captain who the woman singing was, and Miller told him.

"What's her problem?" Ryan asked.

"Her lover left her, and everywhere she looks, she sees his face."

"That'd do it. . . . Want a swig?"

"Sure."

Ryan tossed Miller the canteen, and the captain lifted it to his lips with a shaking hand that the private noticed.

"You all right, sir?"

"Just keeping rhythm," Miller said with a wry smile, and tossed the canteen back.

Ryan studied Miller for a while, then asked, "Is it true what they say about you?"

"Now, you'll have to narrow that down."

"That you're a schoolteacher?"

"Yep."

Ryan shook his head. "That's something I could never do. Not after I saw what my brothers and me put those poor sons of bitches through. No way, sir."

Miller glanced at Ryan and saw that the private

was lost in thought. The kid was grabbing his moments of grief wherever he could find them, wherever those moments could be spared.

"You know," the boy began, "I'm having trouble."

"Yeah. I can understand that."

"That's not what I mean. It's . . . I'm having trouble seeing their faces. I keep trying, but I don't have any pictures with me, you know, photos, and my memory—do you believe it? I can't see 'em. Can't make 'em form in my head."

"Gotta think of them in some context or other."

"What do you mean, sir?"

"Don't try to think of their faces, try to remember some thing you did with them, someplace you went together. What I do, when I want to think about home, is think about lyin' in my hammock in my backyard, or my wife bendin' over, pruning roses in my old gloves. I do that, and I'm right there."

Ryan sat back and seemed to think that advice over. Then a smile lighted his face, and his eyes were suddenly elsewhere.

But his voice remained in the ruined building, reporting to Miller: "One night, well after dark, Tom and Pete dragged me out of bed, sayin' they had something to show me in the barn. Somethin' really special. I was afraid maybe it was some kinda practical joke on me. . . . I mean, you wouldn't believe some of the stuff older brothers can pull on ya, particularly on a farm. . . . Anyway, we sneaked up into the hayloft, and Tom and Pete make these hand signals down. I peek over and so do they, and Alice Jardine, who's this blonde who looks like Lana Turner only better, is in the back of the haywagon with Danny. Danny has her sweater off and he's about to undo her bra, which was pink and looked like a couple of really pointed artillery shells, and then she hears somethin' and looks up and sees these three guys looking down at her with their tongues hangin' out. And brother, does she scream bloody murder, runs the hell outa there. Danny, he's so pissed he chases after us with a pitchfork, knocks over a lantern, and then the hay's on fire. He's gotta bury the hatchet, though, and help us put out the fire before the whole damn barn burns down."

Miller smiled and said, "Better not let Reiben hear that one. He's got a thing about ladies' underwear."

"Danny went off to Basic the next day," Ryan said. "I sure hope he caught up with Alice Jardine that night; hate to think he went off without . . . well. That was the last time the four of us were all together. Two years ago."

Miller nodded. Edith Piaf was still singing.

"Long record," Ryan noted.

"Yeah."

"How about you tell me one. Tell me about the hammock, why don't you?"

"Okay. It's in the backyard."

"You said."

"Yeah. So I'm lying there, half asleep, listening for the sound of breaking glass. And that's all it takes to take me back home."

"Why? Why breaking glass?"

"You gotta understand, I got the best house in all of Addley. Not the biggest house, or most expensive, but it's got the best damn windows a baseball coach could ask for. See, we're right next to the junior high, or that is, we're behind the junior high baseball field. The garage windows face left field. Guy who owned the place before me put screens over the windows, but the first thing I did after I bought the place was take those damn screens off."

"Why?"

"Well, think about it. It's three hundred twenty-two feet from home plate to my garage windows. Takes one hell of a junior high baseball player to hit a ball that far, that high. I look at my garage windows as my baseball scouts, lookin' out for the junior high kids that are gonna pave my way to a state high school championship. Every time I hear breakin' glass when I'm lyin' in that hammock, I just smile and smile . . . knowin' I'm that much closer to a winning season."

Ryan was smiling. "That was swell, Captain. Now, how about your wife, and those roses?"

Miller pondered that. "I don't think so. . . . I think I'll keep that one, just for me."

The needle was scratching across the label, the record over. Miller was gazing out the window, listening to the silence, smiling, enjoying the afterglow of Ryan's memories and his own.

Then his smile began to fade. In the church bell tower, Jackson was perking up, too, and all around the village and on the bridge, paratroopers and Miller's men heard it now: the deep rumble of diesel engines, heading their way.

"Here they come," Miller said, sitting up. "Sweet Jesus, here they come."

18

All around the ruins of Ramelle, the Americans heard the rumble of the approaching tanks, a sound they greeted with relief and dread. Cocking their weapons, sighting down muzzles, crouching in debris, ducking past broken shutters, the welcoming committee watched as diesel fumes rippled over rooftops, the air distorting with heat haze, as if ghosts were invading the ghost town.

From Miller's position near the bridge, those fumes weren't yet visible, but the mechanical groan of tanks growing ever nearer told him battle was imminent. Sarge and the demo man, Toynbe, hustled into the roofless building where Miller and Ryan were dug in, Sarge tossing the captain a pair of binoculars.

Miller went to a former window with a view of the bell tower and brought Jackson, in his perch, into focus. He could see Jackson peering off through his rifle scope, to get a fix on what exactly was coming their way.

In that bell tower Jackson was telling Parker, at his machine gun, "I see Tigers. Two of 'em."

Through his binoculars, Miller could see Parker holding up two fingers, then making a "T" with his hands. Then the machine gunner patted the air with both palms, signaling Miller more information was forthcoming. Soon Parker held up two fingers again, this time holding up one hand sideways and straight and bringing in his cupped other hand to form a "P."

"Four tanks," Miller told the men around him. "Two Tigers, two Panzers."

Mellish and Henderson, at their machine-gun post in another crumbled building, also had a view of the bell tower and had seen the signals.

"Tigers," Mellish said, rage and fear quaking through him. "Shit, it would have to be Tigers. Why didn't they just send fuckin' King Kong?"

The ground under Mellish, and everyone else in Ramelle, began to vibrate, as if an earthquake were issuing warning tremors. Bits of plaster and rock and stone began shaking loose, hellish dandruff drifting from the rafters of roofless buildings onto waiting Americans.

Looming into view around the curve of the main street was a Royal Tiger, sixty-eight-point-six rumbling, clanking tons of tank, monstrous of size, monstrous of mien, carrying an 88-millimeter gun and a trio of machine guns, shielded by seven-inch-thick armor. With its sloping sides and the hideous smiles of its six steel wheels per side and the probing snout of its cannon barrel, it seemed inaptly named, less a sleek jungle cat than a bulky prehistoric beast, crushing rubble to dust beneath its treads.

Riding the turret was a hawkish-featured S.S. tank commander, a major, who was surveying the ruins of Ramelle with the haughty expression of a conqueror, even though this destruction had been the friendly fire of the Allies.

Another Tiger shadowed the first, and on the heels of the larger tanks clanked the pair of much smaller Panzers, twenty-three tons each. Trooping along in the dust-stirred, diesel-fume-shimmering wake of this impressive armor was a company of elite troops, Wafen S.S. from the Das Reich Division, perhaps a hundred men strong.

"Lord grant me strength," Jackson said in the bell tower, peering down at the procession passing awesomely below.

"Ask Him to save me some, too," Parker said breathlessly.

But back in the building near the bridge, Miller, peering through his binoculars, was smiling a little. "Looks like we've caught one break," he said. "Those tanks are heading down main street. . . ."

Half a dozen men, Reiben and five paratroopers, had been selected to bear the sticky bombs. They lay hidden in various positions at the outskirts of town, each man ready to emerge and play rabbit to draw those tanks down the main street. But that part of the plan was unnecessary now—the shuddering steel beasts were rolling down main street of their own volition—and the men, conveying the bombs, big gooey bizarre globs of grease that sprouted fuses, scurried to new positions on either side of main street.

Miller was watching through his binoculars, waiting for that lead Tiger to reach the rubble-clogged impasse between husks of buildings. Toynbe at a detonator, eyes riveted on the captain, waited for the word to throw the switch. Miller's hand was raised, poised to give that signal, as the captain watched and waited, watched and waited.

The hand lowered, Toynbe threw the switch, and the parade of tanks and men down main street was greeted not by confetti and cheers but a thunderous hell of exploding Hawkins mines, walls erupting in flying stone shards, fire and shrapnel streaming in a horizontal deluge of death. A dozen S.S. troopers fell shredded, dead. The rest scattered, seeking cover, reeling with concussion, choking with smoke. Both machine-gun nests opened up, raking the street in intersecting angles of slaughter, sending the German infantry yelling, screaming, scrambling for cover, dying in rubble, as lead hammered at them from seemingly every direction.

The machine gun in the bell tower, manned by Parker, threw its own thunderstorm of bullets down onto the street, spraying lead at the S.S. Jackson had drawn a bead on the tank commander, the major's head fixed in his crosshairs. But just as Jackson squeezed his trigger, the major—bullets flying all around him—ducked down into the turret, pulling the hatch shut, Jackson's slug whanging off the metal.

The tank rolled on, leaving its dead infantry behind, impervious to the machine-gun fire. Staying low, Reiben and the five other men bearing black globs, trailing smoke from lighted fuses, swarmed alongside it like insects. They hurled their gooey packages at the treads and steel wheels, then veered away, bats out of hell, scrambling this direction and that, finding rubble piles to duck behind.

The second Tiger spotted the fleeing saboteurs, the tank's forward machine gun nailing one of the runners, tearing him to pieces, dropping him like so much debris.

When the sticky bombs went off, it was like six cannons firing one after the other, and gouts of blue and orange flame blew sideways over both sides of the street, as if the tank had sprouted fiery wings, which promptly disappeared, leaving black smoke . . .

. . . and a Royal Tiger tank that was still rumbling along.

Reiben, crouched behind wreckage, said, "Damn!"

thinking their efforts, and the life of a man, had been wasted.

Then the tank's treads separated and peeled off the idler wheel, and the big machine skidded, skewing to one side, a staggering drunk, steel wheels spinning. The tank tried backing up but even more tread unspooled, and it jerked to a gear-grinding halt.

Now, as Miller had intended, the huge tank was a sixty-eight-ton roadblock, creating a traffic jam with the tanks following it, their brakes whining, treads and wheels groaning as the other three tanks were caught at the barricade of the first.

But that wrecked tank was still a fighting force to be reckoned with. Its turret, and those of the three tanks clogged behind it, cranked and swung around, muzzles leveling at the surrounding, surviving buildings where the attacking Americans were hiding. The big guns began blasting, thunderclap muzzle bursts that punched holes in some buildings and turned others into storms of deadly hurtling debris.

Even in his relatively remote position, Miller had to duck, Ryan, too, fragments flying, as the tanks pounded away. Americans posted about the village scrambled behind rubble piles, diving for cover. Reiben watched as a paratrooper got in the way of the methodical blasting of the tanks and blew apart like a human bomb.

The S.S. infantrymen were scrambling for shelter, too, pulling their wounded off the street, herding behind half-walls and trash heaps, their spiffy uniforms spattered with dust and blood. When they had taken cover, they began returning fire as the three tanks at the rear of the stranded Tiger seemed to desert them, backing up, blasting away as they went.

From behind rubble Sarge jack-in-the-boxed into position, a bazooka shouldered. He let go, and his projectile whooshed toward its target—the middle tank—only it deflected off the turret, exploding against the freestanding wall behind it, demolishing that wall, collapsing it, a ton of fragmented stone dropping down on the tank in an avalanche.

The stricken tank lurched, backing up, doing its best to get clear of the debris, muzzle cranking toward where Sarge had fired, and Horvath ran for his life.

From his position, Reiben saw this happen, saw the rubble pile behind where Sarge had fired go up in a cloud of smoke and flame and fragments. When the smoke cleared some, there was no sign of Sarge, and Reiben couldn't be sure if Horvath had made it or been blown to atoms.

The tanks lurched forward, clanking, wheezing, veering off in various directions, down side streets, leaving the main street and the stranded Tiger, heading through the havoc, making their way toward the bridge as best they could.

This was exactly what Miller had hoped for, and— seeing these results in his binoculars from his forward position—he shouted to Ryan and Toynbe, "Let's go!"

In the killing zone of main street, the machine-gun nests at their opposite stations were hurling lead at the S.S. troops. The Americans had hit them hard, the crossfire costing the Germans dearly, but the sheer numbers of the enemy, pressing forward in the demolishment, carried the threat of those nests getting overwhelmed.

Privates Lyle and Fallon knew it was time to displace, and used rags to pick up the machine gun, its barrel boiling hot, charring the cloth. Upham, like a man without an umbrella trying to duck raindrops, zigzagging through singing bullets and airborne rubble, delivered a pair of fresh ammo belts even as the nest was moving out.

Terrified, the world around him getting shot to pieces, Upham moved on to the other nest, where Mellish and Henderson were hauling their griddle-hot machine gun off its rubble-pile perch, too.

"Displacing!" Mellish yelled redundantly.

He and Henderson were already frantically falling back under heavy fire from advancing infantry. Upham, hugging the ammo belts, trailed after them as they found new cover and slammed their machine gun down, and again started blasting.

In the church bell tower, Parker was blazing away with his machine gun, and Jackson's eye was pressed to his sniperscope, picking off Germans like carnival targets, never missing, thinning the infantry ranks with deadly precision.

Then bullets impacted the balustrade Jackson was leaning against, chewing up the wood, spitting it out into splinters. The sharpshooter ducked back, none of the bullets catching him. He flashed a look at Parker, who flashed one back.

"Those Nazi ground pounders finally figured out we're up here," Parker said, hunkered over the big weapon. "Let's hope they don't tell their friends in the tanks. . . ."

One of the smaller tanks was plowing through what had days before been some family's living room, shattering plaster and lathe, grinding furnishings to garbage. But then the Panzer got bogged down, hitting a stone wall that didn't want to give, grinding against a pile of rocks, struggling to push through.

Flattened against a wall nearby, Miller noted this and motioned privates Rice and Garrity (David, twenty-one, Harrisburg, Pennsylvania) to the attack. From the rubble the two privates raced and bobbed, sticky bombs in hand, heading for the struggling Panzer.

Private Ryan began to follow them, but Miller grasped his arm, saying, "Not you."

Ryan might have argued if advancing S.S. troops hadn't taken precedence. The private and the captain laid down cover for the two sprinters with bombs in hand, Ryan with his M-1, Miller with his Thompson, sending the Germans scrambling for safety, pinning them down.

The Panzer was doing its best to maneuver out of the dead end, grinding, whining, groaning, and seemed about to batter through that wall when Rice and Garrity reached the tank, pausing to get their fuses going . . .

. . . and one of the homemade bombs went off, a premature detonation that made the two soldiers vanish like a magician's assistant. Only this puff of smoke had a reddish tinge accompanied by ghastly splattering human shrapnel. The wall the Panzer had been caught against became a hailstorm of stone fragments, and the blast slammed both Miller and Ryan to the ground, hard.

And the Panzer lumbered on, unfazed—in fact, aided by the bomb, which had helped dislodge the tank.

All around, a battle was raging in the rubble of Ramelle, smoke and dust creating a wicked fog through which German infantry emerged like materializing ghosts, ever firing, pushing forward by inches, by yards.

Still the machine-gun nests pummeled away at the S.S., continually getting pushed back by their sheer numbers, falling back to a new post, and pummeling away again. Through this nightmare of gunfire and smoke and dust and screams and blood mist, Corporal Upham shuttled ammo to both teams, keeping up with their new positions, running like an escaped lunatic through the devastation.

A squad of Germans advanced on Mellish and Henderson as they were displacing, the big hot gun in their hands. Then Private Trask stepped out from behind a wall, wielding a flamethrower, and bathed the charging S.S. with flame streaming like water from a fire hose. Men turned orange and blue and danced to their deaths in a hell of mushrooming smoke.

While the S.S. fried and died, the tanks rolled inexorably along, plowing through walls, battering down buildings, crushing rock and rubbish, turrets swinging, picking targets, firing, taking down any obstacles in their paths.

Grinding through the decimation came the second Panzer, an invitation for Reiben and Toynbe to run and attack it. And they did, each slamming a pair of fuse-lighted sticky bombs onto the treads and steel wheels, then scurrying away like naughty children. In their wake they left multiple explosions that were like a thunderous firing squad, as gouts of flame and tufts of smoke shot from the tank. The blast knocked Reiben ass over teakettle, asprawl on a rubble pile.

Dazed, Reiben raised up on his elbows, ears ringing, trying to clear his head. When he looked over at the tank, to admire his own handiwork, he saw that goddamn thing was rolling right along, unharmed!

The fucking tank swerved toward him. He scrambled on the rocks, desperately, trying to get out of the Panzer's path, but still reeling from the concussive impact of his own bombs and stumbling and tumbling. . . .

From where he scrambled, Reiben couldn't see the bazooka projectile give the tank a flaming enema, blowing out its engine. But he did hear the tank stutter and hitch and groan to a halt.

Reiben glanced back and saw the stopped tank, and saw, too, a soot-covered Sarge, smoking bazooka in his hands, perched on a pile of rocks. Their eyes met, and Sarge winked, smiled, and took off running, ducking out of sight behind a half-wall.

Relieved, Reiben turned his eyes back toward that tank, where the turret hatch lifted, and a Panzer crewman popped out, Luger in hand. From that perch the German picked off Toynbe, where he was hunkered behind a trash heap.

And the Luger was panning Reiben's way when a bullet blew through the crewman's chest, sending him flopping over sideways on the turret, out of the war.

Stunned, Reiben whirled and looked up, knowing that shot had come from the bell tower—knowing Jackson had saved him. Like Sarge had saved him . . . his life saved twice within seconds by two of his brothers. . . .

In the bell tower Jackson was already working his

rifle bolt, turning away from the tank, eyes to the sniperscope, searching out more targets.

" 'Blessed be the Lord my strength,' " he muttered, " 'which teacheth my hands to war, and my fingers to fight. . . .' "

Paratroopers emerged from the ruins to attack the crippled Panzer, Reiben leading the charge. When a second crewman popped up past his dead comrade, Reiben shot the bastard with his .45, then joined in as pins were popped and grenades tossed in and down. The GIs scrambled away as behind them the concussive blast shook the tank. Black fire-laced smoke puffed from its turret as if from a volcano.

In the bell tower, Jackson at his Springfield was searching out another target, and he was saying, praying, " 'My goodness and my fortress; my high tower, and my deliverer; my shield and He in whom I . . .' "

In his sniperscope sights now was the crippled Tiger, which still blocked the main street. Its turret was cranking around, the muzzle raising.

Right at the bell tower.

" '. . . trust,' " Jackson said, pulling his eye back from the scope, allowing himself a heartbeat of stunned horror. "Parker! Git outa here now!"

Jackson was already at the trapdoor, and Parker was behind him, but they both knew they'd never make it, and Jackson said, "Jesus," a prayer, not a curse, right before the tank's thunderclap blast turned the bell tower into a fireball of hurtling debris.

The tank lowered its muzzle and blasted again, and the rest of the church was blown to smithereens.

From their latest machine-gun position, Mellish and Henderson had witnessed this, had watched Jackson die in church, and watched the church die, too.

"Jackson," Mellish said, staring in horror. "God-damn it, Jackson!"

"Knocking the treads off that bastard ain't enough," Henderson said. "We gotta take that Tiger out."

Mellish fired a burst and sent some S.S. scurrying for cover.

"Yeah?" Mellish said, still reeling from the loss of Jackson. "And how in hell you suggest doin' that?"

"I got an idea," Henderson said, and plucked a grenade off his webbing.

"You fuckin' nuts? That's a Tiger! Grenades bounce off those fuckers like Superman!"

Henderson's grin was a little boy's. "Didn't ya ever hear of kryptonite? Keep me covered. . . ."

And he dashed into the street, weaving through the ravagement, as behind him Mellish kept the machine-gun rattling, keeping the Germans pinned down, giving Henderson the cover he needed to get close to that crippled tank.

Henderson crouched behind a rubble pile near the stalled Tiger, pulled his grenade pin, holding onto it tight, waiting, waiting, waiting. Then the muzzle turned, adjusting, seeking a new target. Henderson pressed his forearms to his ears, in anticipation of the thunderous muzzle blast—when it came, that was his cue. He lunged from cover, running straight at the tank, jumping up and hooking his arm around the muzzle, hanging like a monkey, hurling the grenade straight down that barrel. . . .

Henderson dropped to the street and kept low, yanking another grenade free, popping its pin, holding down its lever, waiting, not long, for the tank to shudder from the blast. Then he scrambled up onto the tank, and the hatch opened, smoke billowing, the hawk-faced S.S. major pushing up, coughing, ears and nose bleeding, glazed with shock. Henderson stuffed the grenade down the major's blouse and leaned hard against the hatch door, stuffing the major back down into the tank.

The next blast opened the hatch rudely, sending Henderson flying off the tank, depositing him on the street.

Mellish paused in his firing, amazed by this feat. Henderson didn't seem at all injured, was picking himself up, grinning, running back toward Mellish, energized, exultant.

"Did you see that?" Henderson yelled. "Did you fuckin' *see* that?"

And from somewhere, German machine-gun fire stitched across the corporal, spinning him around, slamming him to the street, before he even had time to scream, before he even had time to take the triumphant smile off his face.

Mellish had time to scream, though, and he did. He screamed and he kept firing and screaming and firing with the machine gun, raking the German positions with bullet after bullet.

And then Mellish's ammo belt ran out. Upham had delivered the last of the machine-gun ammunition already. The S.S. wasn't out of bullets, though, and lead was spattering against the rubble around him, driving him down. Mellish grabbed his M-1 and fell back, running for his life.

19

On the move, the clank and wheeze of the remaining Royal Tiger building in their ears, Miller ran with Ryan tagging after him. They ducked to take advantage of the cover of half-crumbled-away walls, and almost stumbled over Sergeant Horvath, who was lying in wait for that tank, bazooka propped over the edge of a half tier of brick.

"Gotta aim for the treads!" Sarge yelled, and demonstrated, the fiery projectile streaming toward the oncoming Tiger, which was in the process of plowing through a stone wall like it was papier-mâché. The bazooka round connected, exploded resoundingly . . . and the tank kept coming, ramping up, slamming back down again. . . .

"Fall back!" Miller shouted. "Fall back!"

"Go," Sarge yelled, "Go! Go!"

The Tiger was crashing through, bearing right down on them, and they took off like bandits. Sarge abandoned the bazooka, which with the half-wall was soon crushed under the massive treads.

Nearby Lyle and Fallon, in the remaining of the two machine-gun nests, threw blistering rounds at the tank. The gun swiveled, chattering, but got nowhere with the Tiger, which was in the process of rolling over a wounded paratrooper, grinding him under.

Seeing this, the machine gunners began screaming as they fed and fired. They knew they were on their last ammo belt and would have to fall back—only they didn't have to. A potato-masher grenade came spinning toward them and exploded before it landed. By the time the smoke had cleared over the shredded remains of the two Americans, the Germans were overrunning the position.

Mellish, on the run, saw Upham up ahead, confused, disoriented in the haze of smoke and dust.

"Upham!" Mellish yelled, and Upham looked back at him. "The bridge is straight ahead! Run!"

Barely had Mellish said this when a young S.S. trooper darted from the battle fog into Mellish's path. They faced each other in a frozen moment, like two gunfighters poised for a fast draw. But they were not gunfighters, they were boys serving their respective countries, though one of them *was* faster: the German.

While both their weapons raised at once, the German's Schmeisser submachine gun belched bullets before Mellish's finger could squeeze the M-1 trigger. Hot rounds slammed into him; a bloody stitch-work pattern appeared across the private's belly as he tumbled backward, dead before he hit the ground.

"Mellish!" Upham cried.

And the German whirled, turning the Schmeisser toward Upham, who froze, staring down the black empty eye of its barrel. The corporal knew this to be his last moment, but it wasn't: the martial music of a B.A.R. punched one, two, three holes through the German's chest, absurdly massive wounds that sprayed blood and bone and tissue and leaked sunlight. The Schmeisser belched again, this time at the sky, as the German arced back into a rubble pile where he lay staring, shocked to be dead.

Upham, on the other hand, was shocked to be alive, and when Reiben—his B.A.R. in his hands—appeared next to the corporal, saying, "C'mon, Upchuck, we gotta fall back," Upham was slow to move.

So Reiben dragged him along, firing the big B.A.R. one-handed, covering their retreat. Rally point was the detritus-choked town square, and they scurried down a side street in that direction.

Miller, zigzagging through the devastation with Ryan and Sarge tagging after him, was headed for the same spot. They could hear the Tiger nearby, bashing down walls, bullying what was left of Ramelle out of its path.

Trask had the Tiger in view and hosed it with flame, fire and smoke mushrooming, but the tank couldn't be bothered, and Trask was soon out of fuel. He shrugged out of his harness, ditching the now useless flamethrower, and hightailed for the town square.

They all made it there more or less at once—Miller, Ryan, Sarge, Trask, then Reiben and Upham—and now they raced for the steel-and-stone span over the sparkling blue river. Up ahead they could see Private Weller—one of the paratroopers who had saved Miller's squad when they'd arrived at Ramelle—already hunkered in behind the sandbags of the machine-gun nest near the bridge entrance, racking the big gun's bolt.

But behind them, the Tiger's cannon blew a wall apart and the tank came thundering into the square, treads grinding. It made a massive turn, its forward machine gun blasting flame and bullets, swiveling, tracking the men running toward the bridge.

The head start the Americans had was enough to beat the tank's bullets to those sandbags. Every one of them went hurtling over, ducking down into safety, half a moment before the machine-gun fire tore into the sandbags, ripping the bags apart, sending up clouds of sand.

The remaining Panzer was joining the bigger tank in the square, and both tanks began to close in on the bridge and its defenders. The remaining S.S. troops—their numbers well thinned—were plodding alongside.

As Weller opened fire with the machine gun, Ryan snatched up one of the two remaining bazookas. Laying it over the lip of the shredded sandbags, taking aim at the oncoming Tiger, Miller loaded, pounding the private on the helmet to indicate the bazooka was ready to fire—which Ryan did. But the projectile exploded off the tank treads, with no discernible impact.

"Reload!" Ryan called.

"Reiben and me'll take it," Sarge told Ryan, then looked pointedly at Miller, reminding him why they'd come. "You two fall back!"

Miller nodded, grabbing Ryan by the arm, saying to Horvath, "You can't maintain this position much longer—follow right behind us!"

"Yeah, right, go!"

Ryan and Miller snatched up all the armaments they could, and left the forward emplacement, dashing across the bridge.

Sarge leveled the bazooka up over the sandbags while Reiben loaded. Then Reiben tapped Sarge on the shoulder. Sarge blasted away, this projectile also exploding off the Tiger treads to no effect. Upham and Trask were firing their rifles, trying to pick off the S.S. troops, with only occasional success.

The Tiger and its tagalong Panzer kept coming, ever nearer, and Sarge yelled, "Fall back!" as he and Reiben and the rest snatched up whatever they could and ran for it. Only Weller stayed behind, blasting away with the machine gun. He tagged some of the S.S. troops at least, providing cover as the sergeant and three privates sprinted toward the sandbags at the far end.

Seeing the Tiger swiveling its muzzle toward his sandbagged position, Weller jumped from the machine-gun nest and scurried after Sarge and the others. But the thunderous blast from the tank's cannon exploded the emplacement into a swirling ball of flame, sand, and debris. Too close to the blast, Weller got tossed like a rag doll, slamming facedown into the brick pavement, breaking many bones, but he was already dead, his back pulverized by shrapnel.

Miller and Ryan had reached the sandbags, throwing themselves over. The captain grabbed the final bazooka, yelling to Ryan, "Connect those wires! We can't let the bastards take this bridge!"

While Ryan frantically connected wires to the detonator, spinning wing nuts, Miller laid the bazooka over the sandbags, aiming at the bridge where the tank would be coming. Through the fog of smoke and dust and sand, though, first Sarge, Reiben, Trask, and Upham emerged, on the run.

And looming right behind them, seeming vague at first in the haze then taking terrible shape, came the Tiger, clanking and whining and lumbering.

"Shit," Miller yelled, "Run! Goddamn it, run!"

The tank's forward machine gun opened up on

them, first ripping up the brick pavement, then catching up with the runners, who were hurling themselves to either side of the bridge, looking for something to hide behind. Trask caught a slug in the leg, and Sarge, not missing stride, plucked him from the pavement and hauled him behind a buttress.

"Get down!" Miller called.

And he fired the bazooka. A projectile rocketed down the center of the bridge past the two men huddling behind the buttress and over the heads of Reiben and Upham, who lay flattened on the brick. Then traveling the length of the bridge, it exploded harmlessly on the sloping front of the tank.

As Miller desperately reloaded the bazooka, Sarge, hauling Trask under the temporary cover of smoke, called to Reiben and Upham, "Go! Go!"

And they joined Sarge, helping him drag Trask toward relative safety.

The tank's forward machine gun opened up again, and a pair of slugs ripped into Sarge, in his back, and he dropped.

"Sarge!" Reiben screamed.

"Goddamn it!" Miller said, resting the bazooka on the lip of the sandbags, aiming again. "Down, down!"

And Reiben and Upham hit the deck, next to the fallen Sarge and wounded Trask, Miller firing another projectile over their heads, flaming its way to the Tiger, where it exploded to no avail.

The noise and smoke, however, encouraged Reiben and Upham to jump to their feet. Reiben dragged Sarge, and Upham dragged Trask, giving the effort everything they had—but it was like running in mud, running in slow motion. Then the Tiger fired that 88 cannon, and the explosion seemed to tear the world itself apart, to rip the air to shreds, flinging heat and shrapnel in all directions, sending the running men and the wounded they were lugging to the pavement with heads spinning and ears ringing. . . .

Miller wasn't as close as those men were, but the monstrous discharge had deafened him, much as another explosion had on Omaha Beach. It was as if all the sound had drained from the world, with the exception of faint, disembodied sounds that somehow worked their way in. . . .

Not sure where the 88 shell had finally found purchase, Miller knew only that he was alive and that the bridge was standing. And, yes, Private Ryan was alive, tossed like rubbish within the tumbled mess of the sandbagged emplacement, where everything lay strewn and smoking. Battered, stunned, head reeling in a manner that seemed to slow everything down, Miller could make out, in the nearly silent world, the muffled sound of the clanking, crunching Tiger pressing toward them.

He peered up and saw, through the swirling dust and smoke, the sprawled corpse of Sergeant Michael Horvath. He didn't scream or weep; there would be time for that only if he himself could survive these next minutes, perhaps moments. He saw Upham crawling like a baby, looking down at the dead Sarge, as Reiben—huddled behind a bridge buttress, half of his face blackened like a minstrel who'd removed only some of his makeup—motioned frantically for Upham to get off the middle of that bridge.

The Tiger was materializing again through the smoke, and its muzzle was pointed toward Miller's encampment, above the childlike crawling figure of Upham as he moved toward Reiben and the cover of that buttress.

Ryan reached for the toppled .30-caliber machine gun, and Miller joined in. The captain glimpsed Reiben grabbing Upham's hand and pulling the private to some seconds of safety, anyway. The two clung together, like scared children, brothers fearing a scolding for some mutual shenanigan.

Together the captain and private slammed the big machine gun atop the sandbags. Ryan worked the bolt, its echoing *clack-clatch* signaling the gradual return of Miller's hearing. They opened fire, and strangely, Miller could barely hear that, though the bolt whacking back and forth seemed clear to him as shells ejected, their faint metallic shriek also audible.

The Tiger rumbled forward, bullets having no effect even though the metal beast seemed to howl in pain. One side of it scraped the steelwork of the bridge. Its forward machine gun swiveled into position, taking aim at the sandbagged nest. Miller remembered the look Sarge had shot him when they'd fallen back to this position—that reminder of his mission. Thinking of nothing but saving Private Ryan now, he threw his arms over the boy, shoving him down out of the path of the bullets.

Those bullets missed Miller, too, but one of the surviving S.S. troops, trotting alongside the Tiger, caught sight of the two figures behind the sandbag and let rip with his Schmeisser.

And these bullets found the high school teacher from Addley, Pennsylvania, two rounds anyway, traveling into and through his chest. Both Miller and Ryan dropped from view, behind the sandbags, but Upham had seen the shooting, had seen it all from behind the buttress he shared with Reiben, who was screaming Miller's name.

Upham had seen it, all right; he had even recognized the German who shot the captain.

And the corporal who would one day record all of this in a novel stepped from behind the buttress, .45 in hand, and looked at the German soldier, the boyish prisoner who liked Steamboat Willie and Mickey Mouse, and who Miller had in his fatal compassion allowed to live.

That soldier, that former prisoner, had not recognized the man he shot; but Upham he recognized. Upham was closer.

"Upham!" the German said, grinning, lowering his weapon for a moment.

That moment was enough. Upham shot the son of a bitch through the heart and let him die smiling.

And as Upham and Reiben worked their way from one buttress to another, trying to make it to the sandbagged nest, the wounded Miller was rising up to play out the rest of the game because he was not, the coach of the Addley High School baseball team was definitely not, a quitter. He didn't hurt, exactly, though the burning sensations in his chest told him he'd been wounded, and he fumbled for the only weapon he had left, his sidearm, his holstered .45.

Captain Miller fired his .45 at that oncoming tank, knowing the effort was futile but pumping that trigger anyway. The pistol jumped in his fist, its loud report faint in his stunned ears, and he ran the magazine down to its final bullet.

He shot the final .45 round at the approaching Tiger, and the tank exploded.

Ducking down, astonished, Miller stared at the pistol in his hand; how the hell could he have done that? How could one .45 slug blow up a Royal Tiger?

Something had: flame gouting from the shell of the beast, a second explosion blasted the Tiger's turret into the air, where it spun like a flaming pinwheel. Then the tank itself seemed to lose balance, slamming into the side of the bridge. Taking steel and stonework with it, groaning, screeching, it crashed into the water like a huge stone, sending wavelike ripples over its blue surface.

Miller heard the splash, his hearing almost back, and he heard something else, too, something that brought his eyes skyward, heavenly voices, a choir of angels whose song built into the throaty roar of a Packard engine. And, as the P-51 Mustang swooped over the bridge, Miller suddenly knew his .45 had not been responsible for that damage.

Reiben and Upham watched from behind the buttress as the tank-buster plane peeled overhead and came around for another pass. The Panzer was desperately trying to back off the bridge and away from the burning shell of its larger brother. The few remaining S.S. foot soldiers were scurrying in retreat. The smaller tank no longer a threat, the two privates left cover and ran to the sandbag emplacement.

They found Miller slumped in Ryan's arms. Tears were streaking Ryan's face; blood was streaking Miller's blouse.

"Captain," Reiben said. "Oh, God . . . Captain."

Reiben and Upham dropped to their knees, as if in prayer. They grabbed on to Miller, took him in their arms hoping to transmit some of their life into him. Reiben was screaming at the sky, curses and prayers. Upham was bawling like a baby.

At the far end of the bridge, the smaller tank exploded into a ball of flame, Mustang roaring past, rising in a steep climb.

Miller was watching the clouds. He tried to say something, but nothing came out. But he did manage to raise a bloody hand—his trembling hand—and point toward the ascending P-51, as it made its damn near vertical climb, straining magnificently at its apex.

"Tank busters, sir," Ryan said, not bothering to brush the tears from his cheeks. "P-51's."

Behind the cluster of battle-torn soldiers in the machine-gun nest, Sherman tanks approached, merging from the tree line, accompanied by waves of supporting infantry.

But Miller wasn't aware of that. He saw only the sky, and the P-51, and the clouds.

"See . . . Wade was . . . right," Miller managed. "Angels . . . on our shoulders. . . ."

Someone's feet on the bridge crunched glass.

Miller smiled distantly. "Winning season," he said.

"Don't talk, Cap," Reiben said.

But his captain was looking up at Private Ryan, the man they'd come to save. The man they'd saved.

"Earn this," Miller said softly.

"Sir?" Ryan asked.

Now the captain repeated it firmly, an order: "Earn this."

His last words.

With the clank and wheeze of friendly tanks in their ears, Ryan and Reiben and Upham carried Captain John H. Miller away from the machine-gun nest to the stonework wall of the bridge and laid him gently there.

"At least it's not shakin' anymore," Upham said, and swallowed.

"Huh?" Reiben said numbly.

Upham nodded toward Miller's limp hand, draped against the stonework. "His hand."

Reiben crouched over the captain, finding something in Miller's breast pocket, removing it, putting it in his own pocket. He said nothing about it, but Upham saw what Reiben had done, and knew Reiben had taken it upon himself to deliver the letter to Caparzo's papa.

And the boys from Mr. Miller's class went back to the war.

EPILOGUE

St. Laurent Military Graveyard
June 6, 1998

James Ryan, seventy-four, Peyton, Iowa, threaded through the perfectly lined rows of crosses until he found the right marker. None of his family, not even his little grandson, could keep up with him.

And that was fine, because he wanted a private moment—that is, a moment between private and captain.

He looked at the white cross and said, "My family's with me today. They wanted to come. Vacation. Me, I didn't know how I'd feel, coming back here."

"Grandpa!" Jimmy was catching up.

Ryan continued to speak to his captain. "Not a day goes by I don't think about what happened on that bridge. About what we did, and what you said to me. And I just want you to know . . ."

"Grandpa!"

Ryan turned and saw Jimmy standing nearby, but sensitive enough a lad to keep his distance. The grandfather patted the air, telling his grandson to stay back, please, for just a little while.

Then Ryan looked at the cross as if it were a person and said, "I've tried. Tried to live my life the best I could. I hope that's enough. I didn't invent anything. I didn't cure any diseases. I worked a farm. I raised a family. I lived a life. I only hope, in your eyes at least, I earned what you did for me."

"Jim . . ."

Now it was not his grandson's voice, but his wife's. His son, his son's wife, the four grandkids, were keeping a respectful distance, just over the rise. Their expressions were touched with confusion, because what this meant was beyond them. So far beyond them. . . .

But not beyond the woman he had lived with, this woman standing beside him now and always. He'd never really told her anything about this place, no war stories, except a few funny ones. Still, this was the woman who had held him, rocked him, comforted him, on those nights, those once frequent, now occasional nights, when he would wake screaming, or weeping. Or both.

So pretty, still so pretty. She took his arm, and looked down at the white cross. "Someone you knew?"

Ryan sighed. "Not really."

"Are you all right, Jim?"

He looked at her, and the tears in his eyes made tears form in hers. "Alice . . . have I lived a good life? Am I a good man?"

"Jim . . . what . . ."

"Just tell me . . . tell me if you think I've earned it."

She studied him, then tenderly touched his face. "Oh, yes. Yes, you have."

Then she left him there, joining the family, giving him as many moments as he needed, to be ready to leave this place.

He didn't need that long. Just long enough to stand erect and give the grave marker a heartfelt salute.

Then walking with just a little military snap in his step, Private James Ryan, winner of the Silver Star, rejoined his family, leaving this well-tended cemetery behind . . .

. . . and the grave of Captain John H. Miller, posthumous Medal of Honor winner, after whom a junior high school in Addley, Pennsylvania, had been named.

Despite a fancy plaque in the school's front hallway, many of the kids there today wonder why.

MAX ALLAN COLLINS has earned an unprecedented eight Private Eye Writers of America Shamus nominations for his Nathan Heller historical thrillers, winning twice (*True Detective*, 1983, and *Stolen Away*, 1991); the latest Heller, *Flying Blind*, explores the mystery of Amelia Earhart.

A Mystery Writers of America Edgar nominee in both fiction and nonfiction categories, Collins has been hailed as "the Renaissance man of mystery fiction." His credits include four suspense-novel series, film criticism, short fiction, songwriting, trading-card sets, and movie/TV tie-in novels, including such bestsellers as *In the Line of Fire, Waterworld,* and *Air Force One.*

He scripted the internationally syndicated comic strip *Dick Tracy* from 1977 to 1993, is co-creator of the comic-book features *Ms. Tree, Wild Dog,* and *Mickey Spillane's Mike Danger,* and has written the *Batman* comic book and newspaper strip. His most recent comics project is an epic Prohibition-era graphic novel, *Road to Perdition.*

Working as an independent filmmaker in his native Iowa, he wrote, directed, and executive-produced the 1995 suspense film *Mommy,* starring Patty McCormack; he performed the same duties for a 1997 sequel, *Mommy's Day,* for which he won an Iowa Motion Picture Award for screenwriting. He also wrote *The Expert,* a 1995 HBO World Premiere film.

Collins lives in Muscatine, Iowa, with his wife, writer Barbara Collins, and their teenage son, Nathan.